MARKED FOR REVENGE

AN ART HEIST THRILLER

JENNIFER S. ALDERSON

Traveling Life Press
Amsterdam

Books by Jennifer S. Alderson:
Marked for Revenge: An Art Heist Thriller
Rituals of the Dead: An Artifact Mystery
The Lover's Portrait: An Art Mystery
Down and Out in Kathmandu: A Backpacker Mystery
Holiday Gone Wrong: A Short Travel Thriller
Notes of a Naive Traveler: Nepal and Thailand Travelogue

Dedication

To my wonderful son and husband for inspiring me daily.

1 Nighttime Flight

August 11, 2018

Marko Antic softly hummed the Dutch national anthem as he cut another watercolor from Vianden Castle's cold stone wall. As the gilded frame dropped into his free hand, he automatically looked to the life-sized portrait of William II hanging at the opposite end of the narrow room, almost sensing the Dutch king's disapproval.

"Will you stop already?" his partner-in-crime whispered.

Marko ceased mid-chorus, the last bar of 'Het Wilhelmus' hanging eerily in the air. He opened his mouth to reprimand Rikard for being such a killjoy when he realized his friend was right. Although the Turret Room was at the back of an unoccupied medieval castle—and the sole security guard had already completed his rounds—they'd do better to be prudent.

Marko slipped the painting into a padded canvas bag, careful not to put unnecessary pressure on the other two watercolors he'd already plundered from the castle's walls. He looked to his friend and saw Rikard was placing the tenth and final painting into his bag. As soon as all of the watercolors were secure, it was time to complete this job. Marko sucked in his breath, excited yet nervous about their exit, inspired by the castle's extraordinary location.

Vianden Castle seemed to grow out of a rocky promontory jutting out into the Our Valley. It was the jewel crowning the tiny village of Vianden—literally. The town's homes, businesses, and church carved into the steep ridge had a thick blanket of tall trees that covered them. A single road led up to the castle at the top.

At first, Marko and Rikard were overwhelmed by the castle's position and the seemingly insurmountably high stone wall built around it. Once inside, they were pleasantly surprised by how easily

1

looks could deceive. The castle itself was the main tourist attraction, and that was impossible to steal. Cameras were trained on the main entrances and exits but were not hung up in each room. During their tour, Marko realized why. Only a few inexpensive pieces of art were permanently displayed, and none appeared to be hooked up to an alarm. But then, his trained eye told him they weren't worth more than a few thousand euros, thus probably not worth insuring. The only additional measure taken to secure the temporary exhibition of watercolors they'd just stolen from was a single camera pointed at the entrance to the Turret Room. One that Marko had covered with tape before entering the space.

Breaking in had been incredibly easy. Because the castle's entrance was literally at the end of the road, there was little chance of a random passerby seeing them return at two in the morning. Marko and Rikard used rappelling hooks to climb over the massive stone wall surrounding the castle and were inside in a matter of seconds. Thanks to the waning moon, they didn't have to look hard to find shadows to climb in. Getting out would entail a different route entirely.

Marko triple-checked his canvas bags before glancing over to see Rikard doing the same. The burglars locked eyes and nodded, then rose and crossed the darkened stone floor.

A door on the left side of the Turret Room led to a wide balcony extending far out over the valley below. As soon as Rikard opened it, a strong wind blew inside, chilling Marko to the bone.

Both men dragged the bags of artwork out onto the balcony then closed the door firmly behind them. Marko knew from their previous visit that the views from here were breathtaking. Because the balcony extended a few feet out over the abyss, visitors could see for miles up and down the valley. Now, a swath of blacks and grays met their eye. The Our river was invisible. A handful of lights—presumably from homes—sparkled through the dense foliage of this sparsely populated region.

Before looting the Turret Room, they had placed two large tote bags on the balcony. Marko opened one and took out a harness shaped like a padded chair. He slipped it over his back and quickly strapped himself in. Then, using a series of bungee cords and carabiners, he secured a crate of artwork to each side. The extra-thick padding should cushion any jarring, and both Marko and Rikard were skilled enough to land softly. Their job depended on it. Once satisfied, he slipped on night-vision goggles, buckled on his helmet, then picked up a small nylon sack with two lines hanging out of it. Marko hooked them into the specially-built loops hanging from his chest. He yanked on each, ensuring they were secure before unfurling the nylon wing. The soft fabric billowed up and out above him. Marko turned on a flashing red beacon attached to his chest and stepped out onto the wide stone railing. The strong winds tugged on the nylon, pulling him forward.

The balcony wasn't large enough for both to jump simultaneously, but Marko could see that Rikard was almost ready. Pulling tight on the controls, Marko waited until his friend had his wing clipped in properly. As soon as Rikard gave him the thumbs up, Marco released the hand brakes and stepped off the ledge, giving in to the wind's desire. Marko's heart raced as his stomach dropped away. For a brief moment, he was plunging toward the earth. Seconds later, his chute grabbed an upward draft and raced up the ridge, jerking him high above the treetops. A smile split his face; he loved the rush. He used his hand grips and weight to control his lateral movements, slowly maneuvering himself away from the tree-covered ridge and back above the river, his night-vision goggles helping him orient.

A minute later, he heard the whooshing sound of another chute catching the wind. He turned his head back toward the castle and searched until he could see his friend's red beacon flashing. Marko's grin intensified when he noticed there were no lights visible inside the castle. The robbery probably wouldn't be detected until morning.

Marko relaxed the tension on his hand grips, allowing his wing to race down the valley, relishing the brief moment of freedom. He couldn't believe his luck. Marko had always loved his work, but since he began working for his uncle a year ago, his job satisfaction had increased significantly. Thanks to years of stealing paintings and antiques from private homes, Marko had developed a real eye for quality. The mental thrill of creating a devious plan and seeing it through was a real adrenaline kick but getting rid of these illicitly gained goods was always such a pain. There was much risk involved. More and more of his associates had been tripped up by selling them to undercover cops. And when Marko did find a trustworthy buyer, they offered minimal payout.

Marko always knew he could count on his family if he ever got into real trouble, but he had enjoyed following his own path. That is until several of his friends were arrested during a recent sting operation. When his uncle Luka offered to take care of all of that hassle, Marko couldn't refuse. And his uncle did pay top dollar, more than he'd been able to organize on his own. From time to time, Luka even supplied him with an interesting theft, to boot. There was no shortage of greedy people willing to pay anything to acquire what they wanted, especially when the object of their desire was entirely out of reach even to people of their financial stature.

He kicked his legs around, reveling in the liberating feeling of flying. Too soon, he made out a set of headlights blinking in the distance. Marko adjusted his direction and relaxed into the harness, determined to enjoy the rest of his short flight.

He looked up to the moon and turned his face into the wind, letting it whip across his cheeks — God, how he loved his job.

2 A Meeting in Marmaris

August 12, 2018

Sunlight sparkled off the waters of Marmaris Bay, turning the ripples into fluid diamonds. In the distance, the green-tipped mountains enclosing the town were hazy purple silhouettes. From his balcony, Kadir Tekin watched Westerners on jet skis churning up the waves as Turkish families splashed in the warm water close to shore. Four-masters decorated as pirate ships sailed further out, heading toward the high peaks of Yildiz Adasi and Keci Adasi, the mountainous islands that separated Marmaris from the Mediterranean Sea.

A servant dressed in a tunic and şalvar trousers unobtrusively came up from behind, bowing slightly. "Luka Antic is here."

Kadir grunted his acknowledgment, keeping his eyes focused south. A large yacht crossed the bay, sail set for Netsel Marina. He watched until the Italian vessel moored and a group of wealthy twenty-somethings scampered off, immediately heading toward the boutique-filled streets next to the marina. He picked up his binoculars and took in their scantily-clad bodies, dark curly hair, and the expensive jewelry hanging around their necks, arms, and ankles. He was planning to lunch along the water after this meeting—he would have to look for them.

Kadir turned and crossed the pink stone marble balcony to the wide-open French doors of his study. Inside stood his Croatian guest. When Davit, a mutual business associate, told him about Luka's specialty and mentioned the Croatian was looking to expand his business interests, Kadir jumped at the chance to meet with him.

Initial contact established that Luka wanted to buy two million dollars' worth of his highest-grade heroin. The Croatian was moving

5

into the drugs business and wanted to make a big splash. Kadir was impressed by his gumption and could easily fulfill the order, but he wanted to meet Luka first. Nothing replaced that initial impression. Besides, he wanted to see the Croatian's reaction when he told him about his rather unusual request. Only then would he know if they could do business together or not.

Luka stood next to Kadir's desk, waiting for his host to approach. Luka was shorter than Kadir's own five-foot, five-inch frame but was studier, broader. His buzz cut distracted from the fact that he was going bald. His face was clean-shaven, but his stubble was already struggling to break through his skin again.

Kadir extended a hand. "Davit speaks highly of you."

"That's good to know. We go way back," Luka replied. The Croatian's raspy voice made Kadir have to strain his ears to understand him.

Kadir sat in one of the chairs across from his desk and signaled for Luka to sit next to him. "Davit told me you are active in the art world."

"That's one way of putting it," Luka responded, his face remaining a mask of indifference.

Kadir leaned over his desk and picked up a newspaper resting atop a stack of coffee table books. He threw it onto Luka's lap. The headline on the English-language paper's front page read 'Brazen Art Theft in Luxembourg.' Photos of Vianden Castle and two painted landscapes were visible above the fold. "This is your work, isn't it?"

The Croatian's jaw tightened as he glanced over the article. "Yes, I organized this," he said, his tone defiant.

Kadir could imagine Luka was not pleased with their friend Davit right now. All successful criminal organizations relied on discretion, and Davit had broken the implied vow of silence by telling Kadir about Luka's line of business. "Frankly, if Davit had not told me about your work, you would not be here."

Luka glared at him then nodded slowly, his irritation dissipating as he accepted his friend's slip of the tongue.

Kadir gazed into his eyes, trying to decide what kind of soul this man possessed and if it was an honorable one. "I am a rich man with prestige, wealth, and a healthy family, yet my hunger for more is sometimes insatiable. I have no interest in working with new clients, but when Davit told me about your current line of business, I realized it was a sign. I can get you the product you desire if you help me realize my legacy. I want to create something wonderful for my children, something that will ensure my family name lives on."

The Croatian looked at him, fighting to keep his face neutral as his mind raced through the possibilities.

Kadir knew his heroin was top quality and available for a lower price than most of his competition. All Luka had to do was say yes. This desire to lay the foundation for his final legacy was gnawing at his soul. Kadir looked away from his guest, almost afraid Luka could sense his desperation.

For far too long, the Croatian remained silent, his eyes studying his host's face. Finally, to Kadir's immense relief, Luka said, "I am listening."

3 Balkan Bandits Strike Again!

August 13, 2018

'Balkan Bandits Strike Again!' screamed the headline of the *NRC Handelsblad*'s front page, now open on Zelda's computer screen. Ten minutes ago, she had finished fact-checking the biographies of Jackson Pollock, Jasper Johns, Franz Kline, and several more American modernists included on the Amstel Modern's website. It was her third read-through, but she wanted to make sure it was perfect before sending the updated texts to her boss. Even though she had always treated her unpaid internships as real jobs, being a paid employee did make her feel even more responsible for getting everything right—the first time. And her work as a collection assistant was both fulfilling and fun. Her coworkers were a blast, and the research, copywriting, and editing work was varied and interesting. She almost hoped the woman whose job she had temporarily taken over would decide not to return to work after her six-month sabbatical ended.

A glance at the clock reminded Zelda that her next meeting was about to start. She skimmed the newspaper open on her screen in the hope of learning more about the audacious robbery that had taken place in Luxembourg two nights earlier. So far, this lengthy article was a summary of what her coworkers had told her during this morning's coffee break.

"Once again, art thieves from the Balkans have pulled off a brazen heist. Late Saturday night, ten landscapes from the Dutch Royal collection were stolen from Vianden Castle in Luxembourg. The watercolors, painted by revered Belgium master Jean-Baptiste van der Hulst, were on display as part of a special exposition celebrating the castle's historic connection to the current Dutch royal family, members of the House of Orange-Nassau…"

Hoping to find new details to share during lunch, Zelda clicked on a television news report posted five minutes earlier. A Dutch news anchor for the *NOS Journaal* recounted the same details as the newspaper, adding, "Two eyewitnesses' statements were originally rejected by police based on the men's high blood-alcohol level. However, camera footage from the castle and local businesses confirm two paragliders jumped off the castle's uppermost balcony and glided to an awaiting getaway car further down the valley."

Geez, last month it was a speed boat and now hang gliders. It seems as if they are trying to score points for ingenuity, Zelda thought. Despite the horror she felt knowing that they were stealing irreplaceable cultural treasures, Zelda couldn't help but admire their audacity.

Still shots of Vianden Castle filled the screen as the newsreader informed viewers about its history and the exhibition currently taking place there. Zelda marveled at its location and architecture. With its turrets and high walls, it reminded her of Camelot, though this one was perched precariously on the tip of a rocky outcrop, high atop a forested ridge. The views from the balcony the thieves supposedly paraglided from made her queasy. It seemed to be suspended over the valley. When the image changed again, video footage from the exhibition's opening night showed viewers the high-profile guests in attendance—including several members of the Dutch and Luxembourgian royal families—all admiring the watercolors that were later stolen.

When the image switched to wide shots of the castle, the reporter said, "Although no suspects have been apprehended, the theft has all the characteristics of a criminal organization based in the Balkans. While several known rings of art thieves are active, the most well-known—the Balkan Bandits—have been evading international law enforcement agencies for the last ten years. Interpol estimates they have stolen four hundred million euros in jewels, antiques, and artwork from European cultural institutions, the vast majority of which has never been recovered. The organization's loosely associated network of freelance thieves spread across Europe makes it difficult for authorities to link members to specific criminal families. These gangs from the Balkans favor smaller, regional museums with less security…"

"Five minutes."

Zelda jerked her head up to find one of the marketing assistants standing in front of her desk. Absorbed in the news report, she hadn't even noticed the woman entering the room. Then again, she shared the space with three other coworkers and had learned not to be distracted every time someone walked in or out of the door. "I'll be right there."

The marketing assistant frowned when Zelda didn't spring out of her chair, but the assistant moved down the hallway just the same. Zelda heard the reporter saying "…as more international law enforcement agencies are able to show a direct connection between art thefts, drug smuggling, and arms dealing, calls for improving museum security are gaining hold in the European Union parliament. However, there is a concern at the national levels about their politicians' ability to secure the funding for such improvements or if sources in the private sector should be responsible for…"

Zelda knew that little would change despite these politicians posturing. As long as museums, orchestras, ballet companies, operas, and the like were considered elitist, gaining broad public support for increasing cultural subsidies would be almost impossible. Many museums were already reliant on private sponsors to fund exhibitions or the acquisition of new pieces for their permanent collections. How much more could they be expected to give? And even if the government coughed up a more significant percentage of the costs, how many museums could they afford to make theftproof realistically?

A few more coworkers rushed by her door, obviously on their way to the same project meeting where she was supposed to be. Zelda clicked her browser shut then gathered up her notebook and the folders containing the project timeline and exhibition plan. *Conversations with American Modernists* opens next week, and the entire museum was on edge. It was the first exhibition organized by their new director, Julie Merriweather, and Zelda knew it had to be perfect. For the past two weeks, Julie led daily project meetings to stay on top of any problems the exhibition team may come up against. Most were nothing more than a rehash of the previous day's rehash. Zelda didn't understand the point, but the new director insisted, and the exhibition was Julie's baby.

Despite her irritation with the meetings, Zelda was as excited as the rest to see works by Jackson Pollock, Jasper Johns, Cy Twombly, Alexander Calder, Lee Krasner, Hans Hofmann, Willem de Kooning, Robert Motherwell, Franz Kline, and Mark Rothko here in Amsterdam. Exhibitions of American modernists were rare in the Netherlands. Back home, Zelda had been spoilt. The Seattle Art Museum had a fine collection of modern and contemporary work, and she had visited it often.

That the Amstel Modern, a provincial museum in Amstelveen, had managed to secure works by prominent American artists for this exhibition had everything to do with their new director. Thanks to Julie, this exhibition would feature the most significant number of works by postwar American modernists ever shown in the Netherlands. She was known for having incredible contacts and a way of sweet-talking private collectors into lending out works they would typically never show to the public. She'd worked her magic again with this new exhibition. Five Jackson Pollocks, three Jasper Johns, and a Hans Hofmann were making their public debut in Amstelveen next week.

Born in London to American parents, Julie had worked on both sides of the Atlantic and was considered to be a rising star in the international art scene. As a former curator at Saatchi Gallery and Tate Modern in London, the Museum of Modern Art in New York and the Los Angeles Art Museum, everyone who mattered was astonished when she accepted the Amstel Modern's offer to become their new director. The museum world was abuzz with rumors—not all favorable—until the press discovered her husband had recently been named the director of the Goethe Museum in Dusseldorf. Amsterdam was a whole lot closer than Los Angeles.

The *Conversations with American Modernists* exhibition was Zelda's first project and a treat to work on. The era fascinated her as well as the selection of artwork, most of which she hadn't seen before. Due

11

to the demands of the insurance company, this exhibition was sketch-heavy. Julie did manage to secure eleven more well-known oil paintings worth a few million apiece, but that was as far as the exhibition's insurers would go. Zelda didn't care either way because the charcoals, line drawings, watercolors, and oil sketches were just as captivating as many of these painters' finished pieces. In many cases, they were more spontaneous and invigorating to look at than the final version of the same scene.

When Zelda saw the ad for this temporary position, she wasn't certain the Amstel Modern would be a good fit. The museum was established in 1972 by diamond trader Henrik Lomak to house his extensive collection of postmodern Dutch art, in particular his paintings and sculptures created by CoBrA artists. Other than Karel Appel, she knew little about CoBrA, an international avant-garde art movement founded by artists based in Copenhagen, Brussels, and Amsterdam that only officially existed between 1948 and 1951. Seeking to achieve direct and spontaneous expression, they were inspired by the creativity of children as well as folk and tribal art forms. The results were always colorful, often surreal and sometimes disturbing.

The position's title and responsibilities convinced her to apply. Not only would *collection researcher* look great on her résumé, but it would also keep her mind occupied while she waited for her master's thesis to be approved. Her university supervisor and the senior Oceania curator from the Tropenmuseum were reviewing her thesis now. They had another month to critique it as well as request any explanations about her sources or methodology. After they gave her their assessment, she would defend it publically before receiving her degree.

Writing her thesis about bis poles and the restitution of colonial-era objects had been therapeutic. She had been able to weave her experiences gained during her work for the *Bis Poles: Sculptures from the Rainforest* exhibition as well as the knowledge she gained during her investigation into Nick Mayfield's disappearance. It had been a turbulent year, one she would never forget. The Asmat and their art still fascinated her. But after a year of being occupied solely with ethnography and colonial history, she was glad for the change of pace the Amstel Modern and its postmodern collection provided.

To her delight, the role and artwork suited her. She was halfway through her six months. Zelda knew the museum's director was considering hiring another part-time researcher. Maybe she would apply for the job when this contract ended. However, once she had her master's degree, she would be able to apply for more senior positions instead of only the assistant roles. After three years of studying art history and museology, she was ready to graduate and start working her way toward her dream role of curator.

But until she had her master's degree in her hand, she was happy to be an assistant *anything*.

Zelda looked down at the exhibition timeline in her hand, wishing Jacob, her boyfriend of eighteen months, could attend the opening. Unfortunately, he would still be in Cologne next Thursday night. They could visit it together on the weekend, she knew, but it just wasn't the same as if he'd been able to be there. Truth be told, Zelda hated attending exhibition openings but knew her presence was required. She never knew who to talk to or what about. Most invitees were there to network with important friends, not look at the artwork on display or chat with museum assistants.

Esmee, Zelda's favorite of the three other collection researchers working on this exhibition, rushed into their shared office and began rummaging around her desk for a pen. "Come on, Zelda. You know how mad Julie gets when anyone's late," she chided.

It was never Mrs. Merriweather but Julie. The new director insisted everyone use her first name. In the Netherlands, using someone's first name was a privilege, not a given. Zelda had grown accustomed to Dutch formality and was irked her new boss was trying to integrate her American ways into their office. Zelda chuckled at the irony that after four years of living in Amsterdam, she was starting to feel more Dutch than American.

She joined Esmee and walked with her to the conference room. "I don't understand why we need to meet today," Zelda grumbled. "Didn't Julie approve the catalogs yesterday? Have you seen them? How do they look?"

"Yes, and they are spectacular. The depth of color is quite extraordinary. The last printer we used made everything look so washed out. I don't think Julie would have stood for it." Esmee was in awe of their new director who had become an instant role model for the young art historian.

"You're right. She is quite the perfectionist. But now that the catalogs are approved, I think we are completely on track for the opening. All the signs and text boards for the exhibition halls arrived last week. Marketing is taking care of the posters and flyers. The website will go live tomorrow. Every item on our list has been crossed off. What else can we do except wait for the paintings to arrive?"

"That's true. But you know Julie. She leaves nothing to chance. I can't say I blame her. It is her debut here and one of the biggest exhibitions the Amstel Modern has ever organized. I can imagine she's feeling a lot of pressure to succeed at the moment and wants to leave nothing to chance," Esmee responded quickly.

Zelda snorted. "What could possibly go wrong?"

4 A Golden Opportunity

August 16, 2018

Ivan Novak hummed *Eine kleine Nachtmusik* by Wolfgang Amadeus Mozart as he slowly flipped through the images on the screen, eyeing each critically. He'd started with a list of ninety potential targets but had eventually whittled it down to a more manageable number. His final selection of forty was a mix of modern and contemporary art by American and European artists. Most were sketches, watercolors, and pastels as the buyer had requested.

When he reached a sketch by Paul Cézanne, he stopped to admire the loose interpretation of a small mountain village, soaking up the simple lines and dramatic color choices. Cézanne was on the verge of discovering cubism, and his geometric renderings of the houses and mountains showed it. Ivan couldn't wait to hold this piece in his hands.

Compiling this list of artwork to steal was a pleasurable exercise of his research abilities, even under such a tight deadline. And the buyer's particularly stringent prerequisites meant he'd gotten a chance to reacquaint himself with the Dutch museum scene. In his older age, he preferred warmer climates and hadn't visited the country in a year.

Based on the auction sales and estimates of similar works, he calculated the total worth of his list to be 20.3 million euro. That gave him three hundred thousand in wriggle room in case the Turkish buyer got greedy and lowballed his estimates. He clicked quickly through the last of the images. His choices were exactly what the buyer asked for.

Luka's call earlier in the week had been an unpleasant surprise, to say the least. And one Ivan had ended abruptly. He'd listened

15

long enough to hear what the Croatian mobster wanted before hanging up on him. It had only taken a few minutes to realize that this was a golden opportunity, and one he could not pass up. Yet it took more than an hour to control his emotions enough to speak calmly and rationally to the man who had destroyed his life.

Most humans wouldn't dare dismiss or ignore Luka Antic—let alone wait an hour to call him back—but Ivan didn't care. *Let the bastard simmer with worry for a bit*, he thought and poured himself a double shot of vodka.

They were once best friends and business partners. Both came from the same small town in the Croatian mountains, yet their lives had taken drastically different turns after they left high school. Luka began working for his powerful family as was expected of him.

After earning degrees in art history and business management, Ivan opened his first art gallery in Split, Croatia's cultural capital. Business hadn't been great that first year until Luka made him a proposition he couldn't refuse. His childhood friend was responsible for overseeing the Antic family's increasingly lucrative art studios. Luka managed a team of artists who forged paintings stolen in Western Europe before both pieces were sold as the original to collectors on the opposite sides of the world.

The Antic crime family was expanding their operation into Western Europe, and Luka offered Ivan the chance to be a part of it. Ivan had said yes without hesitation. Five days later, he began creating paper trails and fake documents to support the forged artwork's fictitious provenance. Months later, he began selling work created by Luka's team of artists in his own gallery. With the help of Luka's family, Ivan was soon able to open galleries in Barcelona, Bern, Amsterdam, Venice, and Paris. The choice of locations was well suited to another task he took on for Luka's family, that of collection point for their thieves to drop off their ill-gotten goods. All he did was store the work while Luka took care of the transportation to and from his galleries.

What Luka's talented team forged, Ivan sold to an endless supply of louche collectors based around the world. Thanks to Luka's investments, he had expanded further. Nowadays, he had galleries in fifteen major European cities and a team of sales associates who represented hundreds of talented artists. He always felt like he was blessed. At least until that horrible day three short years ago when his beautiful daughter passed away.

Looking back now, he could still feel the greed that consumed him in his youth. How he regretted ever saying yes to Luka, stepping so happily into his family's criminal activities, never considering how his actions could affect his future. What a fool he had been. By saying yes, he had sealed his daughter's fate.

Ivan hadn't spoken civilly to Luka since Marjana's passing. He'd broken all contact the day after the funeral, and to his relief, Luka accepted it, allowing him to retreat out of criminal life without any further repercussions. To Ivan, his old friend's uncharacteristic display of sympathy confirmed Luka's guilt.

Since burying his daughter, Ivan had become a shell of a man, haunted by nightmares and consumed with a desire to get revenge. He had dreamt of this day for three years, and in that time, he'd imagined multiple scenarios and schemes but hadn't found a way to hurt Luka without putting himself in mortal danger. And now the object of his rage had presented him with the ultimate opportunity to do so. It was time to stop the nightmares and hurt the man who had destroyed his family.

When Ivan called Luka back, he drove his fingernails deep into his thigh to help keep his voice tempered. "Yes, I accept your challenge. Tell me again the names of the artists your buyer is interested in. Wait. Let me get a pen." A pen and notepad were already laid out before him. Just hearing Luka's raspy voice made his blood boil. Ivan put a hand over the receiver and breathed deeply, his heart racing as anger and sadness surged through his body. Simply speaking to this monster would take all of his self-control. When he was able, Ivan recorded the buyer's list of preferences then hung up.

It took him four days to compile this list of potential targets. He looked at the map of the Netherlands spread out on his dining room table. Red circles surrounded seventeen cities. With three teams, Ivan figured they should be able to complete the robberies within twenty-one days. That was ahead of Luka's already tight schedule and involved more risk, but it was the best way to complete the work he'd agreed to do for Luka as well as execute his own plan. His team would need that extra week. Now all he had to do was figure out a way to convince Luka that the timing, as Ivan had laid it out, was necessary.

But first, Ivan faced a daunting task—convincing his artists to work with him on this rather rushed and unusual assignment. Only then could he call Luka.

Not only did the Croatian crime boss ask him to compile a list of art to steal but he also wanted Ivan to arrange collection points for his thieves to drop off their loot. Instead of using his galleries, as he had done in the past, Ivan decided to use his own artists as the drop-off points. It would save time and keep more distance between his gallery in Amsterdam and the thefts. It would also simplify the execution of his plan.

Luka wanted the originals, and he would get them. But he didn't need to know about the second set Ivan would have created. Several of the artists his galleries represented had copied a piece of artwork for him in the past but never under such a tight deadline. Ivan hoped the extra cash incentive would be enough to help speed their efforts and get everything finished on time.

To assist his flock, he had already prepared packets about each piece, including information about the canvas size, frame, medium, general condition, and paints used. That would be enough to get them started. However, he knew from experience that nothing beat copying the real thing.

He opened one of the folders on his desk and quickly checked that all of the printouts and photos were inside. The Amstel Modern in Amstelveen was about to host an exhibition that was perfectly suited to his needs. For that job, he was planning to use his most experienced and trusted artist, a strong-willed and bad-tempered Croatian beauty named Gabriella Tamic, who happened to live in nearby Amsterdam. Now all he had to do was convince her to take on the assignment. If she agreed, the rest would easily follow suit.

5 A Job Proposal

August 16, 2018

Ivan rang the intercom to Postjesweg 1, apartment number seven. He smoothed back his long, gray hair, mentally running through his approach as he waited for Gabriella to answer. Seconds later, the speaker crackled to life.

"Yes?"

"It's Ivan."

"Come on up."

The door buzzed open. Ivan entered the expansive lobby of Het Sieraad and rode the elevator up to Gabriella's apartment. It shuddered slightly as it reached the top floor. The door at the end of the short hallway was already open, and the bitter scent of turpentine grew stronger as he approached her studio, one of three that he owned in this building.

Ivan had represented Gabriella since she graduated from the Royal Academy of Fine Arts in Antwerp four years ago. She was also from Split and the same age as his daughter Marjana. The girls had been best friends since they first met in primary school, and Ivan had followed Gabriella's evolution as an artist with interest. She was almost as talented as his daughter was. He was thrilled she agreed to let him represent her and promised her widowed mother that he would take good care of her.

Of his current flock of artists, Gabriella was the most profitable, and that was saying something. Last time he counted, his gallery represented three hundred artists residing in the fifteen European countries where his chain of modern and contemporary art galleries were located. This mix of old and new was the key to his galleries' successes, and one born out of necessity.

19

To meet the specific demands of his financial backers and keep all the galleries profitable, he had to get creative and carve out a unique niche. In contrast to most, his galleries showcased expensive masterpieces worth millions alongside works by emerging artists worth tens of thousands. Oddly enough, his unusual tactic worked, and the pieces spoke to each other thanks to his incredible eye and clever placement. To most of his competitors' surprise, his clients bought both kinds of works and proudly hung them in their residential museums-in-the-making. Now, instead of mocking his approach as amateurish, his fiercest critics copied him in style and selection.

Despite the number of galleries employing a similar approach, artists still flocked to him, knowing he was one of the few able to turn them into European stars. He went above and beyond most galleries by providing his artists with studio space, quality supplies, and the freedom to experiment. Being chosen by Ivan Novak was akin to being anointed by one of the gods of the art world.

Long ago, when Luka's crew of forgers became swamped with work, Luka had asked him if some of the more talented artists he represented could help out. At first, Ivan wasn't sure how to approach them or what their reaction might be, but to his surprise and delight, most were so hungry to get ahead they had no trouble completing the work, no questions asked. Especially when they were rewarded with a substantial bonus and a prime spot in one of his galleries.

The few who had refused to play along were quietly removed from his flock and warned never to say a word. And even if they did, he was one of the most successful and respected art dealers in Europe. It would be easy enough to portray them as an artist scorned. Thankfully, he'd yet to have to deal with such an incident.

In many ways, this new job was not unlike his past requests. The tricky part was the timing. His artists wouldn't have the originals in their possession for weeks, but days. And their versions would have to be collected shortly after. When selecting works to steal, the drying time had been a major factor. Ivan had purposely chosen sketch-like works that would not require several layers. He knew creating perfect copies would be simple enough for Gabriella and several others he represented, even within this tight timeframe.

"Gabriella, darling. It's wonderful to see you again."

The young artist pulled him in for a hug then kissed him on each cheek. Her short bob tickled his chin.

"You too, Ivan. It's been too long." She pushed him back, holding his shoulders tight, and eyed him critically.

He attempted a soft, fatherly grin, but it came out more of a grimace. Gabriella was looking at him like his daughter used to when she was worried he wasn't eating well.

Despite her obvious concern, she said, "You look good, much better than you did the last time you visited. The twinkle's back in your eye. What are you up to?"

Gabriella's brow furrowed as if she were trying to understand what could have changed his mood. From her expression, she clearly assumed it wasn't good. He had forgotten that it was no use lying to the girl because she was always able to see right through his lies. But that wasn't why he had avoided Gabriella. When he looked at this vibrant young woman, he saw his daughter—the same talent, self-assuredness, charisma, and passion for life. He saw what should have been, and it broke his heart to be around her for long.

Ivan shrugged as he forced himself to smile. "I've embarked on a new project, and I guess it suits me."

Gabriella finally released his shoulders then plopped onto her overstuffed couch. She patted the space next to her. "Why don't you tell me more about it."

Ivan slowly lowered his old bones onto the soft upholstery and pulled a folder out of his briefcase.

"I have been asked to arrange something extraordinary. However, it is quite a large project, and I need the help of several artists. If you choose to work on it, you must understand that it will demand all of your technical prowess, but you will be highly rewarded for your efforts. Even more than usual." Gabriella was unique in that she could paint convincingly and rapidly in any style. She could easily complete this task if she agreed to do so.

The young woman's eyes widened. "Oh, that's generous! I'm all ears. Ever since my neighbor flew to Indonesia, I can't stop thinking about studying abroad. I've got my eye on a three-month residency in Tahiti. A cash injection is just what I need." She tucked one leg up under the other and leaned forward.

Ivan opened the folder and handed her the four full-color images on top.

She grabbed them greedily, though her enthusiasm quickly faded once her eyes took them in. "Okay, nice sketches. Alexander Calder painted quite a few of these studies, and Franz Kline made a lot of sketches like this one. Hans Hofmann is one of my favorites; his use of color is extraordinary. This Pollock is lovely. You don't see his early drip paintings often in Europe. I take it you need a copy?"

Gabriella was a long-time forger and knew the copies she made for him were sold at a significant profit to gullible buyers. After Marjana's death and his break with Luka, he had resorted to selling forgeries more frequently to keep his galleries profitable. In the beginning, he'd tried to fool her by saying the copies were for clients who couldn't afford the real thing. Unlike the others he represented, Gabriella wasn't content with this obvious lie. If she weren't so talented and hadn't been his daughter's best friend, he probably would have cut her loose after the first round of questioning. Instead, he'd chosen to trust her.

"This assignment is a bit different than the rest. These copies have to be perfect in every way, preferably museum quality."

With the enthusiasm of the young, the artist didn't cringe or become wary but snickered. "You know my work is always perfect."

"Yes, of course," he soothed. "But this time, your copy needs to fool an expert. At least, at first glance. These clients are more, let's say, upscale than usual. More risk means more reward for us both."

Gabriella opened her mouth to respond when Ivan added, "The trouble is, you will only have a few days to complete them."

The artist cocked her head and frowned. "Umm, I've never seen these pieces before. And while your printouts are a good starting point, there's not enough detail here to copy them precisely. Where are the paintings now? In one of your other galleries? Or still with the owner?"

"They will be on display in the Amstel Modern next Friday as part of a special exhibition of American modernists. I'm fairly certain the museum's security will let you sketch with pencils in the hall. At least, they usually do." Ivan held his breath, hoping Gabriella wouldn't bail out now.

Instead, she arched her eyebrows, the first indication she understood there was something different about this job. "What do you mean?"

"A mutual friend wants to remove them from the Amstel Modern. I am arranging the drop-off points for him. I hoped you would agree to be one of them. I need a copy made of all four. I'll let you decide which ones you want to work on. You'll have one to two weeks, at most, to copy them. I was planning to ask Anthony to help you." Ivan rushed his words, praying she would agree to help him. Otherwise, it was going to be nearly impossible to convince the others to take this big of a risk.

Gabriella's face grew increasing ashen as he spoke. "You don't mean Luka Antic, do you?" Her voice was a whisper.

"Yes, I do."

Gabriella's body trembled. "Why would you agree to work with that monster again?"

Her outburst reminded Ivan of his youth when the world was still black and white. The shades of gray would come later. "Can we ever say no?"

"Yes, you can! You broke free from all of that. Why would you agree to help him with anything?"

Ivan wanted to grab her and hug her tight, to protect her from the cruel reality of their world. He longed to tell her the truth but knew it was far too risky. No one could know what he was planning. Luka had eyes and ears everywhere. Instead of baring his soul, he sighed.

"I have my reasons. It's a simple job, and we will be well paid for it. Luka wants me to arrange drop-off points for a series of robberies. As far as he is concerned, you are nothing more than an address. It is my responsibility to get the artwork to him shortly after it is delivered to you. You won't have any contact with him. He won't know about the copies you will then make, nor does he need to.

23

They are for me. I can turn two profits from one robbery and help you get to Tahiti. The only problem is a tight deadline. That's why I need my best artists to help me."

"Even after everything that happened with Marjana?" Gabriella asked, tears forming in her eyes.

He frowned. She hadn't been listening to him. Ivan wondered if she was overwhelmed by anger, sadness, or fear. *Probably all three*, he thought. Ivan knew Gabriella was no stranger to organized crime or the ensuing violence. Her father was killed by a prominent Croatian mafia family when she was fourteen years old. Soon after, her mother had immigrated to Luxembourg to get Gabriella away from that life.

Ivan always suspected Marjana had told Gabriella who Luka really was and what she did for him despite being repeatedly warned never to tell a soul. It was only natural. He could imagine Marjana had needed someone to confide in, especially when she was older and her talents made her Luka's prisoner. Did Gabriella also know about his role in Marjana's demise?

"Gabriella, he's unintentionally providing me with a way of building up my pension. I'm not getting any younger, and the galleries eat up most of the cash that comes in."

"Be careful, Ivan. You know as well as I do that you don't want to cross men like him."

"He wants the originals, and he'll get them. What's the problem?"

Gabriella stared at him then started to laugh, a sinister bray that sent chills up his spine. "Are you serious?"

"This is a chance of a lifetime. I cannot say no. And I don't want to." He gathered up the photographs and began placing everything back into the folder. "This job needs to be as perfect as possible, which means I need your help. I'll get you the special brushes and paints that you'll need. If you want to use ovens to dry the layers faster or age the canvas, just let me know. I can arrange one to be brought here or move you to a larger studio with one already in it. I'll let you decide."

Gabriella searched his face as if she expected to find answers in his wrinkled skin for his seemingly rash and unwise decision.

"Once the art is delivered, you will have about a week to finish your copies before I pick up the originals. I will take care of any transport issues. All you have to do is buzz the robbers into your lobby and collect the artwork. As far as anyone else is concerned, they are artist friends delivering a few pieces for an upcoming show. That happens all the time, so no one will look at any of you twice."

"And you think Luka will let you do this because?" Gabriella stared at him.

"What he doesn't know won't hurt him."

"But he may hurt me. And he has a habit of finding things out." Her words carried more weight than they should have. Marjana couldn't get away from Luka despite her immaculate planning. There was no shortage of those willing to rat out another to improve their lot in life.

"He won't hurt you. I will make sure of it." His voice broke as his words sunk in. He couldn't protect his daughter from the Croatian's wrath, and they both knew it.

"But he'll know where I live."

"You're going to Tahiti in a few weeks, right?" Ivan smiled, trying to lighten the mood. Gabriella's somber expression made it clear his efforts were not appreciated. "His team will have your address and a code name. Your only contact with them will be via a disposable phone, one that I will provide, which should be destroyed as soon as the artwork is delivered. Luka will never know that you live here, Gabriella. He'll never know your real name. Once Luka gets his paintings, he'll forget you ever existed."

Gabriella's terse lips told him she wasn't convinced.

"If you want, I'll move you to another studio, a bigger one in another city. Just say the word. But really, we're not in Croatia, and things are different here." Even to his ears, his excuse sounded lame. Of course, there were no land boundaries that could stop a force of nature such as Luka Antic. The man had a sixth sense for betrayal, and his organization had tentacles everywhere in Europe.

Gabriella remained silent, clearly still contemplating his proposal.

"I have chosen smaller pieces that are easy to carry and

25

transport," Ivan pushed on. "The thieves will receive instructions to pack them up so the images aren't visible just in case one of your neighbors stops to chat before you can get them upstairs. No one will be the wiser." He tried to say it casually so as not to upset her. "I'll come by the next day and take whichever pieces you won't have time to copy to Anthony so that we can meet our deadline. You get first choice."

"The most difficult, of course." Gabriella folded her arms over her chest and stuck out her lip.

Ivan smiled. Even fear couldn't temper her youthful arrogance. "Good. Sure. I'll let you choose. It sounds like we've got this all worked out then. Right?"

Gabriella's face was awash with emotions. "Would you have asked your daughter to do this? To work with Luka's men?" she asked, her voice quiet.

Ivan looked stricken. He lay one hand on Gabriella's arm. "Oh, yes. Marjana would approve of my plan. I assure you."

Gabriella gazed deeply into his eyes then took his hands in hers.

"Okay, I'll do it. I trust you implicitly, Ivan."

6 Sleepless Nights

August 17, 2018

Zelda slapped her alarm clock, silencing the incessant beeping for the third time. Rubbing at her eyes, she yawned deeply, sucking in enough warm air to energize her lungs. She'd slept poorly and couldn't quite get her eyes to open fully.

She stretched out on her bed, staring out at the blue skies above. The skylights running the length of the apartment were her favorite feature of this top-floor studio. They even opened, which was a great way to ventilate the strong chemical smells that often leaked into her apartment. Most of her neighbors were oil or acrylic painters and tended to leave their doors open to air their spaces out while they worked, meaning the hallway often reeked.

The only downside of leaving the skylights open was the noise. Depending on where Zelda was standing, it sometimes sounded as if strangers were inside her apartment. The sound was amplified when Zelda lay in her bed, which was built on a makeshift loft only a few feet away from the open skylight. Luckily, Zelda's apartment was at the end of the hallway, meaning she only had one direct neighbor to contend with—a young Croatian painter named Gabriella.

Zelda didn't know what to make of Gabriella when she first met her. It was obvious the girl was talented, but she was so distant that Zelda didn't think they would get along, yet time had proven her wrong. Once she'd broken through Gabriella's icy reserve, Zelda discovered that the twenty-four-year-old was an incredibly warm and generous person, which made it impossible for her to complain about Gabriella's night owl behavior. She knew from her own experience what a wonderful feeling it was when creativity flowed through her veins. It was only too bad her neighbor's happened mostly at night. The fact she also often had friends over didn't help matters.

Jacob was less enamored with Gabriella's odd hours and the constant stream of visitors. Just thinking about her boyfriend soured Zelda's thoughts. His opinion about their living space was of minor importance. He was in Germany most of the time anyway and only returned home every other weekend.

When Jacob told her he had finally found a full-time research position, she was thrilled even after she found out it was at an ethnographic museum in Cologne and for a year. It was an impressive institution with a long history and varied collection, and Zelda was pleased for him. He had been looking for work for months but hadn't made it past the first round of interviews. There was a glut of qualified researchers all fighting for a tiny number of available positions in the Netherlands. She knew he had recently begun looking and applying for jobs in Germany, Belgium, and France, so his news shouldn't have come as a shock.

She couldn't help being upset that he had said yes before telling her about it. Cologne was a three-hour train ride away, meaning they would effectively be living apart for a year. They had only been dating for sixteen months, and, at first, Zelda didn't know what the distance would do to their relationship, which made Jacob's proposal to move in together even more confusing. There was no reason for him to rent another apartment if he was going to be in Amsterdam only for a few days a month, he reasoned. Zelda agreed wholeheartedly, especially when he offered to help pay part of the rent. The studio she was now residing in was more expensive than she'd planned.

She had been on the hunt for a new place for months and told anyone who would listen that she was looking. When a fellow student's sister won a grant to study in Indonesia, he asked Zelda if she would be interested in subletting her studio for a year. She had jumped at the chance, sight unseen.

Because Jacob was so rarely home, Zelda didn't think he had the right to criticize her neighbor's lifestyle, and she refused to look for another place to live. Neither the chemicals, noises, nor Jacob's disapproval would drive her away. She felt lucky to have found it even if it was only for a year. There was something quite exhilarating about living in an artist's colony.

Her new neighborhood, de Baarsjes, was quiet though petty theft was a problem. An intercom system in her building kept most of the riffraff out. The imposing five-story, red-brick structure was originally built as a trade school. The lower floors were transformed into office spaces for cultural start-ups, and the top floor was converted into studios where artists were welcome to live and create. The woman Zelda was renting from built a small loft in one corner for her twin bed and dresser, reachable with a wooden ladder. Underneath was a tiny kitchen, toilet, and shower. The rest of the space she used as her studio.

The best feature of her new home was the creative vibe. It was almost palpable. Since moving in, Zelda had even taken up working with stained glass again. When she worked at Microsoft, cutting glass and soldering it into colorful objects was her relaxation therapy after long days of staring at the computer screen. The calm, meditative effect of carefully executing steps and following patterns was refreshing after dealing with the chaos of multimedia development, project team meetings, and the like. She was so glad she had given up her old profession to come and study art history here in Amsterdam. Despite some of the more hair-raising moments, her quality of life had improved dramatically since.

When Gabriella saw one of Zelda's abstract windows, she asked to borrow it, claiming it inspired her. Considering how talented she was, Zelda consented without question. A week later, Gabriella returned it. The subtle shading and soft forms she'd added to Zelda's hard edges elevated the window's beauty. It almost looked like a woman in a long dress was reaching up to a glowing sun instead of a random mishmash of shapes and colors. Since then, they'd collaborated on four more pieces. Gabriella had even asked if they could create a few to sell in her next gallery show. Zelda attended her last opening and was impressed by how expensive her paintings were and how many had already sold. She was so flattered by Gabriella's suggestion that she immediately began drawing up a series of ten new windows, all abstract yet complementary to each other in shape and style, which made her sleepless nights *her*—not Gabriella's—problem.

No one else on my floor complained about the noise, so why should I, Zelda thought. She'd even told Jacob that the last time he grumbled about it. Last night, he would have blown a fuse if he'd been here. Gabriella was up partying with friends until four in the morning. The way they were drinking and joking around meant they were clearly celebrating something big. All Zelda could understand clearly was Tahiti. The rest was a drunken jumble.

Zelda was a bit miffed that she had not been invited to the party, but Gabriella knew that she had to get up early for work. She wondered if the party was because her neighbor had scored an international fellowship. It seemed to be the strive for most of the artists in the building. Before she could think up other options, her alarm clock began beeping again. She slowly rose out of bed and shuffled to the shower, hoping the warm water would help wake her up faster. She would need her wits about her at work. She loved her current job at the Amstel Modern, but the mounting pressure of the upcoming exhibition was too much for some of her coworkers who became irritated with the slightest problem or delay. It took all of her energy to remain cheery and not snap back.

Only five more workdays until the official opening then everything will be back to normal, she told herself, then stepped into the soft spray.

7 Time to Get Robbing

August 17, 2018

"Hello, Ivan. How is your assignment working out? All is going well, I hope?" Luka Antic asked. He despised the pleading tone in his voice, but he had been anxiously awaiting this call from Ivan Novak. The future of his deal with Kadir Tekin depended on the art dealer's answer. If Ivan couldn't do what he'd asked, Luka would be forced to find another project manager for this job, and right now, he couldn't think of anyone more qualified to complete the tasks he'd laid out faster than Ivan could.

There was so much riding on this job. Without the artwork, Kadir wouldn't work with him. He had already presold most of the hundred kilos he had ordered. The men he had made promises to were not the sort you wanted to disappoint. The clock was ticking, and it was time to get robbing.

Ivan cleared his throat, breaking Luka's train of thought. "Yes, I've finished my tasks. The locations and contact information your teams will need are in your email. I've grouped the thefts geographically. I figure you'll need three teams to be the most efficient. You will also find the appraisals I used to estimate the works' value. No doubt your client will require that."

Luka walked to his desktop computer and opened his inbox. Ivan's list included several locations he'd never heard of, but the artwork was exactly what he was looking for. Relief washed over him. Despite the extra challenges inherent to working with Ivan, the art dealer was definitely the right man for the job.

"My team will expect to be contacted via SMS when a delivery is imminent. They will be on call for the next three weeks. The order of locations is up to you."

Luka examined the map of the Netherlands Ivan had sent him. Red, yellow, and blue circles were around seventeen cities. It took a moment for the art dealer's words to register.

"Three weeks? You have five to complete this assignment. Why rush things?"

"I have a plan." Ivan's voice remained calm.

Luka could feel his blood starting to boil. "What do you mean *you* have a plan? I told you what the plan was already. Have you changed something without consulting me?"

"No, just adjusted the timing."

"Why?"

Ivan's voice remained neutral. "Two reasons. Firstly, your client's wish list is quite specific. If anything goes wrong with one of the heists, I'll have time to locate a suitable alternative. Secondly, the number of pieces you require means this assignment will bring a substantial amount of attention to your teams and my associates. Whether it happens in three weeks or five, the fact is, the longer we wait to finish the job, the greater the chance security will be improved—at least temporarily—and possibly thwart our effects."

Luka knew he was right. Most art crimes happened under the radar, and the victimized museums usually refused to release information to the media because they didn't want the general public to know they'd been robbed or how. This time, the museums involved wouldn't be able to hide so many thefts from the media. And if the institutions on Ivan's list increased their security, his teams may not be able to complete their assignments on time. And that was the last thing Luka wanted to happen.

"The police will be expecting someone to claim the robberies and demand a ransom," Ivan explained. "If no organization claims the thefts, the police will probably assume criminal organizations are somehow involved. We don't want special teams of investigators on our tail before we have a chance to finish the job. I have thought up a way to divert the attention of the police, media, and the general public. It is of crucial importance that the Robber Hood cards get delivered—no matter how ridiculous you think they are." Ivan's tone made clear there was no room for questioning.

Fear gripped Luka. He didn't like conditions of any kind. "Robber Hood cards? What is this nonsense?"

"I have mailed you a package, which you should receive later today. Once you do, my plan will become crystal clear. Inside, you will find seventeen cards labeled with sticky notes indicating where each should be delivered. It is imperative they are left behind at every robbery."

Luka bit his tongue. He hated that the dealer had thought out the police's response better than he had. Stealing so many pieces in such a short amount of time was new territory for him. He was used to pilfering artwork, forging it, and then finding a suitable buyer for both the real painting and the copy a few months later. His team of forgers and art dealers worked like a well-oiled machine. But now he was stealing a specific list of work for his buyer. The reversal in order was making him nervous and edgy. It also made him completely reliant on the art dealer—at least until this job was complete. Luka hated to be dependent on anyone.

"Okay, I'll do as you ask." Luka hung up as soon as the words were out of his mouth. That simple gesture lessened his feeling of being emasculated, ever so slightly.

8 Late Night Visit to Museum Friesland

August 21, 2018

Tomislav and Sebastijan had plenty of time to get to know each other and discuss their preferred work methods during the long drive through Southern and Central Europe. Tomislav always found it important to discuss such things before working with someone knew. It saved time, and sometimes lives, knowing how his teammate thought.

The two thieves had arrived in Drachten a day earlier. It gave them just enough time to make a quick visit to their first target and buy the supplies they needed to get the job done.

Before they left Split, Luka Antic called a meeting of six thieves in his employ. He divided them into teams of two then gave Tomislav and his partner a map with six locations in the Northern Netherlands and a list of specific targets displayed in each. Luka didn't need to remind them not to deviate from it. They knew how important it was to follow his instructions implicitly, that their futures within the organization depended on it, which made not reacting to the extra instructions even more difficult. Luka had also given each team an envelope full of cards, one of which was to be left behind at each location they robbed. Tomislav accepted the envelope without a word, making sure his face remained neutral as he read through the strange set of instructions. Team Will? Robber Hood? He didn't know what Luka was playing at, but he wasn't paid to think.

Another worrying aspect of this job was the breadth. Luka only made each of the teams aware of the other's presence because this 'project'—as Luka called it—had to be completed within a short period. If any of the teams needed an extra set of hands, they could request assistance by contacting Ivan, their team leader. Tomislav didn't know what this Ivan's last name was or what he did for a living, only that he was their contact on this job. After that initial meeting, it was the intention that the teams never contact each other directly.

But right now, none of that mattered. Ivan and Sebastijan were about to break into their first museum. He had to forget his nagging reservations and concentrate on getting tonight right.

They were able to conduct basic research about all six targets on the drive over. Per usual, they had free rein when deciding the order and timing. The internet, and in particular Google Maps, was a godsend. They could explore the landscape and terrain with the satellite view, allowing them to get a feel for the location.

Still, nothing beat walking around the grounds and through the hallways before embarking on a job. Only then could they see where the cameras were placed and pointed as well as the location of emergency exits and offices.

They chose Museum Friesland in Drachten as their first target because it sat in a large field that bordered a hundred-acre nature reserve. It seemed to be the easiest to break into. At least it did when they viewed the six museums' locations on the internet.

When they visited, they realized that visitors had to follow a single-lane road, which wound its way through a patchwork of protected wetlands to reach the museum. There was not a tree in sight. High winds whipped through the long grass lining the many waterways draining the landscape, flattening it as it crossed the vast open fields. After the robbery, they would be sitting ducks.

Yet once they had a chance to walk some of the trails crisscrossing the fields and test the peaty soil's density, they quickly realized a heavy-duty 4x4 truck would be more than capable of crossing the fields and could thus bypass the twists and turns any responding police cars would be forced to follow. With a well-placed second car, they could leave the 4x4 behind in a residential neighborhood and be heading in the other direction before the police could reach the museum.

Tomislav and Sebastijan had spent the morning getting their

supplies together and stealing the proper vehicles. It was now one in the morning, and the two men stood outside the museum's darkened entrance. The museum's only security guard had left hours ago. They had slowly driven their 4x4 with the lights off over the unlit road, taking care not to drop into one of the many small channels funneling water off the peaty soil. Sebastijan parked as close to the museum's entrance as he dared. They didn't know how far the cameras could see into the parking lot or if a security guard was actually watching the video feed.

They stepped out of the truck, tool bags in hand, and walked quickly across the stone bridge leading to the main entrance. Moonlight reflected off a small pond in front of the museum, lighting up three swans floating in the water. Tomislav tensed up, expecting them to honk before remembering they were lifelike statues created to move with the wind.

Once they reached the main entrance, Tomislav was aware that the cameras now pointed at them. Both men pushed buttons on their watches, starting timers. They figured they had ten minutes to work undisturbed before they should leave the scene. It would take the police at least that long to reach the museum's remote location, probably much longer, but in reality, they hoped to be out in five. Both men preferred to play it safe whenever possible.

Sebastijan quickly picked the lock then held it open for his partner-in-crime. Tomislav recalled that this first door brought them into a central space housing a small café and reading area that overlooked the small pool. On either side of the café were exhibition halls, one for the permanent collection and one for the temporary exhibitions. Sebastijan used the same method to enter the museum's right wing. According to the introductory text, the exhibition showcased a successful businessman's private collection of postwar and contemporary Dutch artwork.

Both thieves had already memorized their shopping list, but Tomislav pulled it out again. Before he cut the wire holding each piece to the wall, he double-checked the titles to ensure they grabbed the correct ones. He wasn't an art lover and couldn't tell the difference between a Robert Zandvliet, Piet Mondriaan, Leo Gestel, or Jan Schoonhoven let alone two pieces by the same artist. Once he'd freed the two sketches on his list, he helped Sebastijan pack them into the padded canvas bags they'd brought along.

According to his watch, they had been inside for almost six minutes. He'd wasted time by checking the names. For this job, it didn't matter, but he would have to memorize the names of the paintings next time. The other locations weren't nearly so remote.

They began to walk back to the front door when Tomislav stopped and spun on his heels, racing back to the exhibition hall they'd just plundered. He pulled out a Robber Hood card and set it in front of the spot the Zandvliet had been hanging in.

He sprinted back to Sebastijan, who glared at him with a questioning look on his face but didn't say anything. The men raced to the 4x4 truck. Sebastijan started the engine while Tomislav secured the artwork in the back. As soon as his door closed, Sebastijan flipped on the floodlights and went off-road. They bounced their way across the fields, scaring many birds in the process. Tomislav turned on the radio scanner he'd picked up yesterday, listening in to the police's response. Only after they'd crossed through the fields and reached their second vehicle did the first police car arrive at Museum Friesland.

9 One Down, Sixteen to Go

August 21, 2018

"It's here. Both pieces arrived safely," Suzanne said.

Ivan murmured his approval, yet internally, he was jumping with joy. One down, sixteen more to go. Ivan wiped the sweat off his forehead. *It must be my age,* he thought. His heart had been racing since the robberies started, and while he usually felt a rush of adrenaline followed by a wave of relief whenever the sale of a forgery went off without a hitch, this was much more intense. As far as he could remember, he'd never been so nervous about a job before. Then again, there was so much more riding on this project than a bit of cash.

He glanced at one of several photos of his daughter, laughing and carefree as every teenager should be. Ivan wiped away a tear, telling himself to get it together. He had to stay strong and focused for Marjana, his little princess.

Suzanne remained silent, waiting for him to respond.

He wanted to ask if she was calling from the disposable phone he'd given her but knew she was a consummate professional. Instead, he said, "Excellent news. Thank you," then hung up without waiting for her to respond.

There was no going back now, he realized, not that he would have wanted to. This was his chance to bring down Luka Antic's empire. With a little luck, his actions would also get the crime boss killed. Ivan reveled in the thought. Would the mobster's death set him free from the pain and sorrow that had engulfed him since learning his daughter had passed? How he regretted the day he had suggested Marjana to Luka. Damn his fatherly pride!

Ivan smashed his fist onto his hotel room's chair, bruising his knuckles in the process. What could have been haunted him daily, but it was too soon to dwell on the future and what might be. He shouldn't get ahead of himself. They still had sixteen more robberies to pull off and a total of forty paintings to forge. So much could still go wrong, and it was early days.

He contemplated how long it would take Suzanne to copy the sketches by Robert Zandvliet and Jan Schoonhoven, mentally running through the various processes she would use to age the paper and final product. Suzanne wasn't nearly as fast as his daughter had been, but she was good enough. And she knew how to get in touch with him if she needed any extra equipment or assistance. He had to be patient and not pressure her to work faster. That was how mistakes happened. Instead, he pushed the copies out of his mind and mentally prepared himself for his next task.

It was time to call Luka and tell him the good news.

10 Conversations with American Modernists

August 23, 2018

Zelda walked around the Amstel Modern, her feet barely touching the floor. The *Conversations with American Modernists* opening party was in full swing and quite busy.

She squeezed around a couple debating the merits of Karel Appel's later works to get closer to one of her favorite paintings by Jasper Johns. This later version of his iconic *Flag* was a small sketch-like image painted in green and black stripes with stars floating on a field of orange. Johns had worked so quickly that the canvas was still visible in places. Next to it hung a colorful and dreamlike work by the Danish painter, Asper Jorn. The square oil painting was almost as tall as her five-foot, ten-inch frame and was saturated in thick layers of color. The contrast between the two—reserved and linear versus explosively expressive—worked well, elevating both pieces. It did indeed seem as if the two artists were chatting with each other about the use of color or the lack thereof.

She turned to her left where an oil painting by Eugene Brands hung next to a sketch by Hans Hoffmann. Brands' wispy clouds reminded Zelda of a softer version of Hoffmann's harder, edgier composition, rendered with the same vibrant intensity. The simultaneous contrast—what Hofmann called 'push and pull'—of complementary colors side by side made the squares and rectangles dance on the canvas.

Up ahead was a Franz Kline paired with an Armando, both large canvases filled with bold, sweeping strokes of black and white. Close by hung a Cy Twombly. His canvas was filled with colorful, otherworldly scribbles hidden under a fog of white and gray. The way it was positioned next to Corneille's bold colors and childish shapes, it appeared as if the mist on Twombly's canvas had dissipated, and the images underneath had been captured by the Dutch painter.

In the center of the hall hung an early drip painting by Jackson Pollock next to a disturbing, surreal painting by Lucebert. The Dutch artist's canvas was a mess of linear scratches and slices of color breaking through a field of black. Paired together, the Lucebert looked like a linear version of Pollock's chaotic work.

Zelda was thrilled to see pieces by these American masters hanging next to works by their Cobra counterparts. Their similar yet different styles of expression, as well as their use of color and form, exhilarated her.

She wandered among the guests attending tonight's official opening party, feeling invisible. Most were already laughing a bit too gregariously, a reminder that booze had been flowing freely all night. And why shouldn't they celebrate? The exhibition's opening was a resounding success. Perhaps more importantly, it was also a chance for these museum professionals and the cultural elite to forget about the spate of robberies. Two Dutch museums had been hit in three days, and everyone had the feeling they could be next.

From afar, she observed the Amstel Modern's curatorial staff, marketing team, and director standing in the center of the exhibition hall, ringed by the most important people in the Dutch cultural scene. All had wide smiles plastered on their faces as guests greeted and congratulated them. Considering this was the first time so many American modernists were being shown in the Netherlands, the exhibition was almost guaranteed to be a success. The number of reporters from newspapers and television stations around the world was a testament to that.

In one corner, a small group of directors from other regional museums were huddled together with their heads close, all glaring critically at a wall full of drawings made by American and Dutch abstract expressionists. Their haughty facial expressions were a combination of envy and contempt.

Zelda slowly walked to the bar all the while observing the who's who of the Netherlands social and cultural elite. She had no idea so many actors, writers, dancers, and television personalities would want to attend. Most stood clustered together in small groups, chatting away and only occasionally glancing at a painting or, at least, the majority of guests.

She'd almost reached the bar when she noticed two men in the crowd who seemed to be interested in the artwork—extremely so. Their ill-fitting suits and weathered faces stood out among the perfectly coifed and dressed cultural elite circling the room. She watched as the two men moved through the hall, chatting animatedly about the color and design of each painting, sketch, and watercolor before moving to the next. Her curiosity piqued, Zelda walked closer to them so she could hear what interested them so much. She had taken a few steps toward them when she noticed how the chubby one smiled at a hostess passing out the champagne. It made Zelda shiver. She veered away and headed for the crowded bar instead.

A tall man in an expensive suit pushed his body a bit too close to Zelda's as he squeezed past her. His lecherous smile made her tug at her dress's hemline, ensuring it hadn't slid up again. She was already feeling uncomfortable in this too-short green dress and chastised herself again for not wearing opaque tights under it instead of pantyhose. Her new stiletto heels were killing her feet, and she felt like she could topple over any second. Luckily, she was able to wrestle her long hair into a tight bun, which made her feel sophisticated enough to be here.

Zelda ordered a red wine then wandered through the crowd again, recognizing several highly-placed coworkers who pretended not to notice her. As a lowly assistant, she was not a desirable conversation partner, at least from a networking perspective. She couldn't blame them for ignoring her because tonight was about being seen with the right people. A bright flash on her left made Zelda blink. A professional photographer snapped a shot of the marketing director with her arm swung over the shoulders of a famous Dutch television presenter, their loopy grins perfect for Instagram. A lucky few would make it into the online media's society pages, important blogs, and social media channels as well as traditional newspapers.

She was almost at the back of the exhibition hall when she spotted several fellow collection researchers and marketing assistants huddled together, looking as uncomfortable as she was. She waved, and Esmee made a beeline for her.

"Phew, it's busy tonight," Zelda said.

"Yeah, it looks like everyone who was invited showed up this time." Esmee's words were a bit slurred. Zelda wondered how many spritzers she'd already had.

"Do you think it will be a blockbuster?" Zelda asked, knowing the museum always had a target number of visitors in mind that, when reached, meant the exhibition had made back its costs.

"I sure do. Look at the turnout! Nora from marketing said the opening is going to be splashed all over the Dutch media tomorrow, as well as several other countries. That's never happened before. I hope we have enough capacity. I can already imagine lines of visitors snaking out into the square." Her eyes twinkled with glee.

"That would be pretty cool," Zelda responded, feeling her joy intensify as she thought about all those visitors reading her texts and learning from her research.

"The only thing that could stop us now would be if the place burned down," Esmee said. As soon as the words were out, she turned pale. "God, that's a horrid thought. Time for another spritzer. Do you want one?"

"Sure, thanks." As she watched her friend saunter away, wobbling only slightly on her stiletto heels, Zelda couldn't shake the feeling that this exhibition wasn't going to work out as everyone hoped.

11 Opening Night

August 23, 2018

Marko and Rikard sipped their free cocktails, taking in the busy opening night. Marko's fake beard itched, and the fat pads that covered his skinny frame were making him sweat. He glanced over the *Conversations with American Modernists* flyer again before pocketing it. Despite his discomfort, he was grateful Ivan Novak managed to secure them invitations to this exclusive event. They didn't have much time to plan and needed this opportunity to study the museum's layout and artworks' location.

Rikard nudged his side, drawing his attention to a blond, middle-aged man standing a few feet away. Marko's eyes widened as he realized it was private investigator Vincent de Graaf chatting with one of the Amstel Modern's curators. Thankful for his disguise, Marko swiftly changed direction and followed Rikard away from de Graaf and toward the bar. The detective had investigated several thefts that both Marko and his uncle Luka were involved with, but in every case, they had managed to slip through de Graaf's fingers—along with the artwork they had stolen. The Antics were almost solely responsible for blemishing de Graaf's otherwise spotless record, so Vincent would surely recognize him despite the beard and fat suit.

As they moved through the crowd, Marko noticed a younger woman in a green dress and stiletto heels. She didn't appear to be one of the invited guests; she was too young and nervous to be someone of significance. His gaze was drawn to her hemline, which barely reached her mid-thigh. The dress seemed to be meant for a shorter woman, though it did show off her long legs. *Too bad her hair was tied back in a librarian's bun*, Marko thought. *She might be stunning if she let it loose.* He looked down at his pudgy body and stopped criticizing.

He watched as she made her way to a group of shabbily dressed younger people, giddy with alcohol, hanging out at the back. *They must all work for the Amstel Modern*, he thought. They all seemed to be happily observing the party yet not really a part of it. None were important enough for the invitees to want to interact with.

He and Rikard had already walked around the exhibition hall twice and had inspected the artwork as well as the windows and doors for security tape or other triggers. They would have to case out the museum tonight and see when the security guards left and if a night shift replaced them.

The staff offices adjoined the exhibition hall, but the door was only accessible by key card. Marko realized they might need to sweet-talk one of the museum's staff members to find out if a security guard was snuggled up behind a bank of video monitors, although experience told him it probably wasn't worth his time. In most museums this small, video security was monitored off-site.

Even if a few guards were only a few feet away, both he and Rikard knew that most museums had a strict 'no contact' policy when it came to thieves. The on-location security personnel were supposed to call the police and monitor the intruders' actions but not intervene. They weren't cops, and most museums' insurance policies didn't cover the death of staff members while on duty.

If he and Rikard timed it right, they should be in and out within three minutes, meaning they would be leaving with the artwork before the police could arrive.

Luckily, their targets were clustered on the walls furthest from the office door and close to the main entrance. Two glass doors opened onto a steel staircase, which connected the second-floor exhibition hall with the permanent collection downstairs. The stairs ran along the glass wall covering the back of the building. From here, visitors had a perfect view of the Amstel Modern's collection of kinetic sculptures floating in a pond below.

Based on photos they'd found of the building online, their original plan was to break in through the service entrance, which was secured with a ridiculously easy-to-pick lock. But once they arrived, they realized that was impossible. The museum was in a busy part of Amstelveen, situated at the edge of a large shopping center. The front of the building looked out onto shops, cafés, bars, library, and a theater hosting nightly shows. On its left was a bank and five-story parking garage, covered in security cameras. The right side, where the service entrance was located, butted up against a busy four-lane street leading to the freeway. Even after hours, three sides of the museum were busy with foot, bike, and auto traffic. The chance of a passerby spotting them was huge.

Only the back of the building was quiet. It faced the small pond, surrounded by high grass. A poorly-lit, single-lane street paralleled the water.

"Being on the second floor does complicate matters, although the ventilation shafts have potential," Rikard said softly and casually as he gestured toward Jackson Pollock's *Study Number 5*, an early version of his famous drip paintings. To a casual observer, it seemed as if he was commenting on the artist's bold use of color.

The roof of the two-story museum was flat, providing them with more options. They might be able to climb up to the roof from the back of the building or even swing over from the taller parking garage next door—as Rikard pointed out earlier. The small road running between the garage and museum made it more challenging yet not impossible. They might be able to secure a zip line. There were always ventilator shafts and air vents they could take advantage of to get inside, but there was no guarantee the artwork would fit through the air ducts.

Marko cocked his head and studied the sketch. "I think we need to keep looking." His eyes flickered briefly upward. "Might be a tight squeeze on the way out."

Rikard nodded in understanding and continued scanning for options. As they passed by the large windows lining the back of the building, both men stopped to watch the sculptures in the water dance in the wind. As a strong gust sent the grass waving and the flying pig twirling, a smile broke across Marko's face. He squinted his eyes and realized the pond was not a pond but a canal. The long waterway was encased in high reeds and virtually invisible from the road or sidewalk. Marko followed the narrow channel with his eyes, seeing how it ended two streets away.

"Rikard, I know exactly how we're going to pull this off."

12 A Moonlight Paddle

August 25, 2018

Four thieves paddled a flat-bottom boat along a channel running parallel to Heenvliet Lane, directly behind the Amstel Modern in Amstelveen. The darkened street was lined with old trees and regal homes surrounded by expansive walled gardens. Not that the thieves could see the houses or street clearly through the walls of reeds lining both sides of the waterway. The moon helped to light their way, making their night goggles unnecessary. They had launched the boat from a small dock at the opposite end of the two-block-long canal. A few strokes later and the back of the Amstel Modern was visible. The glass façade glistened in the moonlight as they approached the canal's low brick wall butting up against the museum's concrete foundation.

Rikard looked over to his teammate Marko, then Tomislav and Sebastijan. The four men had never worked together before, but so far, things had gone smoothly. He was grateful that Ivan, their project coordinator, was able to arrange for Team Will to assist so quickly. This job would have been impossible without them.

Sebastijan untied the rope holding a foldable ladder to the deck. Tomislav held on to the bricks and kept the boat steady as his partner tilted the ladder into the foot-deep canal. The water only reached the first rung. The ladder, painted matte black, almost disappeared into the night. Sebastijan stepped out onto it, forcing the metal legs deep into the muddy bottom before extending the ladder to its full thirty-foot height. He then carefully leaned it up against one of the wide silver metal bars holding the six-foot-wide glass panes into place. Once he was satisfied it was secure to climb, he nodded to Team Tuck and stepped aside. Marko and Rikard, both swathed in black, scampered up.

Once they were at the top, Rikard took four suction cups with loops of steel attached out of his fanny pack. He fastened one set to the glass pane just below him and the other to the window in front of him. Then he pushed a thick wire rope through the loops, tugging to make sure everything held in place. After cutting through the pane with a battery-powered saw secured to his belt, he carefully pulled the pane outward. Holding his breath, he waited for the scream of an alarm, Rikard relieved it didn't go off. Nothing was more distracting than a siren in your ear. And tonight, they needed to remain focused. Their getaway was risky at best, and every second counted. He lowered the pane down until it hung loosely against the building's façade. The suctions cups held.

As soon as he released the pane, Rikard heard Tomislav in his ear, "Timer starting now."

Rikard slithered into the opening and landed on the metal staircase leading up to the second-floor exhibition hall. After he checked that his earpiece was still in place, he stepped aside.

Moments later, Marko was by his side. As soon as they entered the exhibition hall, each man heard, "Thirty seconds." Tomislav would continue counting off until he reached three minutes. By then, both he and Marko should be heading back down the ladder. It didn't sound like much, but Rikard was always amazed at what could be done in a few hundred seconds given the right motivation.

While Rikard unfolded two hard-shell cases, his companion ran to their prey and began cutting the wires that held the artwork captive before propping them up against the wall. As Marko removed the fourth, Rikard heard "one minute thirty" in his earpiece. He scurried behind Marko and laid a Robber Hood card on the floor before gathering up the freed artwork and carefully packing it into the padded cases.

As soon as all four pieces were secure, Rikard raced back down the stairs and lowered the artwork to his companions in the boat. He waited for a tug on the rope before letting go. Rikard and Marko climbed swiftly down the ladder and sprang into the boat just as Sebastijan shoved off. Police sirens were rapidly approaching the front of the museum. Their companions paddled them away as fast as their oars would allow. Rikard's nerves were jangled. He wished they had stolen a motor but knew it wasn't an option. The noise would attract the police's attention to their position.

Just before they rounded a slight bend in the short canal, Rikard looked back and saw a single flashlight, its ray whipping back and forth across the exhibition hall they'd just plundered. *They must have night guards, or their security company was there in record time*, he thought, a sinking feeling of dread working its way up his spine. To his relief, the light did not point down toward the water.

After they reached the other end of the canal, Rikard noticed several flashlights climbing the same stairs they'd just used to enter the exhibition hall. Before the police discovered the missing glass panel, the thieves had loaded the artwork onto two waiting scooters and were speeding away into the night.

13 Broken Glass

August 26, 2018

Marko and Rikard drove around for hours, switching from residential roads to freeways and back again. The police response to the robbery had been much heavier than anticipated. After dropping Tomislav and Sebastijan off at a nearby tram stop, they dumped their scooters in the Amsterdamse Bos and continued their journey in a stolen Volvo, circling Schiphol Airport then heading north.

They'd gone through one roadblock without incident before having to backtrack to bypass a second. The artwork was hidden in the trunk's wheel well where the spare tire should have been. It was a miracle the cops didn't search the car thoroughly enough the first time. Neither man's nerves could handle taking that chance twice. Despite the fact they'd already sent a message to their contact, saying they were en route to the collection point, neither dared go to the drop-off point until they were confident no cops were following them.

It was only after several hours on the road that they felt safe enough to head back to Amsterdam. They stopped at a truck stop outside of the city to fuel up and settle their nerves. After ingesting pastrami sandwiches and a few beers, they finally felt ready to complete their last task for the night.

They'd driven farther outside of Amsterdam than they realized. When they finally approached the drop-off point, the sun was beginning to rise, turning the sky into a watercolor of pink and lavender.

A few blocks away, Marko sent another SMS to their contact, letting 'G' know they were almost at their door. All he knew about his drop-off points were their address and a letter, not a name. He looked at the dashboard clock and realized it was five in the morning. He hoped G hadn't dozed off while waiting for them. He was ready to get this artwork off his hands.

When they arrived, Marko had to buzz the intercom twice before anyone responded. It was the only apartment number without a name next to it. Marko hated feeling so exposed, standing outside this monumental building with two bags full of stolen artwork for all the world to see. He was double-checking the apartment number when a sleepy female voice answered.

"Yes? Who is it?"

"Hi, G. It's Team Tuck." He felt so stupid saying the words aloud, but he did as instructed.

"Fifth floor," was the mumbled response before the door buzzed open.

By the time Marko and Rikard knocked on her apartment door, their contact was fully awake and clearly not in a good mood.

"Where were you? You should have been here hours ago." The tiny young woman pouted as she threw her hands onto her hips. Her hair hugged her face like a 1920's flapper though her torn jeans and paint-splattered T-shirt were anything but elegant.

Marko held his hands up and smiled. "More police responded than we expected. We wanted to make sure no one was following us so we took a tour of the Dutch countryside until we were confident we wouldn't be leading them straight to you. I apologize for not letting you know." He kept his tone humble and his eyes downcast even though he wanted to slap the bitchiness out of her.

His contact's eyes narrowed as she studied him for a moment before nodding slowly. "Do you want coffee? I know I need one before I check the work."

"Yes, thank you. That would be great," Rikard responded quickly, stepping between them.

While she prepared their drinks, Marko glanced around the small studio, which was the dictionary definition of chaos. A wobbly bookshelf flowed over with art books while cans of paint, chemicals, and brushes filled another. Canvases were stacked up against two walls, making the room seem much smaller than it was, a third wall

52

completely bare, save several strategically placed nails. Paint splatters outlined the spaces where canvases had recently hung. In the middle of the room was an easel. Something about the canvas resting on it caught his eye—it seemed familiar. Whatever it was, it was clearly a new work in progress and not much more than a series of seemingly random lines and paint splatters. He started to rise to get a better look when G returned with a tray holding a pot of coffee, milk, sugar, and three cups.

She set it onto a table, poured herself a cup, then said, "So, let's take a look."

One by one, the woman removed the four stolen pieces and examined their condition. Rikard and Marko fixed their own cups, took a sip, and smirked at each other.

"Disgusting," Rikard whispered without moving his lips. Marko bobbed his head slightly. Both set their coffees down on the table and ignored them.

Marko sank onto the couch and let his eyelids close. It had been a long day, longer than intended, and he couldn't wait for this cranky artist to finish up so he and Rikard could go to their hotel and crash. As soon as he was in his bed, Marko figured he would sleep the day away.

Except for the occasional grunt, the woman didn't say a word until she reached the final piece. "Hooligans! You broke the glass! If it damaged the paint..." She didn't complete her threat but did keep her eyes on the artwork, lightly brushing the area of concern with her fingertips. It was a study in oil by Jackson Pollock that Marko didn't find particularly appealing. He was not a fan of Pollock's drip paintings. Marko sat up straighter and watched the woman intently as she examined the artwork. He couldn't see any damage, at least not from his position on the couch. After a long silence, she finally said in a stern voice, "I don't see any damage, but it is going in my report."

While she noted down her findings, Marko rolled his eyes. They'd had mere seconds to steal the art and had done their best to protect them. Too irritated to doze off, Marko stood up and stretched while the woman reframed the Pollock, *sans* glass. He gazed at the canvas on the easel in puzzlement. Where had he seen that piece before? Only after he'd finished stretching did it click. Marko stared at the work in progress, his eyes wide in recognition. Of course, the piece looked familiar—it was an incomplete version of the Pollock she'd just berated him about. But why would she be copying it? Marko knew his uncle Luka wouldn't try to cross his Turkish contact by delivering copies instead of the real thing. Was he planning on doubling his profits by selling the forgeries abroad? It seemed foolish, and his uncle was anything but. And even if his uncle Luka was planning to attempt something so crazy, why wasn't he using his own team of forgers?

"Okay, you can go now." The woman's command broke his train of thought. She stood next to her front door, her hand on the handle.

Her sudden dismissal caught him off-guard. Had she noticed him staring at the painting on the easel? Rikard was already standing next to her, clearly wanting to get away from the bitchy woman. Marko wanted to ask her about the work in progress on her easel but couldn't think of a way to do it without making her suspicious. And until the paintings had been picked up by their contact for transport, he didn't want to risk doing that. The last thing they needed was for her to get spooked and disappear with the artwork.

Marko pulled the door shut firmly behind them, resolving to tell Luka about her painting. His uncle instructed them to report any anomalies, no matter how trivial they seemed. For all Marko knew, the woman had been to the Amstel Modern exhibition and simply liked the work. She was obviously an artist. Yet he had learned at an early age to trust no one. That was the Antic way.

14 Branching Out

August 26, 2018

Luka Antic gazed out across the thick forest in front of him and inhaled deeply, reveling in the soft breeze gently scented with pine as the moon created shadows that danced in the green grass. After a long day of chopping wood and tinkering with the cabin's unreliable plumbing, he enjoyed sitting outside on his porch, rocking in his swing with a vodka in hand. Yet physical labor and alcohol weren't enough to ease his troubled mind. The Robber Hood thefts were by no means the most complicated job he had organized, but they were one of the most worrying. He had come so far in twenty years of hard work, mostly because he never got greedy or rushed a project, yet to meet Kadir's demands, he had to do both.

Since saying yes to Kadir, he'd had to continually fight the feeling that he was about to lose it all. Not just this sprawling cabin in the foothills of the Dinaric Alps or his many legitimate businesses but also his entire operation.

With his family's blessing, he had started his own art theft and forgery ring twenty years ago, and it had expanded exponentially since. The key to his success was utilizing a large network of thieves, forgers, and dealers spread across Europe. He used team members irregularly so that their connections to each other—and him—remained loose. For larger jobs, he always used a middleman to isolate himself even further. His money bought their loyalty in case they were caught. He preferred to use Balkan-based thieves so that he could put pressure on their loved ones if need be. Few dared to talk out of turn about Luka Antic.

He also owned many aboveboard legitimate businesses, yet, until recently, forgeries made up the majority of his profit. His team of artists could replicate almost anything to near perfection. But since the late 1990s, when art prices skyrocketed and record-breaking auction sales made international news, more and more gangs began specializing in art theft. With all of the new young bucks breaking into the market, the competition was fierce, and it was a challenge staying on top.

To make matters worse, there were too many players willing to accept increasingly less. Artwork was worth whatever the sucker was willing to pay, and the profit margin was decreasing rapidly. That's why he was following his brother's advice and branching out. Heroin was an item that never goes on sale.

The rest of his family had already given him their blessing. When his friend Davit told him about his Turkish connection and the exceptionally high quality-to-price ratio, Luka couldn't believe his luck. He knew it usually took time and a better network to be able to purchase high-grade heroin. And Kadir Tekin's product was consistently the best available on the market today. The Turk rarely took on new clients, but he had developed a taste for Western artwork, and his men were often spotted at auctions buying postmodern works for him. Asking Davit to mention him and his art theft operation to Kadir was a stroke of genius. A day later, the Turk had gotten in touch and soon requested a face-to-face meeting. This kind of chance would not present itself twice. Luka had to make this deal work. And right now, that meant trusting Ivan Novak.

Deep down, Luka knew, unless he was able to break into this new market and succeed, he would no longer be able to afford the luxuries in which he had become accustomed. Like most who had fought for everything they owned, losing it all was his biggest fear. Of course, there were other heroin dealers he could contact but none with such impressive merchandise as Kadir. His own family was involved with cocaine, something he had no interest in dealing. The profit margins were almost as unpredictable as artwork.

Luka took a deep calming breath, infusing his lungs with the musty scent of the forest floor. The smell reminded him of Ivan Novak's daughter, Marjana, and the heavy perfume she favored. Since contacting Novak, Marjana had been at the forefront of his thoughts. She was the best forger he had ever had on his team, and he felt her loss daily. He didn't dare steal anymore early Renaissance masters, for example. He didn't have the right kind of artist to copy one effectively, not anymore. That was precisely why he couldn't let her go.

Luka stared out into the forest, his mind slipping back to that horrible night three years ago. He should have sent a smarter bunch to get her back, but she'd taken off so suddenly that he wasn't prepared. Not that he would ever admit that to Ivan. He had invested so much in her education, provided her with the most advanced studios and any supplies she desired. He even allowed Marjana to sell her own work through her father's gallery, a right none of his other forgers enjoyed. Why couldn't that have been enough for her? Luka gulped down the last slog of vodka. *What's done is done*, he told himself. There was no point reminiscing about past events. You couldn't change them, only learn from them.

Now it was time to think about his future. The first four robberies had gone off without a hitch. Only twelve more and Ivan Novak would be out of his life. Perhaps then he could sleep soundly again.

He hoped this was the only time Kadir would expect so many pieces of art as payment. Next time, he would try to talk him into accepting a few masterpieces instead of several dozen lesser works. But right now, Kadir was most interested in—perhaps even fixated—on expanding his collection as quickly as possible. If Kadir demanded art in lieu of cash again, he would find another dealer to work with. He had plenty to choose from, but none were as knowledgeable as Ivan Novak. He had needed this job to be perfect and given the number of thefts involved, Ivan was the only realistic option for it. But in the future… Ivan may be the best, but he was not irreplaceable.

His mobile phone's ring interrupted his thoughts. Luka looked at the incoming number and frowned. It was his nephew Marko, his favorite brother's son and one of his most professional and creative thieves. Marko was one of the few people on the planet who Luka trusted implicitly, not that he would ever tell the boy that, which made this call even more disturbing. Marko knew better than to contact him directly when a job was in progress—that was Ivan's role. Telephones were still the easiest way for the police to intercept their conversation or trace his location and possibly connect him to the crimes. At least, Marko knew not to call unless there was an imminent problem he needed to deal with personally. Or one that involved Ivan Novak.

"What?" Luka answered, his voice gruff.

"We might have a situation, sir," Marko spoke quickly, knowing better than to wait to be asked. "The person we delivered to last night had a copy of one of the goods."

Luka thought a moment, trying to unravel the cryptic nature of their conversation. "A copy?" His frown intensified. "I didn't order any copies." *Not this time,* he added in his mind. It was his usual practice to have his own team to make a copy of all stolen works immediately. That gave him two 'originals' to sell to nefarious collectors on either side of the globe. He learned early on how easy it was to double his profits from a single theft. Best of all, his clients were in no position to go to the authorities even if they later discovered they had paid top dollar for a forgery. It was tempting to do so again, but he didn't want to risk one of the copies ever coming to the Turk's attention, no matter how small the chance.

Marko continued, pulling Luka out of his thoughts. "She is an artist, and the opening did get a lot of press coverage. Maybe she visited it and got inspired?" Luka could tell from Marko's tone that his own words did not convince even him. His nephew sighed. "It might be a coincidence, but I know how you feel about coincidences, Uncle."

"You're right. They don't exist." Luka's mind whirled with possibilities. The drop-off point was an artist? What was Ivan playing at?

Did the art dealer have the same thought he had—was Ivan having copies made so he could sell them off later? Was that why he wanted to leave the paintings at the collection points for a whole week after the last robbery? Ivan said the extra week was to allow the media to concentrate on other things and forget about recovering the artwork. It would be easier to move the pieces that way, he'd said, but now Luka wondered.

In some ways, Luka didn't care if the art dealer was copying the artwork. Ivan was getting close to retirement age, and Luka knew how much money his chain of galleries ate up. Luka was surprised his galleries had survived so long without the Antic family's financial support. He could imagine it would be difficult for Ivan to pass up on such an opportunity.

But would Ivan be smart enough to sell them abroad and long after Luka's deal with Kadir was complete? That was the rub because without asking Ivan directly, he couldn't be certain. And even then, the art dealer may lie to him.

Luka could feel his blood pressure rising as he began fretting. Nothing could jeopardize his deal with the Turk. Should he interrogate Ivan now? If he did, there was a large chance the art dealer wouldn't coordinate the final thefts or delivery of the stolen artwork. And if Ivan refused to cooperate, he wouldn't have enough time to organize another string of robberies. No, until his artwork was in Turkey, he and his men had to leave the art dealer be.

"Should I question Ivan?"

"No, leave him alone," the Croatian snapped. If Marko dropped by, no matter how innocent his questions were, the dealer might get suspicious. Yet this artist was a new player. Once Ivan picked up the pieces she'd collected, she would be unnecessary. Was it worth having Marko break into her apartment and get a better look at the painting on her easel? Luka quickly weighed the pros and cons, deciding to err on the side of caution. They knew nothing about this G person nor her patterns. They would have to wait and watch. Patience was always rewarded, not rash action.

"The artist you mentioned. Follow her when you can, and familiarize yourself with her routines, but don't question her—at least, not yet. We don't want to spook her into alerting Ivan. If she does anything you deem suspicious, call me. But don't forget that your jobs are your priority." Marko had five more robberies to plan and pull off. Luka needed him to concentrate on those. They'd worked together enough times that Luka knew he could trust his nephew to make the right decision.

"Yes, sir. No contact and surveillance only when time allows. Understood."

Luka hung up. He looked out again across the forest draped in moonlight, his thoughts now less jovial. All he could see were sinister shadows, toppled trees, and sickly branches. The smell of decay filled his nostrils. The beauty he had experienced minutes earlier was hard-pressed to find.

15 Artnapping or Theft-on-demand?

August 27, 2018

"That doesn't make any sense," Julie Merriweather, the director of the Amstel Modern, said with an uncharacteristic frown. She felt haggard and knew she looked it. This exhibition was supposed to be the crowning glory of her first six months as director of the Amstel Modern, not end up as a police investigation. She quickly made eye contact with the insurance agent, curators, security personnel, and marketing team, all clustered around the museum's largest conference table. She knew they were all looking to her to lead them, but she didn't have a clue as to what to do first. In her fifteen years as a curator, she'd never worked at a museum that had been burgled.

"I know, but that's what they stole. One pencil and three oil sketches by Jackson Pollock, Franz Kline, Alexander Calder, and Hans Hofmann," Berit, the senior curator, said with a shrug.

"Well, that's a small relief," Julie responded. She could feel her shoulders relaxing automatically.

Ruben Meyer, the bespectacled man representing the museum's insurance provider, cleared his throat loudly.

"We still have four missing pieces to contend with," said Nora, the head of marketing and public relations, the whine in her tone making it clear she was shocked the others were reacting so casually.

The insurance agent bobbed his head in agreement. "The works stolen were thankfully not the most expensive pieces in the exhibition, but they still have a combined worth of two million euros. And the museums and private collectors you loaned them from do consider this devastating news."

"Yes, of course. I don't mean to downgrade the robbery. This is every museum's nightmare." Julie's voice and face radiated genuine concern. "It's just hard to fathom why any thief would leave the oils by Robert Motherwell, Mark Rothko, and Jasper Johns behind. Those three pieces alone are worth fifteen million euro. The thieves' choices are, in my mind, quite surprising."

"Frankly, I don't care if it was due to poor taste or a lack of knowledge, but I am glad they left the oils alone," added Liam, the junior curator, slapping his hands on the table for emphasis. "All three are important pieces, but Johns' *Flag* is one of his most iconic works. I can't imagine the world losing access to it."

Berit rolled her eyes. Julie ignored Liam instead. The young curator loved to add drama to every meeting, and she had no desire to fuel it further.

The insurance agent raised an eyebrow. "The thieves' choices are curious. But to us, it doesn't matter which pieces they stole. We want to do all we can to help get the artwork back." Julie knew his proverbial 'we' referred to the museum's insurance provider.

"One way to do that is to figure out what the thieves' motives are," Ruben explained. "The fact that no one has demanded a ransom for the pieces' return leads us to rule out artnapping. At least for now."

Julie knew a commonly used ploy by thieves was to steal artwork and then ransom it back to their owners. Most museums did everything in their power to keep such thefts and payouts out of the news, not only out of fear of losing sponsors but also to avoid encouraging other thieves to try the same trick. In this case, no one had contacted them directly, but the thieves had left a message behind. "And the Robber Hood card? They have some nerve robbing us and leaving a note with 'your security needs improving' on it," Julie pressed. "I wouldn't be surprised if they did demand a ransom of some sort. Otherwise, why let us know who took them?"

Ruben shrugged his shoulders. "I know Robber Hood's message indicates they are a group concerned about the protection of cultural heritage, but so far, they have not made any specific demands for the artworks' return. Until they do, we cannot consider this an artnapping case."

Ruben continued, addressing the table, "What we do know is that four museums have been robbed in the last eight days, and in all the cases, the thieves stole several pieces of modern art, all valued at eight hundred thousand euros or less. Our assessment is that the more expensive oil paintings were not taken because they are listed in international art registers and, therefore, would be more difficult to sell."

Julie put her head in her hands. Ruben didn't seem to notice, continuing his monologue in his dry, nasal voice.

"Another theory is that this was a theft-on-demand, instigated by a rogue collector. Considering the eclectic selection and the high number of targets, we cannot rule out that possibility. And most of the pieces stolen are part of a museum's permanent collection, which means they won't ever come up for auction."

Julie's stomach began to churn. She knew Ruben was paid to think of everything that could go wrong, but it was still depressing to hear it all spoken aloud.

"When you combine this knowledge with the fact that police have identified one of the thieves as a member of an Eastern European criminal organization specializing in art theft, we are concerned that the mafia is involved. Whether they are stealing the art for a rogue collector or intend to use the artwork in an underworld transaction, we cannot say. No matter which scenario you choose, we are concerned the artwork will be moved out of the Netherlands and disappear in the Balkans long before the police capture the Robber Hood gang or figure out what their real motive is."

"Wait—what are you saying?" Julie asked. Her stomach shot a stream of acid up that took her breath away. She wasn't sure if she was going to survive this next week without developing an ulcer. "You think the mob robbed our museum?"

"Yes, we are beginning to believe so," Ruben said.

"Why?" Julie cried out. Any robbery was bad, but if a criminal organization took the artwork, it was as good as gone. *Just like my job*, she thought.

The insurance agent took her *why* literally. "Art crimes are the third most profitable crime committed by criminal organizations. Stolen artwork is often used as collateral for drug deals, money laundering, or arms dealing. Several of these Balkan-based groups forge them as well, selling off their copies to dealers or collectors as the real thing."

"I know all of that. I mean why do you think a member of a Balkan gang is involved?" Julie was exasperated. The police promised to keep her in the loop. "I spoke with Detective Prins of the Art and Antiquities Unit this morning. His team was still busy checking fingerprints pulled from the scene against those of our staff, as well as viewing all the video footage taken by security cameras in the vicinity. That's how they were able to figure out how the thieves got away so quickly…"

"I told you that canal was a security risk!" The museum's head of security interrupted to scold the director.

"The canal was there when I took the job, Aart." Julie scowled at him until he bowed his head.

"As I was saying… how could they know someone working for an Eastern European criminal organization was involved?" *And not call me immediately*, Julie added in her mind.

"I called Detective Prins right before our meeting started, and he told me they just had a small breakthrough," the insurance agent said. "He'll relay the details to you later today."

Julie folded her hands on the table and breathed in deeply through her nose. "Why don't you enlighten us?"

Ruben shifted in his chair. "They found the scooters the thieves used to flee the scene. One had been reported stolen a few hours before the robbery. It was parked across the street from a convenience store. When the police checked the store's surveillance footage, they discovered the robbery had been caught on camera and the thief's face is clearly visible. They were able to match him to Marko Antic, a member of the Antic family, a criminal organization based out of Split, Croatia. Marko is a suspect in several art thefts in Switzerland, France, and Luxembourg, all most likely ordered by his family."

"And the Robber Hood card?" Julie pressed. "Why would the

mafia leave a calling card behind?"

"I agree. We need to find out more about this Robber Hood before we can make any assumptions as to the thieves' identities or motives. A card has been left at every theft. All of the messages chastise the museums' poor security, yet no one has contacted any of the institutions affected with demands for their return. There are similarities between these robberies and the theft of Edvard Munch's *The Scream* in 1994. The thieves claimed to have stolen Munch's work to raise awareness about the poor security of Norway's museums. Ultimately, Norse police discovered the thieves had ties to the Eastern European mafia, as well."

Julie threw her hands up in the air. "Good God. Can it get any worse?"

"Let's hope not," the insurance agent responded. Julie couldn't tell if it was meant wryly or if Ruben was serious. "The police are actively pursuing the Robber Hood gang and a few forensic clues left behind during the robberies. However, I would like to bring in a local private investigator, Vincent de Graaf, to look into the Eastern European connection. He is an art recovery expert with a strong network of informants in the Balkans. If the Croatian mafia is involved, de Graaf will be able to find that out for us."

"Is it prudent to call him in if the police are still investigating?" Julie mused aloud.

"I did ask Detective Prins' permission to do so, which was why I contacted him earlier. When I told him about our suspicions, he agreed wholeheartedly. The Dutch police force just doesn't have the resources to track down so many stolen pieces, especially if the artwork has already been transported out of the Netherlands."

"I don't know..." Despite her reservations, Julie knew it was important to act swiftly. And if the insurance agent wanted to bring in a detective, so be it. It was just so extraordinary to think the mob might have robbed her museum. She was having trouble wrapping her head around the idea. Then again, she hadn't slept since the break-in two days ago, and her mind was muddled. Even though she'd only been the director for six months, she had already decided the Amstel Modern was where she was going to leave her mark.

Being a big fish in a little pond made it so much easier to make an enormous splash. New York and Los Angeles were filled with highly qualified professionals vying for the same fifteen minutes of fame. Here, she was a rising star, envied by many. Whatever happened, she had to do all she could to show the board of directors she was a woman of action. No matter what happened, she could not lose this job.

Ruben's watch started to beep. He turned it off and addressed the room once again. "I have another meeting to get to, so let's wrap this up. Our position is this—whether the thieves stole this work for a gang or a rogue collector, we have to assume these paintings will disappear if we don't find them soon," Ruben said. "Of course, if we are lucky, Robber Hood is a protest group, and after they've made their point, the art will be returned unharmed. However, we prefer to take a proactive approach and operate from a worst-case scenario. We want to get an art detective working on this case straightaway while the Dutch police continue following up local leads and connections. There are a few good ones based in Europe, but Vincent de Graaf has worked on several cases involving Balkan-based criminal organizations and has recovered many pieces. He has better connections to the Eastern European mafia than any of our in-house investigators."

Julie noticed a few heads nodding in recognition.

Liam piped up, "I know him. In fact, I spoke with him at the opening. He helped my wife's grandmother recover two paintings taken from her father during World War II. He's good."

The insurance agent continued, "With Julie's permission, I would like to contact him this afternoon and arrange a meeting."

"If we do meet with him, will you let us open our doors again?" Nora from marketing asked Ruben.

Julie answered instead, "The police should be finished with their on-scene investigation this afternoon. A new glass pane will arrive tomorrow morning. I also have a team of cleaners on standby. Liam, Berit, once we get the okay, we will need to decide how to rearrange the remaining pieces to fill the walls better. We aren't the Gardner Museum, so I'm not leaving empty frames up. I want as few reminders of the robbery as possible. I hope we'll be able to reopen in three days."

"Some opening week," Liam grumbled.

Nora responded evenly, "No, it's not ideal, but my department is doing all it can to spin this to our advantage. If anything, the robbery has raised our social media profile significantly. We're getting ten times the amount of shares and likes that we normally do. I'm positive we will have an influx of lookie-loos once we reopen."

"Pretty expensive marketing campaign if you ask me," Liam quipped.

Julie wished he would give it a rest, just this once.

"We'll see what happens when we crunch the numbers at the end of the exhibition," Nora stated without batting an eyelash.

16 The Audacity of Art Thieves

August 27, 2018

Zelda rushed through her lunch, keeping chitchat to a minimum so she could spend a few minutes reading *The Art Investigator*—a new blog everyone in the Amstel Modern was talking about—before her next meeting started. Her coworkers were shocked by the blogger's take on the recent spate of museum thefts in the Netherlands. Even though the mainstream media had reported on all four robberies, they had not connected them. Apparently, this blogger had proof they were linked.

The buzz around the watercooler also speculated on the blogger's profession, a man known only as Nik. Most figured it was someone with a high-level position in the Ministry of Culture while others thought he was a senior curator at a prestigious museum. A few suspected it was one of the Netherlands' three art detectives. Whoever it was, Nik was privy to information most of those who worked in the Amstel Modern were not.

It didn't help that the Amstel Modern's director and department heads were being incredibly tight-lipped about the police's investigation and any leads they may have. Rumors were already circulating about the message written on the Robber Hood card found at the scene, the same message the museum's director refused to acknowledge. Just like her colleagues, Zelda was eager to know more about their museum's theft and its possible connection to a more sinister complot.

Zelda shoved the last bite of egg roll into her mouth and cleaned up after herself while chewing. She waved goodbye and dashed off before anyone could ask where she was going. Lunches and coffee pauses were sacred in the Dutch museum world, and it was not okay to rush back to work during officially sanctioned breaks. If too many people did that, their right to take so many might be revoked.

Zelda plopped into her office chair and surfed to *The Art Investigator* blog. On the homepage was the latest post, entitled, "The Audacity of Art Thieves."

> This week, four Dutch museums were robbed of nine works of art. That much you probably already knew from reading the mainstream media. What you may not know is that a group calling themselves Robber Hood organized all of the thefts.
>
> I now have confirmation from the burgled museums that small green cards were left at the scene of each crime. On one side 'Robber Hood' is printed in embossed gold letters. On the other side are these messages—'Thanks for your poor security,' 'Too bad you can't afford a better security system,' 'Protect what you love,' and 'Your security needs improving.'
>
> Sources working in three of the museums were able to share photographs of the messages left behind.

Zelda glanced at the images, all poor-quality snaps made by a smartphone, probably taken on the sly.

> These Robber Hood cards haven't yet been reported in the mainstream media. Why not? Are the police asking the museums' staffs to keep the presence of the cards quiet? To what end? If an audacious group of morally emboldened thieves is targeting our cultural institutions, doesn't the public have a right to know? As taxpayers, we do fund the majority of museums in this country.
>
> Who are Robber Hood, and what are their motives?
>
> The messages left behind suggest they are stealing to draw attention to the poor security of our public art collections. Yet if they are cultural crusaders trying to draw attention to the vulnerability of our cultural institutions, they are doing a pretty crappy job of it.

Why aren't they on social media broadcasting their manifesto and flaunting photographs of their daring crimes? Why aren't they contacting the traditional media directly and explaining their motivations? How do they expect to grab our attention and spread their message if they do not?

When we look critically at the work they have stolen, the thieves seem to have a preference for sketches, studies, and watercolors. None of the stolen works are on par with the Night Watch. Why haven't they stolen the most expensive pieces in the museums they've broken into, artwork so ingrained in our collective consciousness that its theft would enrage a nation and band the public together?

After the embarrassingly easy theft of two multimillion-euro paintings from the Van Gogh Museum in 2002, the Netherlands' top cultural institutions invested heavily in their security. Pieces like the Night Watch are virtually impossible to steal. Yet smaller regional museums don't have access to the same kinds of funding and subsidies that the big boys do. Robber Hood's week-long spree has affected cultural institutions across the nation. If their tactic is to enrage as many cultural lovers as possible, this is a good second best.

So if Robber Hood is trying to send a message to those responsible for safeguarding our nation's historical, cultural, and artistic heritage for future generations, why haven't they spoken up yet? Why haven't they made demands for the art's return? Or are there more thefts on the horizon? Could they be waiting until their spree is over to reveal their identity and demands to the museums from which they stole?

Time will tell, though the police maintain they still have no viable leads into the whereabouts of the stolen artwork nor Robber Hood's true identity.

Zelda couldn't believe it. The Robber Hood cards meant these weren't random robberies but committed by the same organization.

It seemed so strange and unbelievable.

Zelda clicked on the About section. A Dutch culture-lover named Nik started this blog three months ago. His profile photo was of an average-looking, middle-aged man turning away from the camera as the photo was taken. Zelda doubted she would recognize him on the street even if she walked right past him. She scanned the scant details about his life, scrolling down to read about his motivation.

Why do I blog?

In the topsy-turvy world of art crime, nothing is ever as it seems. My blog is dedicated to reporting on art thefts and forgery cases in the Benelux, especially those crimes often ignored by the mainstream media. And trust me, there are many. Knowledge is power. We can't sit back and do nothing while the mafia, profiteers, and misfits steal our culture—our history—for a quick buck.

17 The Art Detective

August 28, 2018

Vincent de Graaf leaned back and folded one knee over the other, his broad shoulders filling the conference room chair. He flicked a piece of lint off his pant leg then looked up at Julie Merriweather. His sapphire blue eyes pierced her soul and took her breath away. "You do realize how unconventional it is to call me in so early? This is still a fresh case, and the police are actively pursuing leads." His voice was deep and booming. Julie could hardly believe the man could ever work undercover.

"Yes, of course, I am. I have already discussed your involvement with the lead investigator, Detective Prins, and he supports our decision." Julie leaned forward, trying to infuse her voice with authority. But in the face of this private investigator's oozing self-assuredness, her voice sounded weak and whiny. The Dutch police had already assured her that Vincent would also be given access to all the information available about the Robber Hood thefts once he agreed to investigate this one. That was a big *if*—Vincent de Graaf was known for being picky and not swayed by emotional pleas. If he didn't think he could locate the artwork, he wouldn't bother to waste his time and energy on it. So far, this meeting was not going as she'd hoped. Vincent seemed uninterested in investigating any Eastern European connection to their robbery. She sucked up her breath and tried again.

"The Dutch police are concentrating on tracking down several local leads. However, there are indications that at least one of the thieves involved is from the Balkans. The police are open to you investigating any connections outside of the Netherlands and tracking down the artwork if necessary. They know as well as we do that if a criminal organization took the art, the longer we wait to follow up any viable lead, the less likely it will ever be recovered. And if it does end up an artnapping case, it may be preferable to have you negotiate for the insurance company instead of the police."

Julie looked to insurance agent Ruben Meyer, seated to her left, for confirmation. He locked eyes with Vincent. "We believe—"

The art detective ignored him, and instead asked Julie, "Why exactly do the police believe criminals from the Balkans are involved?"

Julie sat up straighter, knowing this was the moment of truth, that this was the information that would either interest him in the case or not. She pulled a photograph out of a manila folder lying on the table and passed it to Vincent. "This is a still-frame capture from a security camera in Amstelveen. This man is stealing one of the two scooters used to flee the Amstel Modern robbery. Police were able to use footage from home security cameras in the area to place it at the scene. Our insurance company put us in contact with Interpol, who was able to match him to a Croatian criminal named Marko Antic. My museum's security team is now reviewing our video feeds in the hopes of finding a record of him visiting the museum."

Vincent de Graaf startled visibly when he heard the name. "Marko Antic? We've crossed paths before. If Marko is involved, then the chance is quite high that the artwork will find its way to the Balkans. Your insurance provider is right—the police don't have the resources or connections to investigate this possibility further. But I do." By the end of the sentence, he had uncrossed his legs and was leaning forward, making eye contact with both Julie and Ruben.

Julie was overwhelmed with relief. That was precisely why the insurance agent had recommended him. Not only did Vincent have a vast network in Eastern Europe but he also had a good working relationship with most of the national and international police forces involved. For the first time since entering the room, he seemed interested in listening to what they had to say. There was hope he would take the case, after all.

Vincent picked up the photograph and examined it carefully. Julie's hands shook in her lap as they waited for him to make his decision. After what felt like a lifetime, the detective said, "I will take this case as a consultant. I can't guarantee I'll find Marko, but I think I know where to start."

Julie had to bite her lip to stop herself from crying out in joy. The police were not making much progress, and with more robberies happening every day, the Amstel Modern theft was already old news. The insurance agent believed this detective was their best hope at recovering any of the art, and for the first time since the break-in, Julie felt a spark of hope. Perhaps her new position as director was not in jeopardy. She might have a chance at leaving her mark on the museum world, after all.

Vincent whistled as he unlocked his bicycle chained to a rack outside the Amstel Modern. How many times had he crossed paths with the Antic family? And how many times had he gotten stung for it? While he made a point of always putting the art's recovery before anything else, where Luka Antic was concerned, it was personal. Evidence found in three cases he'd been working on linked Luka and his criminal organization to the crimes. Each time, he had been so close to recovering the artwork only to have it yanked away and disappear forever.

Three months ago, one of his informants had his throat slashed, his body laid out where the final meeting was supposed to be taking place. Vincent knew the dead man's wife and three sons as well. Since that cock-up, several of his regular informants refused to work with him, fearing for their lives. Considering his plans to open an office in Split, he needed as many of his Croatian contacts on his side as possible. And proving himself more formidable than Luka Antic may be the only way to do so.

Luka was an elusive figure, who could never be tied to any art-related thefts. Vincent, as well as several of his colleagues, suspected Luka of being the brain behind the Balkan Bandits. But this time, they'd found evidence that his nephew Marko was directly involved. In contrast to his powerful uncle, Marko was still young and prone to making mistakes. He'd even been caught on camera during several recent robberies. Though he was incredibly adept at vanishing into thin air when the police came looking for him, there was a higher chance of catching Marko than Luka. And if Vincent could pull that off, there was a chance he could break the young thief, thereby reassuring his Croatian network that he could protect them, especially if Marko implicated his uncle—assuming Luka was the ringleader behind the Robber Hood crimes. Or was Marko or another young buck trying to butt in on Luka's market... Vincent's mind reeled with possibilities as he biked through the residential neighborhoods of Amstelveen toward his home on the Amstel River.

18 Creating a Legacy

August 29, 2018

Kadir Tekin always enjoyed his brother-in-law's company. Not only did Yusef marry Kadir's favorite sister but they were also roughly the same age, had ten children, and were successful businessmen. They always had much to talk about and often had the same opinions about world events as well as the resolution to family squabbles. So when Kadir decided to start selling cocaine and heroin in his hotels, he had turned to Yusef. His brother-in-law was one of Istanbul's best suppliers of wholesale product, shipped straight in from Afghanistan and Columbia on his overseas transport company's many ships.

"How far have we come, eh? Thirty-five years ago, you were a tour guide in Dalyan, and I peddled miniature mosques to tourists in Istanbul. Now we own empires." Yusef punched him lightly on the shoulder before taking a long drag of the hookah placed between them.

Kadir nodded. They were indeed blessed, and he knew it. He had risen from his humble beginnings as a tour guide on the Dalyan River delta to become the owner of hotels, nightclubs, bars, tour companies, and a fleet of rental yachts. Nothing had come easily to him, first as a child working ten-hour days to serve Western tourists' every whim, and then later as the owner of so many ventures that he had to bring in several trusted relatives to help him run them all. Now, everything he touched seemed to turn to gold.

He had accomplished so much, yet as he approached fifty years old, Kadir's mind often turned to the legacy he would leave his children. He had his many bars and hotels to thank for his enormous wealth, more than a simple fisherman's son could ever dream of. But that was not the lasting legacy he wanted to create. Kadir wished to leave behind something that would earn the Tekin name everlasting respect. "It is important to leave a mark on the present and future. Don't you agree, Yusef?"

"Oh, yes. I am grooming my sons to take over my import-export businesses and transport companies. I want them to own good, reputable businesses they can be proud of. They won't have to deal with the same scum I do."

Neither man wanted his children to have to go through the same hardships they had. Kadir had earned enough in his short lifetime that none of his ten offspring would ever have to engage in the same criminal activities that made him so rich. Just as any father, he wanted his children to have a better life.

Yusef held his tea up to his lips then added with a laugh, "But you, Kadir, you have the Midas touch. Your accomplishments dwarf those of your brothers and uncles. Perhaps, one day, you will also be buried with the kings in the cliffs of Dalyan."

Kadir snorted. "They would never allow the grave of a fisherman's son to be carved into those cliffs, my brother." But the thought alone brought a smile to his face. His birthplace was known for its turtles and the royal tombs carved into the cliff faces in the Dalyan River's delta. "Besides, without your connections, I would have never made it this far. Perhaps there is room for two graves."

His brother-in-law bowed his head at the compliment. Both sipped their tea, contentedly.

It is true, Kadir thought, *without my brother-in-law's help, I wouldn't have been able to expand my businesses so rapidly*. Since he started selling hard drugs in his clubs and hotels, his total profits had tripled, allowing him to invest in even more ventures geared toward Westerners. He'd learned at an early age that tourists were always on the lookout for substances to enhance their vacation. As a young boy, their requests offended and disgusted him. Nowadays, he was happy to fulfill their whispered requests for marijuana, cocaine, ecstasy, and heroin. Every bar and café in Marmaris offered water pipes, but he'd built his reputation on providing the best party drugs in the region, but temples to drugs and alcohol were not the legacy he wished to leave his children. There was more he wanted to do with his money, and he'd recently discovered another way to garner the respect he desired.

Yusef was one of the few people he trusted implicitly. He hadn't told a soul about his plan, and his desire to share it with someone was overwhelming. If he had anyone he could talk to about it, it was Yusef. Kadir sucked up his courage and said, "Brother, since my fifth son was born last year, I have been contemplating my legacy — and not one carved in Dalyanian stone. I want my family name to have the respect it deserves. To be important to all Turkish people, even those snobs in Istanbul."

His brother-in-law laughed. Those who lived in the capital were often considered arrogant elitists by the rest of the country.

"Ever since Omer's boy, Taner, returned from studying art history in The Hague, he's been teaching me about Western art. I must admit that the more I learn, the more fascinated I become. The longer you look at a piece, the more it speaks to you." He glanced at his brother-in-law, wondering if Yusef could understand how he felt, feeling foolish talking about it. Yusef listened attentively. Kadir dared continue. "I want to be remembered for more than my dance clubs, bars, and boats. Taner has shown me how the rich and powerful of today create their legacy by collecting and protecting cultural treasures. In Western lands, important families like the Rockefellers, Guggenheims, and Gettys have all been sponsors of arts and culture, and their names adorn the museums they funded. Taner has also shown me the websites of new museums being built in Saudi Arabia, China, and Mexico and how their collections combine local and Western art. Yusef, I want to see the Tekin name on such a monument. Maybe then those elitist snobs will accept us as one of their own."

Yusef's eyes widened as he looked to Kadir, a puzzled look on his face. "Are you building a museum here in Marmaris? "

"Of a sort. Taner is now my art advisor. He has recently helped me purchase several Western paintings at auction, which is a start. But Taner has explained to me that a museum must have many pieces and should include earlier works that show development in

78

style and artistic expression." Kadir hoped he was recounting Taner's words correctly. Though he was fascinated by the art world and the status it could give his family name, he still had much to learn.

"That sounds like quite a project, Kadir. Luckily you have a long life ahead of you to fulfill your dreams." Yusef sipped his tea, watching his brother-in-law closely.

"It may not take as long as that, my brother," Kadir responded.

Yusef grinned slyly. "Ah, you have found a way to get what you want faster. Does this have anything to do with the large purchase you wish to make?"

"As a matter of fact, it does. Taner has also taught me that the better pieces of art do not always come onto the market."

Yusef laughed. "Oh, oh. Are you planning on doing something naughty?"

Kadir laughed along with his drug-dealing brother-in-law. Naughty was par for the course. "Yusef told me something interesting recently. During a class in Culture and Law, he learned that the Netherlands is the only country in the world where stolen art can become the rightful property of a thief."

Yusef's eyes widened in astonishment. "How is that possible?"

"The statute of limitations on artwork stolen from a Dutch museum collection is only thirty years. After that, the piece is considered the property of whoever has it even if it is the person who stole it."

"Oh, that is quite stupid of our Dutch friends to have such a law."

"Yes, it is. Ever since Taner told me about it, that tidbit of information has fascinated me. I can have anything stolen for me—that is not an issue—but this collection should be a source of pride, not controversy. When it is revealed to the public, I do not want my children's ownership contested. This shortsighted law offers me a loophole, and I intend to exploit it to my advantage."

Kadir paused to take a sip of tea and wet his throat. "You asked why I want to buy more heroin than usual this time. The product you are supplying me with will be used to expand my collection exponentially. By the end of the month, I will have the foundation of my museum secured."

Yusef clapped him on the back, smiling broadly. "You are truly blessed, my brother!"

"Çok teşekkürler! Many thanks, Yusef. I am a lucky man."

19 Seeing Double

August 31, 2018

Zelda pushed the heavy door to her apartment building open, whistling a jaunty tune. She was enjoying trying out all the bars and cafés in her new neighborhood. Since discovering two of her coworkers lived a few streets away from her new apartment, they had been meeting for drinks every Friday night at a different location. Tonight, they also had dinner together. It was a great way to forget the work week and get to know each other better. Both of her coworkers seemed like fun people who shared similar interests. And as Zelda had learned from her previous experiences, the museum world in Amsterdam was small. Even though she was only going to be at the Amstel Modern for six months, there was a real chance they would work together again one day.

Zelda's heels echoed off the tiles of her apartment building's lobby as she walked past the staircase to the elevator. The businesses on the lower four floors were already closed for the night, leaving only the few residents living on the top floor. Zelda pushed the up button next to the elevator, and the door immediately opened. Gabriella was inside, crumpled up in the fetal position. Zelda rushed to her friend. Gabriella's breathing was ragged.

"Gabriella, can you hear me?" Zelda yelled as she gently slapped her friend's face, hoping to wake her out of this trance. Her neighbor was a diabetic who often got so absorbed in her work that she forgot to eat or sleep during her long painting sessions. In the three months since Zelda moved here, she had seen Gabriella go through two insulin dips, one of which landed her in the hospital. Zelda was pretty certain the artist's coma-like state was due to her illness, and she only hoped a shot of insulin would be enough to snap Gabriella out of it. Otherwise, she'd need to call the ambulance straightaway.

When Gabriella moaned slightly, Zelda breathed a sigh of relief and pushed the fifth-floor button. She searched through her neighbor's jacket pockets until she found her keys. As soon as the elevator doors opened, she carried Gabriella to her apartment, depositing her friend gently on her oversized couch. Zelda didn't know whether to give her the insulin shot first or call the ambulance. She picked up her phone to dial 1-1-2 when Gabriella roused a little and muttered, "Insulin pen."

Zelda sprinted to the refrigerator and grabbed the medicine. When she returned with it, Gabriella pulled down her pants and shoved it into her thigh. Moments after the insulin entered her bloodstream, Gabriella's eyes fluttered open. "Orange juice."

Zelda ran back and poured her friend a glass. When she reentered the room, the painting resting on Gabriella's easel caught her eye and stopped her in her tracks. It was as if a kaleidoscope of color had exploded onto the canvas. Lines danced across the surface, interwoven through the thin layers of oil. Zelda cocked her head, studying its composition. The painting seemed so familiar, one she'd definitely seen before. But then again, Gabriella's living room was a jumble of ongoing projects set aside until inspiration struck again. Last week, she had been working on ultra-realistic cityscapes. This was much looser and spontaneous. It reminded Zelda of the studies Jackson Pollock made for his early drip paintings, the ones that she'd researched for the Amstel Modern exhibition.

Gabriella groaned, and Zelda rushed to her. She helped her friend take a few small sips of juice, then set it on the table when Gabriella lay back and shut her eyes. The artist's breathing grew heavy, and soon, she was snoring.

Zelda looked again at the easel and noticed it was positioned in front of another piece hanging on the wall. It also seemed familiar. Curious, Zelda rose and walked closer, examining both pieces. Her forehead creased in concentration. She leaned in closer when the truth made her eyes pop. They were two versions of the same painting. And they weren't reminiscent of Jackson Pollock—the finished piece on Gabriella's wall *was* a Pollock, his *Study Number 5*.

The same sketch that had been stolen from the Amstel Modern last week.

Zelda felt limp and dizzy. She had to tell someone but didn't dare leave Gabriella in this comatose state. She turned away from her friend and pulled out her phone. But who should she call? The police? Or her employer? And what should she say about Gabriella's involvement?

Before she could decide who to call or what to say, Gabriella's eyes open and she groaned. "Oh, my head. Could you get a bar of chocolate out of the cupboard? There should be a bunch on the third shelf."

"Sure, Gabriella. But what happened? Why were you passed out in the elevator?"

"I pushed myself too hard and forgot to eat today," she mumbled. "I went downstairs to order some takeaway but never made it outside." She shrugged then closed her eyes. "It sometimes happens, especially when I'm in the flow."

"But why…" Zelda wanted to ask about the Pollocks but didn't know where to start. And considering Gabriella's current condition, she doubted the artist could explain herself coherently.

Instead, she got her friend a chocolate bar, then excused herself to the toilet. She needed a minute to collect her thoughts. Zelda turned on the sink and stared into the mirror. Was there a stolen Pollock in Gabriella's living room? She wasn't an art expert but did spend weeks studying the piece. As much as she wanted to believe it was all a big misunderstanding, she had to tell someone about it. Should she call the Amstel Modern or police first?

Before Zelda could make up her mind, a soft knock disturbed her thoughts. From inside the bathroom, she could hear Gabriella's front door opening.

"Hello, Gabriella." A man's voice rang out. His accent was clipped and formal.

Zelda figured he must have a key because Gabriella was in no state to open the door so quickly. Was it her boyfriend? Gabriella hadn't mentioned having one before. Zelda heard footsteps enter the living room, and then the man called out in Croatian. She couldn't understand the words, but the man's concern was evident.

Zelda opened the door to make her presence known, and a "hello" was halfway out of her mouth when a flash of motion made her look up. Her knees buckled as her head exploded in pain. Just before she passed out, Zelda saw an older man standing over her, his wrinkled face and gray hair looming closer. Then, only darkness.

20 Beer and a Book

August 31, 2018

Marko sat in a bar across the street from Het Sieraad, enjoying a Heineken and his book, the latest adventure by Clive Cussler. To his delight, they served *bitterballen*, a Dutch delicacy made from deep-fried beef ragout that he couldn't get enough of. Preparing for Team Tuck's next job had taken less time than anticipated. While Rikard rounded up a few last-minute supplies, Marko decided to see what the artist was doing. Staking out her apartment was easy enough since there was only one entrance, and from his seat by the café's front window, he could see through the skylights that her apartment lights were on. As he waited for his second portion of *bitterballen*, he gazed outside and up at the moon. Fall was already settling in, and the drop in the temperature caused Amsterdam's trees to shed. In the evening light, the leaves swirling in the strong winds reminded him of snow flurries.

His eyes were drawn to a fast-moving vehicle, speeding toward the small cobblestoned square in front of Het Sieraad. The van slowed just before it rode over the sidewalk and stopped a few feet from the front entrance. Marko lay down his book and watched with interest. Seconds later, an older man exited the building, pushing a trolley stacked up with canvases. The van's driver opened the back door and loaded them inside.

Marko had seen several artists going in and out of the building, so the men's actions didn't raise any alarms. Still, habit made him take out his phone and snap pictures of both men and their vehicle, making sure the van's license plate was visible. He then picked up his book and read a few pages, glancing up now and again at the men loading the van. They made four trips, each time bringing more canvases and painting supplies down. Marko figured the vehicle was filled to the brim by now.

He had just taken a large swig of beer when he noticed the older man had made a fifth trip. This time, he was half-carrying a young woman toward the van. He couldn't see her face clearly, but she did seem to be the same size and have the same flapper haircut that the artist had. The second man helped him get the woman into the passenger's seat, then both men jumped inside and sped off.

Marko felt his drink catch in his throat, choking him as he grabbed his phone and dialed. As soon as Luka picked up, Marko blurted out, "Uncle, you aren't going to like this."

"What now?" Luka Antic sounded irritated, not concerned.

Marko glanced around and realized the café was full. This was not the right place for this conversation. He placed a fifty euro note under his half-full beer glass and stepped outside.

"I'm outside that artist's apartment now. Two men just drove away with her and a bunch of paintings. I don't know where they're going, and it happened too fast for me to follow them. But I did take photos."

"Send them now," was the terse reply. A few moments later, Luka said, "The older man is Ivan Novak. I don't know the other one."

"That's Ivan?" Marko had never seen him before but knew he was project managing the Robber Hood job. Ivan Novak had arranged for Team Will to help Marko and Rikard pull off the Amstel Modern theft. "I thought you said that none of the work would be moved until after we finished?"

"That was the plan, yes." Luka growled into the phone. "What happened exactly?"

Marko knew how important this deal was with the Turk. In hushed tones, he told Luka everything that had happened. Just as he was finishing up, Marko heard sirens in the distance.

"What is that noise?" Luka asked.

Marko stared wide-eyed as the small square in front of the artist's building filled with vehicles, all with lights blazing and sirens blaring. "Four cop cars and an ambulance just showed up."

"What's going on?"

"I'm not sure. Several officers and ambulance personnel are rushing inside the artist's building. I can't tell you much more without attracting attention to myself."

"Do what you need to do but find out."

Marko was silent a moment before saying, "I will do my best, but I would hate to jeopardize my other projects. The next is slated for tomorrow."

"Of course, you're right. See what you can find out tonight. Otherwise, I have friends on the Dutch police force I can ask."

Marko noticed a crowd of onlookers had already begun to form in the square. He joined them, keeping to the back as much as possible. Ten minutes after the police arrived, the ambulance personnel wheeled a stretcher outside with a young woman laying on it. Marko could see an oxygen mask on her face, meaning she was still alive. He didn't recognize her but took a picture anyway. Could this woman's injuries be related to the artist's exit minutes earlier? Or were the two incidents unrelated? Marko knew he needed to find out.

He ran back to his car and followed the ambulance to the VU University Medical Center.

Unfortunately, the woman was already inside by the time he parked and made his way to the emergency room's reception desk. He inquired about the woman, stating that he knew his neighbor was brought here, but not knowing the woman's name didn't help matters. The nurses refused to tell him anything, and the hallways were only accessible by key card. He wouldn't be able to find out more without risking imprisonment.

Marko went outside, lit up a cigarette, and pulled out his phone. "You said you know somebody in the force? Maybe you can call in that favor…"

21 Welcome Back

September 1, 2018

Zelda opened her eyes slowly. The light felt like knives stabbing her brain.

Her mouth felt like sandpaper stuck together with dried saliva. She glanced around, desperate for anything to drink. A pitcher stood on a white table next to her but too far away to reach without sitting up.

On the bed, close to her arm, was a call button on a long white cable. She moved her hand toward it and noticed a tube sticking out of her wrist. She pushed the red button in, trusting someone would respond quickly.

Her head felt heavy. She gingerly touched her forehead and felt a thick bandage. Her hand followed it around her head and found it seemed to cover her entire scalp like a helmet.

Moments later, a nurse rushed in, her smile bright. "Well, well. Welcome back." She raised Zelda's bed into a sitting position, and while the movement was gentle, it still caused her whole body to shake in pain.

"Welcome back?" Zelda asked, but the words stuck in her parched throat and came out as a nasty cough.

The nurse instinctively poured a glass of water and stuck a straw in before placing it between Zelda's cracked lips. "Try drinking this—small sips."

Zelda drank greedily, feeling the liquid rush through her body. Water had never felt so good. She leaned back against her pillow, momentarily refreshed. "What the heck happened to me?" Her voice sounded strangely deep. "The last thing I remembered was being in my apartment... Or was I?"

A frown crossed her face as she rubbed her temples, careful not to move the bandages wrapped around her head. Her memories were flashes of unconnected images.

The nurse rolled a table up next to Zelda's bed and put the glass on it. "You've had a hard hit to the head, which resulted in a fairly serious concussion. Your memory may be a bit unreliable for a few days. Try not to worry too much. You should be your old self quite soon."

Try not to worry? Zelda felt helpless. She hadn't seen the inside of a hospital since she'd had her tonsils out as a young child. And she'd never been knocked out before. "Where am I?"

The nurse hesitated. "VU University Medical Center in Amsterdam. Let me get the doctor for you."

A few minutes later, a serious-looking woman, not much older than Zelda, entered. Despite her solemn demeanor, her smile lit up her face. "Nice to see you again." She half sat on Zelda's bed and shook her a hand. "I'm Doctor Maring. We met yesterday evening, but I doubt you will remember since you were still unconscious. How are you feeling?" She searched Zelda's face as she waited for an answer.

"My head really hurts. Actually, everything hurts."

The doctor nodded. "It will take a few days before the intensity of the pain lessens. You have been receiving a low-level dosage of morphine intravenously. I'll adjust the dosage to help take the edge off. I have to say you had us all worried."

Zelda automatically touched the bandage swaddling her head. "Really? Is it that serious?"

"You have been unconscious for twenty-nine hours. Your vitals were strong, so we didn't suspect brain damage, but the wound is deep. Luckily, you've got a thick skull." Doctor Maring smiled as Zelda's face drained of color.

"That's what my mother always says." Zelda chortled nervously. *I've been unconscious for a day? How could the doctor think this is the moment for a joke*, she thought.

A knock on the door made the doctor rise. "The police asked me to inform them as soon as you regained consciousness. I imagine that's them."

Zelda could feel herself tensing up.

"You don't have to talk with them for long, but they are concerned for your safety." Doctor Maring took her hand. "Zelda, if that wound had been an inch deeper, we wouldn't be talking right now. Anything you can tell the police about your assailant may help them find whoever hurt you."

Zelda dipped her head slightly, not wanting to set off another stab of pain. "Of course, I'll do my best. But it hurts to think."

"I've already warned them that you will need a few days to regain your memory completely. Tell them whatever you can remember now. They can always come back once you're feeling better."

Zelda's visitors knocked again, and Doctor Maring opened the door. "Please, come in."

A man and woman, both in uniform, entered. They exchanged handshakes with the doctor before approaching Zelda, smiling as they did. The woman introduced them. "Hi, Zelda. I'm Officer Vos, and this is Officer Landhuis. How are you feeling?"

"I've been better," she mumbled.

Officer Vos chuckled politely. "We understand you need to rest, but we would like to ask you some questions about Friday night. Do you think you could try to help us?"

"Yes, I want to try."

"Excellent. Can you walk us through what you remember about that night? When did you get home? Why don't we start there?"

Zelda closed her eyes and concentrated hard. Scenes from that night began flashing through her mind, but not in the correct order. She rubbed at her forehead. "I got home late from work. A few of us from the Amstel Modern had drinks and dinner at a café close to my apartment. I was tired, so I took the elevator. When the door opened, my neighbor Gabriella was inside. She was passed out on the floor but was breathing. I know Gabriella has diabetes and keeps insulin pens in her refrigerator, so I took her back up to her apartment."

The female officer touched Zelda's foot to interrupt. "How did you know Gabriella has diabetes?"

"We're friends, and it's happened before. When she's working on a new painting, she forgets to eat, and her blood sugar dips too low."

Zelda suddenly looked up to the officer, a jolt shooting through her neck. "Wait, where is Gabriella? Is she here at this hospital, too?"

"You mean Gabriella Tamic? The woman who lives next door to you in apartment number seven?" Officer Landhuis joined the conversation, double-checking his notepad as he spoke.

"I don't know her last name, but she's the only Gabriella in the building."

"And you live there with your boyfriend, Jacob Dekker?"

"Yes, how did you know that?"

"We got in touch with Jacob after you were admitted to the hospital. It took us a day to find him because, according to the landlord, you are not officially renting the apartment, a woman named Renee de Vries is. She gave us your names."

Zelda swore under her breath. She had promised Renee that she would not get in touch with the landlord under any circumstances. Technically, Renee wasn't allowed to sub-rent her studio for more than three months at a time and didn't want him to know about Zelda's year-long lease. She hoped there wouldn't be repercussions for the young artist or herself. She loved that apartment.

"Jacob returned from Cologne yesterday," Officer Vos added. "The nurse tells me he was here all night and only left to go home to sleep about an hour before you woke up."

Zelda felt tears welling up in her eyes. Jacob came back as soon as he heard. She couldn't wait to see him.

She started to pick up the phone next to her bed when Officer Vos said, "You can call him in a minute. We are almost done."

Officer Landhuis took back the lead. "So you found your neighbor in the elevator and rode up with her to the fifth floor. Then what?"

"I carried her to her apartment and laid her out on her couch." Zelda's voice was more assured now. Simply knowing Jacob was here was such a relief. And talking about that night was bringing it all back. "Her eyes were open, but she wasn't all there if you know what I mean. She asked for an insulin pen. I went to her kitchen and got her one out of the refrigerator. She shot up and sort of fell back onto the couch in a trance. I sat next to her for a few minutes. I thought she'd fallen asleep, but then she asked for orange juice. I went to the kitchen and poured a glass for her."

Zelda hesitated, momentarily not trusting her memories. "There was something odd. I noticed it when I walked back to the living room." She stopped talking and frowned. What was it again that caught her attention? She closed her eyes and willed her thoughts to clear.

The officers waited patiently for a moment, then the woman asked, "Zelda, what was unusual? Was it a photograph? Or a letter? Was someone else there, perhaps hiding in the room?"

"Wait! It was a painting. No, two paintings that were the same— that was it."

"She had two pictures hanging on her wall that were similar?" Officer Vos asked in confirmation.

Zelda blushed. Her memories were all jumbled together and she didn't know if she trusted them or not. "I know it's not odd that she was painting, I mean, she is an artist. It was the paintings themselves. They were identical. Or almost."

Vos nodded encouragingly. "Okay. So she was making two versions of the same painting. Do you know if she was preparing for an exhibition?" Her tone made clear she didn't find Zelda's observation strange or out of place, especially in an artist's studio space.

"You're going to think I am crazy, but the paintings looked just like Jackson Pollock's *Study Number 5*. It was stolen from the Amstel Modern last week. That's why they caught my eye."

After a long pause, Officer Landhuis asked, "Are you saying that your neighbor was painting two copies of a painting that was stolen from an exhibition at the Amstel Modern?"

"No! Listen to me." Zelda's head felt as if it were about to burst. "There were two copies of the Pollock in her living room. The one hanging on her wall was finished and perfect. The second one, the painting on her easel, was almost finished. It was like she was making a copy of the one hanging on the wall, the original Pollock."

Both officers looked up at Zelda in surprise. "So let me get this straight. You think you saw a painting stolen from your employer in your neighbor's studio. And that she was making a copy of it?" Landhuis asked.

"Yes! I mean, no." Zelda realized she was accusing Gabriella of stealing and forging a Pollock and wanted to backtrack before she got her friend into real trouble. She still didn't know what Gabriella was doing or why the original Pollock was in her living room. "Yes, I saw two paintings that seemed quite similar to the one that was stolen, but I don't know for certain either was actually painted by Pollock. I didn't have a chance to examine them thoroughly, and I'm not an expert. Why would they be? I mean, Gabriella is a successful artist in her own right."

The officers both seemed puzzled by her change in attitude. "Do you believe Gabriella was involved with the Amstel Modern robbery?" Landhuis asked.

"God, no. She's as apolitical as they come. I doubt she would ever take part in a protest action."

"Why do you think the theft was a protest action?"

"I thought that's what the news was saying, that the Robber Hood gang are trying to get museums to secure their collections better? At least, that's what my coworkers think."

Both officers stared at her, expressionless. Officer Vos finally asked, "Ah, yes, your coworkers. We understand you were one of the research assistants for the exhibition that just opened in the Amstel Modern. And that you were responsible for writing the texts about the American modernists, including the stolen Pollock. Is that correct?"

"Yes," Zelda responded, unsure why they were asking about her work.

"And in the course of your research, did you look at the Pollock often?"

"Of course! I helped write the text boards and biographies of all the American artists in the *Conversations* exhibition. I guess I got to know all the artwork fairly well."

The officers exchanged cryptic glances before Vos said, "Zelda, your doctors warned us your memories would be unreliable. I believe you did see two paintings similar to one stolen from your employer, but unless we have reason to believe Gabriella is an art thief or forger, I think we should set this aside for now. Why don't we talk about the Pollocks again once your memory has improved? We're here today because we want to find the person who hurt you. Can you tell us what happened after you brought Gabriella her insulin pen?"

Zelda glared at Officer Vos, wishing she wouldn't use such a condescending tone. As much as she wanted to argue with the officers and make them understand why they should take her seriously, she wasn't entirely certain she believed it herself. Gabriella's paintings were often colorful and loose, so what if her shattered memory intertwined the Pollock, robbery, and her attack? But why did she want to call the police? A stab of pain overwhelmed her, almost as if her brain was telling her to take a break from thinking. Zelda shut her eyes tightly until it subsided.

"Zelda, can you tell us what happened next? Or should we come back tomorrow?" Officer Landhuis asked.

"No, it's fine. Let's get this over with." Zelda took a deep breath and concentrated on that fateful night. "I brought Gabriella the orange juice and helped her drink it. She seemed to feel a bit better. Then she wanted a chocolate bar. After I got her one, I used the bathroom. When I was inside, a man knocked on Gabriella's door and entered her apartment. I heard him walk into the living room, and he started yelling, which I assumed was because Gabriella was passed out on the couch."

"What did he say, Zelda?"

"I don't know. He wasn't speaking in English. I think it was Croatian."

"Okay, then what?"

"When I opened the bathroom door, I saw an older man with bushy white hair standing there, swinging something at my head. The next thing I know, I'm here."

"Would you recognize him if you saw him again?"

"I guess so? I mean, I remember his eyes. They were a dark

brown. And his hair was long. And white."

The officers asked a few more questions, but Zelda couldn't remember much more and got frustrated.

Officer Vos finally said, "I think you need to rest now. When you feel better, give us a call, and we can talk more." When she pulled out a business card, Zelda grabbed her arm.

"Wait, how did you find me?"

"Emergency services received an anonymous call that a woman in Gabriella's apartment needed medical attention. Gabriella's door was partially open when the first responders arrived. The trail of blood indicated you had been attacked in the bathroom, just as you remember, then dragged through the living room and into the kitchen, presumably out of the assailant's way," Officer Landhuis stated matter-of-factly.

Zelda could feel her stomach convulsing. Doctor Maring, who was standing in one corner listening, rushed forward with a garbage can. Zelda threw up bile, retching horribly as she thought of the trail of blood her body had left behind.

"I think you should go now, officers," the doctor said, nodding toward the door.

"No, wait..." Zelda tried sitting up. The sudden movement made her howl. "Please, what if he comes back? What should I do if he visits Gabriella again?"

"I don't think you will be seeing either one of them anytime soon."

"Why not?" Zelda asked, fearing the worst. "Did he hurt Gabriella, too?"

"We don't know. Gabriella vanished along with all her personal effects and artwork. The only thing left inside her apartment was you."

22 What Day Is It?

September 5, 2018

Zelda hugged Jacob as hard as she could. Deep in her heart, she already knew she was important to him, but the fact he had rushed back from Cologne to be by her side made her feel so loved that she was afraid her heart might burst.

When she released her grip, Jacob stroked her cheek. "Oh, Zelda, I am so glad you are going to be okay. I was so worried. The doctors didn't know what to think..." He looked away and wiped away a tear before adding in a whisper, "I don't know what I would have done without you."

She ran her fingers through his hair. "I'm not planning on leaving you anytime soon." Since regaining consciousness four days earlier, each reunion was an emotional affair. They kissed again so passionately neither heard the nurse enter.

"Okay, lovebirds, break it up. It's time for Zelda's breakfast."

The nurse brought a tray of runny scrambled eggs, a banana, and yogurt over to her. "Do you want one, too?" she asked Jacob, grinning widely.

He took a look at the plate and grimaced. "No, I think I'll pass. Thanks," he said, then winked at the nurse. He'd gotten to know the hospital staff pretty well this past week, perhaps better than Zelda had.

After the nurse left, he pulled a chair close to Zelda's bed. He watched her eat for a moment, then folded his hands into a steeple under his chin. He did that whenever he was afraid to tell her something. Zelda set her fork down.

"My boss called again." He looked up at her expectantly, obviously wondering if she was going to freak out or not.

"Oh, I didn't know he'd been calling you. Is everything okay?" Zelda kept her tone level.

"Yeah, it's just I have an important project meeting Friday afternoon that he doesn't want me to miss. I'm supposed to be presenting the last three months of research and my preliminary findings to the grant committee," Jacob said apologetically.

"What day is it today?"

"Wednesday."

"Oh, darling, you have to go. Please. I would feel terrible if your project didn't get its full funding."

"Really?" Jacob cocked his head and squinted his eyes.

"Of course!" Zelda laughed and touched his arm. "I'm not going anywhere."

Jacob considered her words. "I could get the night train Friday night and be back early Saturday morning. I'll ask the doctor what she thinks. I want to be here when you're released."

"I can't sit up without my head exploding. Trust me. I'll still be here Saturday. Besides, the bigwigs might want you to wine and dine them. Don't rush back here on my account. Securing your funding is more important."

"Well, if you're sure..."

"I am!" She took his hand and kissed it. "Now go call your boss."

Jacob seemed so relieved. She loved him so much, and she would hate to hold him back from doing what he enjoyed most. And considering how long it had taken him to find this job, she would never forgive herself if he lost it because of her.

He pulled out his phone and stood up. "I'll book a train ticket for the morning. But first, I'll call my boss. He will be so glad to hear that I'll be back in time for the meeting." He kissed her eyebrow and nuzzled her nose with his. "Be right back."

As soon as he left, she lay back in bed and closed her eyes, no longer interested in her meal.

23 Practice Makes Perfect

September 7, 2018

Gabriella practiced sweeping her hand loosely across the canvas twice before picking up a wide brush and plunging it into the black oil paint. With one fluid motion, she swiped the hairs against her work in progress, pulling the brush swiftly down then up again. It left behind just enough paint to create the swirl she wanted without it being too dense to see the underlying layers.

Gabriella stepped back and eyed her work critically as she compared it to the original Alexander Calder hanging on the wall in front of her. The sketch was a dance of yellow squiggles, blue dots, red dashes, and black swirls. Her first swirl was perfect. Only fifteen more to go.

Calder's *Study Number 9* was as fluid as his kinetic sculptures. He didn't restrict his movements or try to make each shape precisely the same. That was what she felt when she looked at the original and knew her copy needed to convey the same emotion. It was far more difficult to replicate spontaneity than precision. Luckily, she loved a challenge.

After practicing how to recreate the impulsiveness the piece breathed, it had taken her a day to copy this Calder. She used a hairdryer between layers to dry the paint rapidly and force it to form *craquelure*, microscopic cracks on the paint's surface that occur naturally over time.

The black swirls—sixteen giant curlicues spread randomly across the canvas—were the last layer. At least, Calder's version was random. Before painting the next swirl, Gabriella used a ruler to check the distance between each of the black shapes to ensure her copy was as accurate as could be. She knew Calder didn't sketch out his ideas on the canvas in pencil first but painted according to feeling and emotion. It was so tempting to save time by penciling in all the black curls at once, but she didn't want her copy to get tripped up by something as silly as a pencil mark showing through. To any art expert familiar with his loose style, that would be a dead giveaway that they were looking at a forgery.

She dipped her brush into the black paint for the second time just as the doorbell rang. She looked up at the clock hanging over the door. *Right on time*, she thought.

Moments later, Ivan Novak entered, carrying a large cardboard box. "Hello, my dear. I come bearing gifts," he said cheerily before kissing her on the cheeks. He set the box of paints down then studied her critically. Gabriella knew he was still worried about her health. And perhaps rightfully so because when she was working on a strict deadline, she had a bad habit of losing track of time. When she was in a creative surge, it wasn't unusual for her to work for thirty-six hours without a break. Her diabetes always flared up when she was in one of these moods. And locked up in this studio made it even more difficult to remember to stop and eat food as a normal person would.

That was why Ivan asked Anthony to stay with her in Maastricht and assist her with the copies. He was two years younger than her twenty-four years yet almost as talented. She figured working together, they would be able to copy all four pieces before Ivan's deadline. It was also reassuring to know someone was keeping an eye on her.

Since bringing them down to Maastricht, a thriving city on the Netherlands' southern border with Germany and Belgium, Ivan had made a point of stopping by every two days. He claimed it was to check on their progress, but Gabriella knew her insulin dip rattled him, and he didn't trust Anthony completely to take care of her. Ivan had always treated her more like a daughter than an employee. Considering the terrible shape she was in, Gabriella was grateful for his extra attention even though she knew it meant he spent several hours on the road just to visit her. He'd taken them to one of his studios in Maastricht because it was pretty much as far away as you could get from Amsterdam and still be in the country. The last thing either one of them needed right now was for the police to find her. As soon as they did, they would want to question her extensively. And their deadline was looming. She didn't have time to sit in a police station. Once they finish the paintings and Ivan moves them to his warehouse, they would think up a plausible story, and she would go to the police herself.

Right now, the police didn't worry her too much, but Zelda's condition did. The American was her only non-artist friend, and truth be told, Gabriella enjoyed hanging out with someone she wasn't in competition with. The stained-glass windows Zelda made were lovely but not interesting or unique enough to be sold in art galleries. To Gabriella's amazement, that didn't seem to bother the American. She seemed to enjoy working with glass for the simple pleasure of creating something. Gabriella missed those days and the joy she once felt when turning a blank canvas into a work of art. Nowadays, a finished painting only brought thoughts of euros to mind.

"I'm glad to see this is full," Ivan called out from the kitchen. Gabriella reckoned he was examining the pantry and refrigerator. "How are you feeling?"

She didn't need to look at Ivan to know how concerned he was. She could hear it in his voice. "I'm fine, really. Anthony started setting a timer for meals, as you suggested, and we make a point of eating something substantial whenever it goes off. My energy level has balanced out, and I'm able to work through the night without feeling any side effects."

"Hmm, I'm glad you are eating better, but you should still get a good night's rest. Do we need to set a timer for bed as well?" Ivan smiled as he spoke, but Gabriella knew he wasn't joking. "I'll let Anthony know. Speaking of which, where is he?"

"Grocery shopping."

Gabriella was glad for the breaks his daily shopping trips provided. Living together in this small studio was quite intense.

"Good. I'm glad he's taking care of you."

"Hey." Gabriella laid a hand on his arm. "You need to stop

worrying about me. I'm doing much better." He started to speak, but Gabriella cut him off. "What I am worried about is Zelda. Why did you have to hit her?"

Ivan sighed. "Gabriella, I told you already. You were laid out on the couch, incoherent and groggy. The Pollock was hanging on the wall, and your copy was on the easel in the middle of your living room. And there was a stranger in your bathroom. I saw my worst nightmare brought to life. No one can know that you have the original Pollock let alone that you're copying it. What did you expect me to do? I got scared, panicked, hit your friend with a chair, and got you and your artwork out of there as quickly as I could. Luckily, Anthony was able to bring his van over right away so we could get all of your paintings, sketches, supplies, and you out of your studio—at the same time. I did call an ambulance for your friend once we were a few blocks away from your apartment building. You were so out of it that you couldn't tell me who she was until we were past Utrecht. And frankly, when you said she worked for the Amstel Modern, I was glad we got you out of there as quickly as we did. Are you positive she didn't ask you about the Pollock before I arrived?"

Gabriella shook her head. "No, she was helping me the whole time. I doubt she even saw them."

"Thank God for that."

Gabriella pursed her lips but said nothing.

Ivan shook his head. "Don't you think she would feel obligated to tell her employer that her neighbor has one of their stolen paintings? And if Luka Antic finds out we are copying these works, we are both dead. You knew there was a substantial risk when you took the job. There is no saying sorry to Luka. This is life and death."

Gabriella's anger subsided, and she nodded in acknowledgment. "Did you kill Zelda?"

"No, she was breathing when I left. Light concussion worst-case scenario."

"How can you be so sure?"

Ivan sat down on a couch overlooking the Maas River from which the city took its name. "Frankly, I wasn't at the time. I was so focused on getting you and the artwork out of your studio that I didn't check her vital signs. Last night, I called the hospital and pretended to be her uncle. They wouldn't let me talk to Zelda, but they did say she had been moved out of the ICU ward a few days ago. So that's good news."

"I guess. I wish I could call and let her know I'm sorry."

"No! You can't get in touch with her or anyone else for that matter. I'm moving the paintings to my warehouse next week. Give me a few more days, and then you'll have your life back and a large bonus to travel with."

"How many more days?"

"The last robbery is planned for next Thursday. That gives everyone one week to finish their copies. After that, you are free to do whatever you want."

Gabriella looked to the floor and blew out her cheeks. Ivan was right. Officially, she was missing. If she called Zelda, the police might be able to trace her location. And as badly as she felt about her friend, she doubted they would ever see each other again. Thanks to Ivan's actions, Gabriella could never go back to her old apartment in Het Sieraad, which was too bad because she loved that little studio and the plethora of skylights. Gabriella looked outside, letting her eyes follow a barge up the Maas River. *The past is the past*, she told herself. Right now, she needed to focus on getting the last two pieces copied. Only after she finished them could she think about the rest of her life.

"Now, let's see what you've got," Ivan said as he walked to the pairs of Jackson Pollock's and Franz Kline's that she and Anthony had already completed. Stacked up in one corner were the crates Ivan brought over the last time he'd visited. As soon as he approved her copies and they had dried completely, she and Anthony could pack them up. Ivan examined each set carefully, moving back and forth between the copy and original as he did.

"This black line is a bit too short. Can you lengthen it by a half-inch?"

Gabriella sidled up next to him and leaned in closer to the Kline. "Wow, you are good," she said. "Sure, I can have Anthony fix that."

Ultimately, Ivan found only three discrepancies, all easily rectified.

Gabriella was thrilled. That meant they only had the Calder and Hans Hofmann to do. Then their work would be done, and she could think about her immediate future—specifically where she would travel to first.

24 A Little Birdie Told Me...

September 8, 2018

Zelda held on to the rolling table for support as she slowly moved from the bathroom back to her bed. For the first time since she'd woken up in the hospital seven days earlier, she was able to walk across the room without it spinning. Her legs still trembled. However, the nurses assured her that was from lack of use, not her head trauma. The constant dizziness she'd been experiencing was significantly less, and the light no longer gave her a migraine. She could even watch a little television or read a book as long as she did so in short sprints.

She lay out on her bed, exhausted from the effort, and scratched at her scalp, free from the swaddling bandages. A large Band-Aid now covered her head wound. She snuggled under the thin blanket and turned on the television. The evening news was just starting. The lead story made her sit up in her bed so quickly that her ears rang. She turned up the volume and listened to a reporter on the scene explain how the Dibbets Museum in Maastricht was the twelfth robbed within the last nineteen days. The thieves broke in through a skylight and rappelled inside. After taking 3.4 million euros worth of artwork, they were whisked away by helicopter.

"What the heck?" Zelda exclaimed. The bed next to hers was empty, so no one responded. *These robberies are only increasing in their audacity,* she thought.

After the short segment ended, Zelda got out her iPad and surfed to *The Art Investigator* blog. If anyone had answers, it would be Nik.

On the homepage was a new post, dated this morning.

Art Detective on the Trail of Robber Hood

Twelve museums robbed in nineteen days! What is going on in the Netherlands?

My sources have provided me with more photos of Robber Hood cards left behind at these most recent thefts. The latest four read:

Why can't you protect what you love?

Isn't your history worth more?

Thanks for the poor security.

You might as well leave the door open.

The police and museums involved refuse to officially confirm these cards' presence at the scene of every robbery. Why the censor? The public has a right to know who is after our cultural treasures and what their motives are because it is our artwork that is being stolen.

Who is Robber Hood?

Is Robber Hood really a radical group stealing from our cultural institutions to raise awareness about their poor security? These messages indicate that they are stealing to make a statement, yet they have not reached out to the general public or media. Stranger still, I cannot find any reference to their organization or motivations online. Even if the police's cyber unit is somehow blocking Robber Hood's website and social media, I should have found some mention of them online.

Assuming this is a protest group acting selflessly, what are their conditions for the artwork's return? Why haven't they made their demands known?

Or is there something more sinister going on?

A little birdy told me something yesterday that makes me wonder if the Robber Hood gang are not the cultural crusaders their cards imply but thugs stealing for profit.

The company responsible for insuring most of our victimized museums has hired Dutch private investigator Vincent de Graaf to assist with the investigation into the robberies. For those of you who aren't familiar with de Graaf, he specializes in recovering stolen artwork—in particular, pieces taken by Eastern European criminal organizations.

Is Robber Hood the latest gang of mafia-sponsored criminals to steal our cultural treasures for use as collateral in their underworld transactions?

When you consider the Van Gogh, Westfries, Kunsthal, and Scheringa Museums were all recent victims of thefts organized by and for the criminal underworld, perhaps bringing in an art detective sooner rather than later is a smart move.

After nineteen days and several ongoing investigations, it seems the police, de Graaf, the media, and I are no closer to discovering the true identity of this Robber Hood gang nor the current location of the stolen artwork.

Which leaves us with the same questions as last time, who is Robber Hood? What are their motives, and why haven't they made them public? And what are the police keeping from us? This cultural lover still wants to know.

What a crazy situation. Was the mob masterminding these robberies? She knew the two stolen Van Goghs were found in possession of the Camorra, an Italian crime family based out of Naples. The Kunsthal in Rotterdam was robbed by Romanians and works taken from the Westfries Museum resurfaced in the Ukraine. Another criminal organization returned two paintings stolen from the Scheringa Museum after they received them as a down payment for a drug deal—on the condition they remain anonymous. Was that why the police weren't telling the public more, because the mafia is involved?

The blog post was only a few hours old but had already gone viral. Five-hundred twenty-three comments had been posted and hundreds of pingbacks from Dutch and international news organizations and bloggers.

Zelda searched for more articles about the thefts and skimmed several. Quite a few of the mainstream media's online sites cited Nick's blog in their articles—in particular, the information he provided about the Robber Hood cards. But none presented new revelations. Why was Nik privy to information they were not? And why weren't the burgled museums talking to the media directly?

Zelda puzzled over the blogger's identity and his sources when a horrible thought went through her mind. Could Nik be Robber Hood? Was this blog just an elaborate ploy to draw attention to the robberies and its protest group's actions?

Zelda contemplated the thefts and Nik's identity until her head hurt but couldn't decide which theory she believed most—that Robber Hood were political activists, a cover for the mob, or simply art thieves.

25 Family History

September 9, 2018

Vincent de Graaf relaxed into his leather couch as he sipped a freshly squeezed orange juice and gazed out his living room windows, meditating on the lapping water of the Amstel River. Swans bobbed on its surface as herons fished in the long reeds lining its banks. Soon, a narrow boat as long as a city bus glided by, powered by eight young women crouching and pushing off in unison. Vincent marveled at their speed and efficiency until their trainer caught up with them on her bicycle. The trainer's tips and encouragement relayed by a megaphone as she biked alongside broke the serenity of the morning.

Moments later, both boat and trainer were gone. The quietness of the morning, along with the wildlife, returned instantly. He chuckled, thinking how lucky he was to be living here on the banks of the Amstel River, just a short bike ride from Amsterdam's city center. The house and art collection—both in his mother's name—was all that remained of his inheritance. The rest had been wiped out by legal fees.

The only thing missing from this perfect morning was his wife, Theresa, currently flying over the Atlantic, destination Mexico City. He knew he struck gold when he met her. Not only was she caring but she was also smart and independent. Her job as a flight attendant meant she was used to being away from home and working irregular hours.

Perhaps, most importantly, she had no desire to have children. With his investigative work, often in foreign countries for an indefinite amount of time, he didn't know how they would have managed them. Theresa loved her job, and her seniority meant she could pick and choose the flights she worked. They even had last-minute access to foreign destinations whenever their hectic schedules meshed, and they could get away together. She was the perfect partner for him.

Vincent flipped through the folder in his lap, containing photos of the twenty-seven pieces of art taken during the twelve robberies to date. He had already downloaded them all onto his iPad, but he preferred a paper dossier. On the couch next to him was a pile of appraisal estimates he'd created for each of the stolen works. After familiarizing himself with each piece, he spread the images out across his couch and coffee table, then stepped back to study them.

The police provided him with these images of the stolen works in the hope that he could create a profile of the thieves' choices and possibly predict which museums might be targets. The fact that they'd asked him to do this told Vincent they were getting desperate. There seemed to be no end in sight with the Robber Hood gang hitting a museum every few nights. The targets were spread across the Netherlands, making their movements even more difficult to predict. The police were operating under the assumption that multiple teams of thieves were active, but so far, no one in Vincent's network nor the Dutch police's local ring of informants was talking. It was as if the Robber Hood gang vanished and reappeared at will, which was why the police wanted to try another tactic and see if they could predict which museum would be next.

Why did the thieves steal these pieces? What connected them, Vincent wondered. He wished he could ask his father about it—the old man was lightning fast when it came to finding visual connections. He recognized patterns others did not. But his father's life choices made it impossible for Vincent to ask him about these thefts. His role in the forgery and theft of several paintings landed him in prison, and Vincent doubted the guards would be amused if he asked his father's advice about an open case.

If his father hadn't committed those crimes, Vincent probably never would have become a private investigator specializing in stolen artwork. As a successful art dealer, his father had sold many a painting to the most prestigious museums in the Netherlands. Unfortunately, as Vincent later learned, several of them had been switched at delivery with a forged copy. It only took one curator to notice a difference and bring down his father's business as well as destroy his reputation. And rightfully so. His father had cheated fifteen museums out of the masterpieces they had paid for and, instead, sold the originals to nefarious dealers and collectors abroad.

As soon as he had his license, Vincent made recovering the museums' lost pieces his first task. He used his knowledge of his father's business and personal life to track down all but two paintings. In the process, he had become friends with many officers and investigators in the Dutch police force, alliances that would prove crucial to future cases. After his spectacular recoveries made national headlines, several more museums hired him to help track down stolen artwork and antiquities. It was then that Vincent became aware of the shadier side of art crimes and their frequent connections with criminal organizations. What made him so successful was his ability to treat thieves and police with the same respect. Thanks to his father's indiscretions, he realized that not everyone who committed crimes was a bad person at heart.

Vincent took the last swig of orange juice and then used his tongue to work clumps of pulp from between his teeth. Pushing his father from his mind, he focused on the twenty-seven images before him. Was it the style, period, artist's nationality, or medium that connected them?

According to his appraisal estimates, all were worth between two hundred and eight hundred thousand euros, were small in format, and sketch-like. These were not the kinds of artwork he'd expected the thieves to take—at least, not if they were looking to make a quick profit by reselling them. Within the mafia and drug circuit, artwork was worth approximately ten percent of its market value. Thus, a painting valued at a hundred thousand euros would only be worth ten thousand in trade. Stealing these artworks hardly seemed worth the effort when you considered the pieces individually, but this Robber Hood gang had taken a total of twenty-seven pieces, so far. Collectively, their net worth was around sixteen million, not a bad chump of change. But it seemed like a herculean effort and risk for a relatively small profit margin. In each of the museums they'd robbed, the thieves had walked past works worth millions to steal a sketch or drawing. On the surface, it didn't make sense, but it did to the thieves. These robberies were too well planned and executed to be spontaneous smash-and-grab jobs.

Think like Robber Hood, Vincent urged his mind, then closed his eyes and considered their motives. That question needed answering before he could know why these pieces were taken. The notes left behind at each robbery seemed to be meant to scare the museums into improving their security. But there was no follow-up demanding a ransom or other condition of return. And Robber Hood didn't exist on social media. If they were cultural crusaders, who thought stealing treasures was the best way to charge up the public to protect them—as their cards implied—why weren't they active online? Why did no one know about them? Robber Hood was unknown in every sense of the word. The police were working with three theories, but Vincent was only concerned with the Balkan connection. And so far, none of his contacts knew who Robber Hood was, or they weren't ready to tell him.

Would his network alert him when the artwork reached the Balkans? With so many robberies happening in such a short amount of time, Vincent imagined it would make more sense to move all of the pieces out of the Netherlands at the same time and not take them back to the Balkans one by one. But where would they store the pieces until then? He made a note for the police to look for an art storage facility in the vicinity of the robberies, though, realistically, he knew there were too many options to search them all.

Until he knew more about Robber Hood and their motivations, everything was conjecture. For now, all he could do was help the police figure out why these artworks were taken and, hopefully, create a list of potential targets. The police didn't have the resources to protect all the museums in the Netherlands—there were far too many. Vincent cleared his mind and concentrated on the stolen artwork again when their simplicity struck him.

The pieces of art covering his couch and coffee table were all loosely painted or drawn, somewhere between abstract and realistic. Most were sketches created by important artists, but none were their most renowned works. Some were painted by Americans, but most by Europeans. All were postmodern works and most created in the last fifty years. The artists used watercolor, charcoal, gouache, pencil, oil, and acrylic to create studies and sketches on paper and canvas. A collector interested in documenting the evolution of postwar modernism would value these pieces far more than the average museum visitor, Vincent realized.

These are exactly the kinds of modern artworks my father preferred to forge, Vincent thought wryly. There was no tempera or mineral-based paints used in their creation, meaning his forgers had easy access to the same sorts of paints the artists had. Everything they needed could be purchased at a quality art supplies store. That made copying the pieces easier and detection more difficult. *Oh God,* he thought with a jolt. *Were these thieves actually forgers?*

So what was their plan? Cry artnapping, and when the museums paid up, they would receive forgeries? It would be easy enough to sell the originals abroad. Or were they destined to disappear into the criminal underworld as a down payment for drugs or weapons? Vincent still had trouble believing that no one in his Croatian network knew who Robber Hood was. He would give anything to be able to connect the thefts to Luka Antic.

Twenty-seven pieces. If they were sold abroad, it would take years to find them all again. Vincent shook that depressing thought off. He promised the police an honest assessment. He now knew what Robber Hood preferred. Could he also predict which museums would be next?

26 An Old Friend

September 10, 2018

"Well, Zelda, there's your taxi. Take care of yourself, and I hope not to see you again for quite some time." Doctor Maring smiled warmly as she held onto the wheelchair she'd used to bring Zelda to the hospital's front door.

"Thank you, Doctor. The feeling is mutual." Zelda grinned back as she slowly lowered herself into the taxi's back seat. Her head spun a little as the driver pulled away. She still wasn't one hundred percent but well enough to be released. This was not how she envisioned her return home after a week in the hospital, but a taxi was the only option. Jacob's meeting had gone so well Friday that the grant funders stayed the weekend so they could tour the museum's research facilities and view the collections Jacob was responsible for documenting. He wouldn't be back until midnight tonight but had already arranged with his boss to work from Amsterdam for the rest of the week. Although Zelda was disappointed he couldn't be here to pick her up, she was thrilled he would be able to spend time at home. If anything, this attack had brought them even closer together. For the first time in her life, she felt truly loved.

The only two friends Zelda knew who owned cars were both unavailable to pick her up, though Esmee from the Amstel Modern did promise to make her soup and bring it over later. Zelda was relieved not to have to worry about food or shopping tonight—she doubted she'd be able to walk to the store without passing out let alone carry everything home.

Walking across the lobby was more draining than she'd expected. By the time she'd ridden the elevator up to her front door, Zelda was feeling faint. Thoughts of stretching out on her comfortable couch motivated her feet forward. She held onto the doorframe for support and then slowly made her way inside. It felt so strange to be back inside her apartment after a week. It was almost as if she were entering a hotel room. Zelda stumbled into the living room and laid out on the couch. Within seconds, she was fast asleep.

Chimes disturbed her slumber, and Zelda woke up groggy. The clock on her living room wall read five p.m. The chimes rang through the apartment again. It was her doorbell. *It must be Esmee with the soup*, she thought. When she opened her door, a skinny man with a pointed beard and long hair pulled back in a ponytail was standing outside.

"Hello, I'm a friend of Gabriella. She's not answering her door. Do you know where she's at?" His English was clipped and off-beat. It reminded Zelda of how Gabriella spoke. With his all-black outfit and hip facial hair, Zelda reckoned he must be one of Gabriella's artist friends. Zelda didn't recognize him, and he seemed friendly enough, but wouldn't her friends know she was missing? Or had she resurfaced while Zelda was in the hospital?

"I'm afraid I don't," she said. She was ashamed to realize she hadn't thought about Gabriella while in the hospital. She'd been in too much pain to think about anything but her recovery. "Sorry. I've been in the hospital all week." She automatically touched the wide Band-Aid covering the two-inch-long wound on her head. "Who are you?"

"I'm Marko. Gabriella and I grew up together. I'm only in town for a few days and thought I'd look her up. I tried calling, but she's not answering. Maybe I have her old number. Is this the correct one?" Marko held up his telephone's screen so Zelda could read it.

"Yes, that's the same one I have," she said, suddenly realizing that he probably didn't know about Gabriella's disappearance last week. But she was too tired to explain the situation in full. Zelda figured he and Gabriella weren't that close if Marko lived abroad. *A little lie won't hurt anyone*, she thought. "Last I heard, she was going to attend a month-long workshop. I think it's in Bali. But I don't know if she's already left or not. Why don't you leave your telephone number, and I'll give it to her when she returns?"

Marko turned red from embarrassment. "I forgot to turn the international phone plan on so I can't call or receive calls while I'm here. I can give you my hotel's front desk, but I'm at a conference during the day. And we are going on several field trips. Could I ask for your number? Then I can borrow my coworker's phone and check in with you later. I'd really love to see Gabriella again. It's been far too long. And her grandmother knitted her a sweater I promised to deliver. I'm dead meat if I don't find her."

When Marko laughed, the hair on the back of Zelda's neck stood on end. Something about his demeanor made her nervous. Who was he exactly? Was this the man who hit her? Zelda studied his face but knew it wasn't. The person who knocked her out was older, shorter, and squatter.

"I don't think..."

"Look, it's more than that," he pressed. "Gabriella's grandfather is quite ill, and I hope to convince her to come back and visit us. She's not much for keeping in touch with her family, but I know she would regret not being able to say goodbye. Are you sure you don't know where she's at or when she'll be back? Or maybe which hotel she's staying at in Bali? Is there someone else in this building that might know?"

Zelda shrugged, "Not as far as I know."

"Do you have any of her friends' phone numbers or addresses? Or could you get in touch with them? I feel obligated to find her but don't know where to look. We haven't seen each other in years."

Zelda waffled. Before she could respond, Marko added, "I promise not to call more than once a day. Just to check in."

His pushiness was unnerving. A wave of dizziness overcame her. She leaned against the wall, wishing this guy would go away so she could get some more shut-eye. She suspected he wasn't going to take no for an answer. A pang of guilt forced her not to shut the door in his face. If Gabriella's grandfather were on his deathbed, she would want to know about it—whenever she returned or was found.

"Sure. Okay." Zelda rattled off her number, adding, "But I have the ringer off most of the time, so you're better off sending a text message." The last thing she wanted was this guy calling her at all hours. Lord knows what Jacob would think.

"Excellent, thank you so much. And you are?" The way he looked at her, almost through her, gave her the creeps.

"Zelda," she said, ignoring his outstretched hand, already regretting giving him her number. "And which hotel are you staying at?" she pressed, trying to match his inquisitiveness.

"The Victoria Hotel across from Central Station." His piercing gaze and broad smile creeped her out. "I'll be in touch."

He reached the elevator just as the doors opened. Esmee emerged, carrying a crockpot. Even from her doorway, Zelda could smell the bacon and peas. Esmee grinned widely at Marko, ogling his wiry frame as they exchanged places. "He's cute," she whispered loudly. "Who is he?"

Zelda stared at the closed elevator doors. "I'm not sure."

27 Peace of Mind

September 10, 2018

Luka knew he was being unreasonable—irrational even—when he told Marko to question Zelda Richardson, the missing artist's neighbor. The knowledge that Ivan Novak was lying to him was driving him absolutely crazy. He wasn't positive Zelda knew where Gabriella was, but the young American worked for the Amstel Modern, lived next door, and in her police report, she claimed to have seen two Pollocks in Gabriella's studio. His gut told him that was too many coincidences for Zelda not to be involved somehow.

Even if the museum researcher wasn't directly involved with the robberies, her testimony confirmed what Marko thought he saw. And his nephew was the most trustworthy person he'd ever met, which is why Luka was grooming him to take over part of his organization. Luka was almost sixty-five years old, an anomaly in his profession, and was considering semi-retirement. Luka knew he had to secure his organization's future by expanding its reach. Although he didn't have children of his own, he still wanted his legacy to live on, and right now, that meant doing everything in his power to find out what Ivan Novak was trying to hide from him.

But neither Marko nor the police could answer his most pressing question—was Ivan having copies of the stolen artwork made or not?

If they couldn't, perhaps through some miracle, Zelda Richardson could by leading them to the artist.

Marko saw Ivan move the artist and her artwork out of her studio and whisk them away in a van registered to a man named Anthony Beek. Luka now knew that the missing woman's name was Gabriella Tamic and that Novak's gallery represented her. But Luka could not confront Ivan about any of it without risking the entire deal.

Where did Ivan take the paintings and Gabriella? And was she busy copying the rest?

Luka longed to ask Ivan about what had happened that Friday night. He'd already pussyfooted around the topic, asking the art dealer during their last call if he had started moving the stolen artwork to a central location yet. Ivan's resolute answer that none of the works would be moved until after the last robbery did not appease him. He needed the peace of mind in knowing what Ivan was up to and how the artist was involved. If he couldn't question Ivan directly about it, he could concentrate his energy on finding the missing artist.

Having Marko reach out to Zelda was him panicking, not taking back control. He knew that, but until Gabriella resurfaced, he had no choice except to use every available resource to find her.

28 People Don't Just Disappear

September 10, 2018

Zelda awoke to Jacob's sweet lips brushing up against her cheek. She smiled and stretched until her back cracked. She'd fallen asleep on the couch in a tight ball.

"Hi, honey. It's nice to see you again and to have you home and out of the hospital," Jacob whispered in her ear.

"Indeed," she murmured and rubbed her cheek against his stubbly chin.

"How are you feeling?"

"Better," she said with a yawn. Esmee's homemade pea soup and lots of sleep had helped.

He rubbed her cheeks with his long fingers. They were soft, warm, and comforting. "I have a surprise for you."

Zelda nuzzled his neck. "You're enough."

Jacob smiled. "On the train ride back, I booked us into a spa in Nijmegen for three nights. I figured it would help you recover faster."

"Oh, Jacob, that's so sweet!" She threw her arms around him and hugged him tightly. Right now, a spa sounded like just what the doctor ordered. All she wanted to do was forget this past week's events and get back to her normal life. She hugged him close before thoughts of Marko made her push him away and sit up. "Something kind of strange happened after I got home. A childhood friend of Gabriella's stopped by looking for her."

"Oh, I'm surprised he didn't know she was missing."

"He said he's only in town for a few days and decided to drop by when he couldn't reach her by phone."

"Okay. That's not strange."

119

"He insisted I give him my telephone number so he could call and check in about Gabriella."

Jacob's brow furrowed. "Your number? What do you mean he *insisted*?"

Zelda reflected on how uncomfortable Marko made her feel. "It's not what he said, it's more how he said it—like there was no other choice but for him to call me. Gabriella's grandfather is sick."

"Hmm. That is kind of weird. But if he's only in town for a few days, I guess he might have come across as desperate."

"So, should we be looking for Gabriella for him?" Zelda asked. After Esmee left, she'd pondered that question until sleep returned. Zelda called Gabriella's number and even knocked on her door but got no answer. She should have told Marko that Gabriella was missing and sent him to the police instead of giving him her number. Next time he called, she would fess up.

"Why would we do that? And how? The police are still searching for her, and they have a better idea of where to look than we would. People don't just disappear, Zelda. I'm sure they will find her if she wants to be found."

"What do you mean?"

"Well, the police still don't know who hit you or why. All of Gabriella's things were taken, even her clothing. Did you ever consider that she wanted to leave? I mean, if she were kidnapped, why would they take her things? Maybe she was behind on her rent and was trying to sneak out in the night."

"But why would someone hit me? Gabriella knew I wouldn't have told the landlord. Technically, we aren't supposed to be renting this place for a year, remember? I hope we don't get Renee into trouble. I'm surprised she hasn't called yet." Zelda felt so tired and confused. It hurt to think, and right now, her brain was in overdrive.

"I don't know why someone attacked you unless they thought you had hurt Gabriella. You did say she was unconscious on the couch. Maybe it was all a big misunderstanding. Besides, I didn't know you were such good friends. Why is she so important to you?"

Zelda frowned. Jacob was right. The police were far better equipped to find Gabriella than she was. She barely knew the woman. They weren't great friends and knew almost nothing about each other's private lives, and if Jacob was right about Gabriella hiding out, she had no chance of finding her.

Besides, Zelda was beginning to wonder if this wasn't a huge mix-up. Maybe Gabriella was at an artist retreat and would resurface of her own accord when it was over. It wouldn't be the first time she'd taken off at a moment's notice. Part of her suspected that Gabriella would get in touch with the police any day now. And if not, the police would surely find her soon.

"Yeah, well, she is my neighbor, and we did hang out a lot when you were in Cologne. It's just so strange not knowing where she's gone or why someone felt the need to assault me in the process." Even to her ears, her reasoning sounded lame. "And I guess Marko made me feel guilty because I hadn't thought about her while I was in the hospital."

"And why should you have? You need to concentrate on getting better, Zelda. Not play detective."

She hugged him tightly. "You're right. Let's go to bed. We have some packing to do in the morning."

Zelda pushed Gabriella and Marko out of her mind. She was in no position to hunt down a missing person. Right now, what she needed most was Jacob and lots of rest.

29 Ode to Modernists

September 12, 2018

Cornelius Kronenburg, director and owner of the Kronenburg Museum, fumed as he read the email from the Dutch police a second time through.

After five years of lobbying, fundraising, and ass-kissing, his dream was finally a reality—his extensive collection of modern and contemporary art now hung in a gorgeous, custom-designed museum bearing his name. It was a wonder of architecture and blended in with the tree-rich environment perfectly. A garden designed by the Netherland's top landscape architect and a perfectly manicured field of grass surrounded his temple to art. Rising behind the museum was a strip of a forest with paths visitors could wander along to reach the North Sea.

Collecting artwork had been a lifelong passion, one he was thrilled to share with the world. Forty years of founding successful software start-ups had made him a multimillionaire. When he retired two years ago, his assemblage of art was considered the most prestigious, privately held collection in the Netherlands. He had spent the last five years securing the land and preparing their new home. With his museum's opening last year, his legacy was secure, and he couldn't be prouder, which was why this email infuriated him so.

According to the police, his permanent collection and current exhibition were the ideal targets for the Robber Hood gang presently terrorizing Dutch museums. And his museum's remote location situated on a nature reserve straddling the dunes of the Netherlands' west coast made it even more attractive.

He was not going to sit back and allow a group of thieves to destroy everything he had worked for. Especially one with such a stupid name. Who did this Robber Hood think they were? Robbing the rich to do what, ransom it back? Had the artwork already disappeared into someone's private collection or, worse, was on its way to Eastern Europe? He read Interpol's annual reports and knew that stolen artwork from Western European museums and galleries often ended up in the Balkans before being further traded or sold. Pink Panthers, Robber Hood, Arkan's Tigers, Groupa Amerika, Balkan Bandits—it was hard to take these groups seriously until you realized that they were responsible for stealing hundreds of millions of dollars' worth of jewels and artwork from private and public collections throughout Europe.

The security system in his new museum was state of the art. *It should be*, he grumbled to himself. The video camera installation alone had cost a half a million to install and fine-tune to his specific space, but the floor-to-ceiling glass windows and isolated location made his insurers nervous. There were no neighbors within miles, meaning no one to help keep an eye on the space at night and report suspicious activities. He had a dedicated phone line to the nearest police station installed as well as discreetly placed panic buttons throughout the exhibition halls. He had even hired an on-site caretaker, a retired cop who lived above the café next door, to help appease their minds and lower his monthly insurance premiums. Still, securing this museum was costing him a fortune.

He was only able to survive thanks to the exorbitant ticket prices and café. Restoring and converting the dilapidated mansion into a café had been a lucrative business decision. Luckily, the newness of such a privately funded institution and the blockbuster exhibitions he was able to arrange brought in busloads of visitors.

His museum was about to celebrate its first anniversary. There was no way he was going to let those Robber Hood jokers tarnish his reputation and destroy his life's greatest achievement.

He wasn't as worried about his permanent collection being taken. The museum was designed to house several of his extraordinarily large pieces—a maze of rusty red steel by Richard Serra, a pair of sunbathing giants by Ron Mueck, and an upside-down swimming pool by Leandro Erlich. The rooms were custom-built to accommodate their size and highlight their beauty.

Most of his paintings still hung in his home. He displayed a few in the bimonthly exhibitions, the chosen works best complimenting or engaging with the art his extensive network of collector friends lent him.

According to the information the police sent in an email to one hundred and fifty museums and galleries spread across the Netherlands, his current exhibition, *Ode to Modernists*, was the perfect target. He was counting on it to draw in new crowds. It was his museum's most ambitious exhibition to date, and several friends had done him a personal favor by lending out paintings and sketches by Kandinsky, Chagall, and Picasso—all pieces never before displayed in a public exhibition. It was the smaller sketches that made his stomach lurch. One successful robbery would mean the end of Kronenburg Museum. No one would ever dare lend him their artwork again.

A fellow museum director had told him about a reputable security-for-hire firm. He requested the two burliest men they had available and was pleased to see they'd taken him seriously. Robber Hood and his gang of thieves had struck sixteen museums in twenty-three days. The police did not have a solid lead to go on and no trail to follow. No one knew how much longer this robbing spree would continue. So far, the thefts had all occurred after hours. It would cost him a pretty penny, but as long as this Robber Hood gang was on the loose, he was prepared to do whatever it took to protect his museum's collection and reputation.

He looked across his desk at the two men the security company had sent over. Both were perfect for the job and available to start immediately. Each man held a copy of the police's email. Cornelius wanted them to know what they were up against. "Your orders are to stop these jokers at any cost."

The guards-for-hire raised their eyebrows. The older man asked, "At any cost?"

"Within the law, of course," Cornelius said, leaning forward to make eye contact with them both. "We don't want to turn this into a murder investigation, but you must understand, these thieves, this Robber Hood gang, they are the bane of every decent museum in the Netherlands." Cornelius paused before adding, "Broken is good."

The guards exchanged nervous glances.

"I will be happy to pay you extra—off the books—for any unpleasantness. Stopping any intruders is of the utmost importance. You will be doing the entire Dutch cultural sector a favor if you intercept and capture them. We all need this problem to go away."

30 On the Road to Recovery

September 13, 2018

Zelda opened her suitcase, and the scent of coconut oil and body butter wafted out. The smells of the spa immediately brought a smile to her face. Their three glorious nights at the Sanadome, a spa resort in Nijmegen, was pure bliss.

Now back home, they were both refreshed, reenergized, and more of a couple than ever. Zelda's wound was healing well, and the stubble around it was already an inch long. Luckily, most of her hair was still intact, meaning she could sweep it over the shaved bit and look normal. She no longer shunned mirrors. Instead, she was happy to see most of the bruising and swelling was gone. Her migraines had subsided to an occasional headache, and the bouts of dizziness were also less intense.

It had been easy for Zelda to put the intruder, Gabriella, and her head injury out of her mind and revel in Jacob's undivided attention. She wished his work wasn't so far away, though she knew he didn't have much choice at the moment. In an intimate moment, she'd said she'd move to Cologne if he wanted to stay there. Her heart jumped for joy when Jacob told her to let that thought go. His research grant was only for a year, and he wanted to move back to Amsterdam as soon as it ended even if it meant searching for academic work. And, in the meantime, he wanted to find ways to be together more often.

Zelda was so grateful because she loved Amsterdam. When she was a child, her family moved often, and she never really got attached to any of the places they'd lived. As an adult, Zelda had spent several years traveling the globe but never felt so at home in any city before. For the first time in her life, she wanted to settle down and root herself to one spot. It was a fantastic feeling, knowing where you wanted to be, but during these past few days, she realized she would move anywhere Jacob asked her to because being with him was more important than where they lived. Still, she was glad she didn't feel forced to choose between him and her new hometown.

Jacob's graciousness and the spa environment had also made her talk with Renee de Vries bearable. Zelda knew it was coming, but it was still a shock to receive her call their first night away. Her landlord was indeed raging mad that Renee had sublet the studio to Zelda for a year. He agreed to let Renee stay on only if Zelda vacated the premises by the end of the month. Given the circumstances, Zelda was grateful she had two weeks to look for another place.

Zelda carried the suitcase into their bedroom and began unpacking its contents. Most of the clothes she threw into a pile on the ground, wanting to get the clothes in the wash before Jacob got back from the grocery store. She was done being the helpless invalid and wanted to do every little thing she could to help out around the house. Jacob had done enough for her these past few days, and it was time to contribute fully again.

She'd finished unpacking one bag and was about to open the other when a familiar beeping noise drew her attention to her night table. *That's where it is*, she thought as she pulled open the drawer. Sure enough, her phone was inside. In their rush to get on the road, she'd forgotten it. When Jacob offered to turn around to fetch it, she'd decided going offline would be better. How refreshing it was to not be constantly distracted by her phone's beeps and rings. However, it was a necessary evil, she realized when she saw thirty unread messages were vying for her attention. Most were from colleagues, wishing her a speedy recovery. Zelda was certain everything she'd told Esmee about her attack and hospital stay had already been relayed via watercooler conversations to the entire staff.

Four messages were from unknown numbers. As she read through them, the calm Zelda had found while on vacation disappeared in an instant. All were from Marko, asking about her progress in finding Gabriella, each more urgent and vaguely threatening than the last. It sounded like he expected her to be searching for the artist. The last message of *ticktock* made her skin crawl. What the hell was that supposed to mean?

Zelda noted each came from a different number. She called the first, but the line was disconnected. She dialed again, only to hear the same grating beeps. The other three were also no longer in service. Wasn't he going to borrow a coworker's phone to call? Why were none in service, she wondered.

Zelda was convinced Gabriella would have either been found or got in touch with the police while they were at the spa. After all, she'd been missing for thirteen days. If she were kidnapped, someone would have demanded a ransom by now, and the country was too small to just disappear. *Oh God*, Zelda thought, *what if she is dead?*

Zelda turned on her iPad and searched for information about Gabriella but to no avail. She couldn't find any news indicating that the artist had resurfaced of her own accord nor any reports of her death. She looked again at the text messages on the phone.

"What have you found out?"

"Where is Gabriella? I don't like being ignored."

"Do yourself a favor and get in touch. Or have you forgotten what we discussed?"

The last, "Ticktock," sent a chill down her spine.

Zelda's concern for her friend grew by the second. Did the man who hit her kidnap Gabriella? The police still had no leads to his identity. Gabriella was practically unconscious from her insulin dip. She could not have packed up her bags and artwork in the state she was in. Whoever hit Zelda, must have taken Gabriella and her possessions with them. But why? If they were kidnapping the artist, for whatever reason, why take all of her things? It must have taken them several trips with the elevator to get all of Gabriella's stuff downstairs. They would have risked getting caught every time they exited her apartment. Or were they just picking her up, and Gabriella went of her own free will? But if that was the case, why did someone feel the need to hit Zelda over the head.

What if Gabriella left of her own accord? Did her disappearance have anything to do with the Robber Hood thefts, or was there something else going on? A week out of the hospital and Zelda was still having reservations about what she had seen in Gabriella's apartment. She'd almost convinced herself that her memories of the artist's studio and her work on the *Conversations* exhibition had merged in her mind. Was Pollock's *Study Number 5* really hanging on Gabriella's wall as she'd originally thought? Or was that a strange figment of her imagination, a twisting of memories induced by the concussion?

Zelda shook her head, immediately regretting the jarring movement. She held her head in her hands and closed her eyes. When she reopened them, she saw the contents of the open nightstand drawer, specifically a single key—the key to Gabriella's apartment. Zelda had forgotten all about it. Jacob had been mad at her for exchanging keys with their new neighbor the first week they moved in. He wanted to wait and see if she was trustworthy enough and assumed she only wanted to swap so she could steal from them. But after Zelda realized the artist stored stacks of her artwork in her living room, paintings worth ten to fifty thousand euros a pop, Zelda was convinced Gabriella wasn't planning to rob them.

She picked up the key, wondering if it was worth going next door and looking for clues to Gabriella's whereabouts. *The police must have picked it over with a fine-tooth comb*, she thought, but if she didn't look, she would never know. Before she could make up her mind, the doorbell rang. She peered through the peephole. It was Marko.

31 Unexpected Visitor

September 13, 2018

Marko felt like a fool standing outside Zelda Richardson's door. He was convinced the woman knew nothing about Gabriella's whereabouts or the stolen artwork. If she did, why did she go to the spa for four days instead of skipping town? When Luka told him to exert more pressure on Zelda, he knew better than to say no. His uncle was so keyed up about Gabriella and any copies she may or may not be making, questioning his orders could prove fatal.

Marko knew Luka had bet everything on this upcoming deal—confident heroin would prove more profitable than art theft and forgeries in the long run. Marko didn't agree but knew it wasn't his place to set the parameters. At least, not yet.

So here he stood, outside Zelda Richardson's apartment. Not surprising, she didn't let him inside.

"What do you want?" she yelled through the closed door.

"Just checking in to see if you had heard from Gabriella yet. You didn't respond to my messages."

"How would you know? Your telephone numbers are all disconnected."

Touché, he thought. He changed phones daily, one of the many things he did to remain as untraceable as possible. "I've been moving around a lot. Look, can I come in…"

"No!"

Marko snickered. "Okay, well, I can imagine you have a lot of washing to do after a long weekend at the Sanadome," he called out.

"Have you been following me?" Zelda yelled back. He could hear the panic in her voice.

"We just want to find Gabriella, Zelda. Nothing more. Don't

make me do anything we'll both regret. If you know where she's at, you need to tell me."

"I don't know where she's at! No one does! Not even the police."

"Hey! What's going on here?" Jacob was back from the stores, full shopping bags in both hands.

Marko held up his hands. "Nothing but a misunderstanding. I'll leave you and Zelda be, for now, Jacob. You let me know if Gabriella surfaces, okay? I'll be in touch."

Jacob puffed up his chest and jabbed a finger toward Marko just as Zelda opened the door.

"Jacob, please come inside!" she cried before glaring at Marko. "And you, will you leave us alone? I don't know where Gabriella is. If you keep bothering me, I'll go to the police."

Marko smiled. "I wouldn't do that if I were you."

Before either Zelda or Jacob could respond, he walked casually past the elevator and down the stairs. Only when he reached the third-floor landing did he sprint down the rest of the staircase and race out of the building.

32 Faulty Memories

September 13, 2018

"What just happened?" Jacob asked, his eyes fixated on the now-empty stairwell.

"That's the guy I was telling you about—Marko! I don't think he's Gabriella's friend."

"Why is that creep looking for her?"

"Jacob, I didn't tell you everything about what happened in Gabriella's apartment." His eyes widened so quickly, she added hastily, "Or rather, what I saw. Come inside, and I'll tell you everything."

Once they were back on the couch, Jacob wrapped his arm around her shoulder. "Okay, what did you see?"

"You're going to think I'm crazy...." She looked up at him sheepishly, but he only hugged her closer.

"Try me."

"I saw Jackson Pollock's *Study Number 5* hanging on her living room wall. It was one of the paintings stolen from the Amstel Modern."

"What? That doesn't make any sense."

"It looked like she was copying it. There was another version on her easel. But I don't know for certain. I mean, many of her paintings are so loose and colorful, it's just... that Pollock was one of my favorites. I even made it my desktop's screen saver. I looked at that thing every day. That's why I'm convinced it was the same piece."

"Darling, you've suffered a horrible head injury. Are you sure you didn't remember it wrong? If you were already concerned about Gabriella and the thefts, maybe your brain transplanted the beloved Pollock piece into her apartment? Didn't the doctor say that could happen?"

Zelda nodded. Doctor Maring had mentioned that her memories would be unreliable for a few days if not weeks. But could she have imagined seeing the Pollock in Gabriella's apartment? It did seem farfetched.

"I thought my mind was playing tricks on me. But what if it's true? That may explain why Marko is trying to find her so he can take the Pollock from her."

"Zelda, we have to go to the police."

33 Securing Storage Space

September 13, 2018

Ivan Novak glanced over the contract in his hand, more stalling for time than out of interest in the rental terms. The storage unit wasn't his responsibility anyway. After what felt like the appropriate amount of time, he flipped to the end and signed the contract, making certain the printed version of his name was legible.

"Excellent," said the storage unit's customer service representative as she grabbed the contract and double-checked that all the appropriate boxes had been checked. This facility outside of Nijmegen was one of the company's thirty that specialized in art storage. Once she was positive it was complete, she smiled and said, "Now all I need is your passport."

Ivan handed it over, smiling widely. "Certainly."

The woman looked at it in surprise. "Wow, you've lost a lot of weight," she exclaimed, then blushed at her indiscretion.

Ivan chuckled. The man in the photo was a lot wider and more muscular than he had ever been.

"I was diagnosed with leukemia last year." Though he had taught himself to speak in perfect British English, he allowed his natural Croatian accent to shine through just as Luka Antic did.

The woman's eyes widened in shock as her mouth formed a tiny O.

"It gave me a chance to try out long hair. What do you think?" Ivan added quickly.

The customer service representative laughed a bit too loudly. "Well, you don't look sickly at all. And I do like your hair better long. That wig suits you."

She finished filling in the required information then handed his passport back. "Thank you, Mr. Antic. I think you'll be satisfied with the space. I will adjust the climate control to your specifications, and the humidity and temperature should be optimal for storage within a few hours. The key code allows you twenty-four-hour access. If you have any concerns, just ask the manager for assistance. There is always one on duty. I will take you over to the office and introduce you after we finish here."

"That would be great." Ivan had trouble keeping his hand steady when handing over enough cash to secure the unit for three months. Renting this space meant he was almost at the finish line. Vengeance was so close he could taste it.

"You can always renew your contract at the same rate," the service representative added as she gave him the keys.

Ivan shook his head. As soon as the last robbery was complete, he would send out the press release and begin moving the artwork. A week later, half of it would be on its way to Turkey. And the rest, well… His plan brought a smile to his lips. "Thank you, but that shouldn't be necessary."

34 Plea for Help

September 15, 2018

"Zelda Richardson, it's nice to see you feeling better." Officer Vos shook her hand firmly. Luckily, both she and Officer Landhuis were available when Zelda asked for them at the front desk of the Amsterdam police bureau on Leidseplein. Zelda figured it would be easier to talk to them about Gabriella and Marko than having to rehash all the details of her assault with someone new.

"Let's sit in interrogation room number three. It's quieter in there than by our desks." After they'd taken seats around a metal table, Vos asked, "What can we do for you? Do you remember something you would like to share with us?"

"I was curious if you had found anything else out about the man who hit me."

Officer Vos shook her head. "I'm sorry, but no. We were able to track the van as far as Eindhoven, but we lost sight of it on the A2."

"Oh. What about Gabriella? She's still not home. Have you found out anything more about what happened to her?"

"No. Another team has been assigned to her missing person case."

"Oh." Zelda bit her lip, unsure what else to ask. She'd hoped the police knew where her friend was so she could tell this Marko guy Gabriella's location and be done with the whole thing.

"Is there something the matter?" Officer Vos asked, her tone gentle and concerned.

Zelda figured she had nothing to lose. "I know this is going to sound crazy, but a guy is pressuring me to find Gabriella. He's convinced I know where's she's at, but I really don't. I think he's been following me—at least, he knew my boyfriend and I went to the Sanadome on vacation last week."

"Did he harm you or threaten you with violence?"

Zelda thought back to her conversation with Marko. "No, it was more how he made a point of telling me he knew where we'd gone. It was creepy. And he sent me weird text messages while we were gone. The second time Marko came by, my boyfriend returned just as he was beginning to get aggressive. I don't know what would have happened if Jacob hadn't of come home right then."

"Could we see the messages he sent?"

"Of course." Zelda passed Vos her phone. She and her partner read through the four from Marko then handed it back.

Officer Vos gazed at Zelda with a frustratingly neutral expression. "They aren't exactly threatening, though the ticktock is kind of strange."

Zelda sighed, exhausted by the past week's events, the police officers' lack of enthusiasm, and her poor health. The spa had helped tremendously, but she still had dizzy spells and dull headaches. "No, perhaps they aren't scary in tone, but I don't know this guy, and I'm not good friends with Gabriella. The fact that Marko came by my apartment twice and messaged so often about her freaks me out."

"How did he get your phone number?" Landhuis asked.

"I, ah, gave it to him." Zelda felt silly saying it aloud. "He came by looking for Gabriella the day I got out of the hospital. He said they were childhood friends, and he was only in town for a few days. His telephone didn't have an international plan so he couldn't receive or make calls. That's why he asked for my number so he could call me from his hotel's phone."

"Hmmm," was all Officer Vos could muster.

Her partner intervened. "The messages are quite vague and not enough to press charges or even pick him up for questioning. Can you describe Marko for us?" Landhuis held pen to paper.

Zelda's eyes shot to the right as she recalled his appearance. "Skinny, tall, and long straight hair pulled back into a ponytail at the nape of his neck. His eyes were dark brown, and he had a scruffy beard—yeah, beard might be too strong a word. It looked like he hadn't shaved in a few days. Everything he wore was black—his jeans, sweater with a hoodie, and high-top sneakers."

"And his voice? What language did he speak in? Did you detect any accent?" The urgency in Officer Vos's voice caught Zelda's attention. For the first time since she'd entered the room, she felt as if the officers were actually interested in what she had to say.

"His voice was kind of high for a man but not feminine. He spoke in English, but the way he clipped his words reminded me of Gabriella. I bet he's Croatian, too."

The two officers bent their heads together and whispered back and forth. Finally, Landhuis stood up and said, "I'll be right back."

Officer Vos smiled but said nothing. Her steady gaze was unsettling.

Minutes later, Landhuis returned with a stack of photographs. "Your description reminded us of a suspect in an ongoing investigation. Can you look at these photos and tell us if you recognize any of these men?"

"Sure," Zelda said, pulling the five mug shots close. She carefully examined all of them, focusing in on their eyes. The second photo sprang out at her immediately. Even though his chin was clean-shaven, and he was clearly a few years younger, but Zelda was positive number two was Marko. "That's him. I am sure of it."

The officers exchanged surprised glances. "That is Marko Antic." They both looked at her carefully, clearly gauging her reaction.

"Okay." The name meant nothing to her.

"I have to tell you, Zelda, I am quite surprised he told you his real name. Marko was involved with the robbery at the Amstel Modern. He freelances now and again but works mainly for his uncle, the head of a powerful Croatian mafia. Are you certain you have never seen him before? Perhaps you worked with him in the past?"

Zelda felt her body go cold. Did the police think she was working with that psycho? "Of course not! Good God, the mafia? What was Gabriella involved with?"

"You tell us. When we talked to you in the hospital, you thought you'd seen a stolen painting in her apartment. Do you think that could have anything to do with Marko Antic's interest in her?"

"I don't know why Marko wants to find Gabriella so badly. All I know is that I can't help him. I'm not you. I don't know the first thing about tracking down a missing person. I have no idea where Gabriella might have gone, and I told Marko that, too. Trust me, I would love nothing more than to find her so she can sort this mess out."

Vos let Zelda's words sink in, nodding slightly. "You have been working at the Amstel Modern for three months, correct?"

"Yes," Zelda said with a start, thrown off by the officer's question.

"How did you find out about the position?"

"One of my professors emailed it to me and about two hundred other museum studies students. I'm on his weekly mailing list of new job openings, which he sends out to students and recent graduates."

"And after you accepted the part-time research position, no one approached you to help them with a robbery?"

"Wait—what? Of course not! Look, I came here today because I am in way over my head and don't know what to do."

"I think that's the first true thing you've said since you arrived, Zelda."

Zelda frowned at Officer Landhuis. Coming here had been a huge mistake. "I am not involved with the Amstel Modern robbery or any of the Robber Hood break-ins."

"You must admit that it is rather odd that you work for the Amstel Modern, live next door to an artist you claim possessed one of the stolen pieces, and you are in contact with a known criminal who is definitely involved with the robbery," Vos pushed.

Zelda wanted to scream. Instead, she closed her eyes and sucked in her breath. "Okay, this is getting ridiculous. I came to you for help. I don't know why Marko is targeting me or searching for Gabriella. How many times do I have to repeat myself before you believe me? Are you sure the missing person team hasn't found out anything about where Gabriella might be? If only we could talk to her, I know she would tell you I am not involved in any of this."

"We are actively searching for Gabriella, but we will not be sharing our investigation with you or your friends, Ms. Richardson," Vos stated.

Zelda gulped. The officer's return to formality scared Zelda more than her chilly tone. When she stood up, her whole body trembled. "Can I go now?"

"You are free to go. For now. We'll be in touch soon."

Zelda nodded tersely. Ignoring the officer's outstretched hand, she turned on her heel and raced out of the station as quickly as she could. Once outside, Zelda had to force herself to walk calmly toward her bike. *What just happened*, she wondered in despair. She went to the police for help and now had the feeling they thought she was somehow involved. It didn't make sense. Worst of all, she was nowhere closer to finding Gabriella or getting Marko off her back.

"What do you think?" Officer Vos asked as soon as Zelda Richardson left the interrogation room. "Was she trying to get information out of us to pass along to her boss? Or is she really the innocent victim she claims to be?"

Landhuis stared at the closed door, briefly lost in thought. "Her story is rather farfetched. Honestly, I get the feeling she can't deliver what she'd promised and is trying to make things right with the mafia."

Vos bobbed her head in agreement. "I wouldn't be surprised to learn she is working with them somehow. She barely reacted when we told her who Marko was—as if she already knew. And it is quite a coincidence, her job, neighbor, and Marko. Maybe she was supposed to be babysitting Gabriella, but the artist made a break for it and took the stolen Pollock."

"You might be right." Landhuis threw his hands up in the air in mock defeat. "What the hell? We don't have a single viable lead. Her name is already on our list of persons of interest, and the Amstel Modern's head of security hasn't ruled out staff involvement. We didn't share Zelda's original statement we took in the hospital with the Amstel Modern staff, did we? Why don't we have a chat with their director and Zelda's coworkers on Monday? I'm curious to hear what they have to say about Ms. Richardson."

Vos snapped her fingers. "Hey, did you see that email from Detective Prins? We should let him know about Zelda and the Pollock, as well."

"You're right. His team did say to pass on any lead."

Vos recalled the email Detective Prins, the officer leading the Robber Hood investigation, had sent to the entire Dutch police force yesterday. He asked everyone to be on alert for any new information about the Robber Hood gang or the stolen artwork.

In his email, Detective Prins asked all officers to share any lead with him, no matter how obscure it may seem. In Officer Vos's mind, this qualified. Zelda's accusations were quite farfetched, but she suspected that even a longshot would be welcome right now.

"Why don't we give Detective Prins a call first?" Vos said.

"That sounds like a plan."

35 Team Will's Last Assignment

September 14, 2018

Tomislav and Sebastijan were looking forward to robbing the Kronenburg Museum. After twenty-four long days of surveillance, bad food, lightning-fast planning, uncomfortable hotel beds, and adrenaline-filled nights, they were ready to be done with the Robber Hood job and go home. They had left Kronenburg as last because it would be a cinch to break in. They could literally pick open the emergency exit door at the back and walk straight into the exhibition hall they wanted to rob. The three pieces on their list were all hanging in one room, located in the center of the building. If they entered the property through the woods, they could easily avoid the gaze of the caretaker, whose apartment was in the attic of an old house to the left of the modern museum. Two quads were already rolled into place and covered with a camouflage net. They could easily cut through the forest and dunes, making them the perfect getaway vehicles. Even after they triggered the alarm, they'd be in and out before the caretaker could find his slippers. They figured they'd be back in Wassenaar before the first cop car arrived.

The two men scurried out of the forest and across the lawn. They kept to the shadows in case the caretaker happened to be looking outside from his apartment window a few hundred feet away.

They raced over to the rectangular building, a mix of glass, stone, and wood. In contrast to most contemporary architectural statements, this one was subdued and elegant and actually fit in with the surrounding field and forest.

Tomislav pushed the building's architecture out of his mind as he and his partner approached a window in the middle of the long rectangle. No cameras were visible, but both men knew they were there. They clambered through the manicured flower beds surrounding the building to get close to the door. Sebastijan turned on his headlamp, briefly shining it inside. They could see their targets from here—three Kandinsky sketches created with pencil and oil. They were still hanging in the same spot as they were last week. He turned off his headlamp and nodded to his companion.

The simple lock was ridiculously easy to pick open. Seconds later, Tomislav was inside and holding open the door for his partner. They operated under the assumption that motion detectors would have just alerted the caretaker to their presence and location. Meaning they had five minutes and counting.

As they entered the exhibition hall, Tomislav pulled out his wire cutters while Sebastijan snapped open a padded canvas bag. When he cut the first sketch loose, vibrations on the wooden floor caused them both to freeze.

Was this a new kind of alarm, Tomislav wondered as a whooshing noise made him turn.

Rushing straight at them were two rugby-sized men, their security uniforms straining against their rippling muscles. Though both were surprisingly silent, their weight couldn't help but vibrate through the wooden floors.

One guard tackled Sebastijan as the other grabbed Tomislav's shoulders, careful not to jostle the Kandinsky in his hands. He dropped the piece, letting the sketch crash to the floor. The glass shattered loudly. Sebastijan was on the ground with a giant on his back. Tomislav knew there was no saving his partner. He had to save himself.

Tomislav broke free from the guard and raced out of the hall. The security man slid across the broken glass, quickly catching up. The adjoining hall was filled with giant orbs and foot-tall vases made of blown glass. When he noticed his pursuer closing in, Tomislav knocked several off their stands to slow the guard down before whipping around the next corner and through a dark entryway. An imposing wall of rusted red metal stopped him in his tracks. He looked up and saw it was at least two stories high. It wasn't a wall, he realized, but a tunnel that curved to the left and disappeared into blackness. Tomislav couldn't see where it led, but he could hear the guard behind him. In a panic, he ran inside, hoping it would ultimately take him into the next room.

As soon as he entered, sounds became muffled, and his breathing and heartbeat flooded his ears. The further he ran, the darker it became. He wasn't crossing into the next room but entering the center of something larger, the walls seeming to bend and contract at will. He ran forward and hit his head hard on the rusty wall. Feeling along the sides as he continued at a slower pace, Tomislav had to fight the growing feeling of claustrophobia as the walls narrowed until it seemed as if they would meet. Noises behind him told him he had no choice but to push on. The walls were so close he could barely squeeze through. His panic rose until they suddenly opened up again, and he was in a wide-open space inside a maze of metal. A surge of euphoria tempered the dread filling him. A large opening to his left was an exit. As he departed the sculpture, he felt happy and light, convinced he'd experienced what the artist had designed it to do.

His elation was destroyed moments later when the security guard tackled him, pushing him back up against the rough surface of the sculpture. Tomislav kneed the guard in the balls, and the larger man rolled off him, doubled over in pain. The wiry thief raced out of the hall and into an area filled with giants wearing swimsuits, lounging under a beach umbrella. He turned left, heading back toward the open window and their quads.

Behind him, it sounded like the guard was closing in. Tomislav turned to see the larger man baring down and then his shoulder slammed into a wall. His body swung left, and he rolled down a flight of stairs. At the bottom, his head slammed against the concrete as his body sprawled out limply. Above him, a strong light shone like a beacon. His eyes instinctively followed the light, turning his head to see a swimming pool floating above him. Tomislav blinked, positive he was hallucinating.

Heavy footsteps descended the stairs. Moments later, the guard stood over him, smiling, and Tomislav lay back in defeat.

36 A Drunken Dare

September 14, 2018

Tomislav couldn't believe his bad luck. This was his fifteenth heist for Luka Antic, and the first time anything had gone wrong. Since starting to work for the Croatian, he'd felt blessed and sometimes even invincible. Unfortunately, in his line of work, that kind of thinking could get you arrested or killed. After taking mug shots and fingerprints, the police brought him straight to this interrogation room. An hour later, three smarmy detectives showed up. Tomislav was so jacked up on adrenaline he had trouble keeping his attitude in check. But he knew from experience that being overly snotty with the police brought on more trouble than it was worth.

"Who is P? Says here that she lives at Apollolaan 22 in Leiden," asked one of the detectives questioning him. To Tomislav, they were all the same.

"Don't know. Some woman I met at a bar last night." He knew it didn't matter what he said because the police were undoubtedly already on their way to her home. Heck, she might be in the interrogation room next door by now. He could kick himself for making such a rookie mistake. If only these jobs weren't so close together, then he would have had a chance to memorize her address. When Luka Antic found out about this, there would be hell to pay.

"She gave you her address, but you don't remember her name? Not very gentleman-like."

Tomislav smiled. "Lots of women give me their numbers. You can't expect me to remember them all."

"Oh, yeah. You're a real Romeo. I bet the girls line up to be with you," another detective said with a snicker.

The third one asked, "Which bar did you meet her at?"

Tomislav shrugged then immediately regretted it. He bruised his shoulder badly with his fall into the swimming pool installation in the Kronenburg Museum. To counter the pain, he began massaging it as he answered. "We went into a bunch of bars in Scheveningen last night. It might have been Bora Bora or The Fat Mermaid. We hit the whole strip."

"And who hired you to rob the Kronenburg Museum?"

"No one. We were a bit drunk and took up a bloke on a dare."

"You broke into the museum on a dare? Funny, we have a video of you and your partner visiting last week. You were consulting a piece of paper. I suppose you memorized that bit of information because we didn't find it among your belongings. Here's a copy to refresh your memory."

A detective tossed an enlarged image of Tomislav holding a slip of paper. Tomislav had to admit, he was impressed. The security cameras at Kronenburg were state of the art. The page was skewed but even zoomed in as far as it was, the names of all three Kandinsky's were legible.

Tomislav looked at the detectives, keeping his face as neutral as possible. "A friend told me to check them out while we're here. He's a fan of Kandinsky."

"That's right. You're not from around here," the detective sniggered, "but you do get around." The policeman showed Tomislav a printout of the file his fingerprints were linked to. "You're Serbian yet have outstanding arrest warrants for burglaries in Italy, Sweden, and Germany. Have you visited any other museums on your travels through the Low Lands?"

Another detective spread out security photos of other museums recently burgled by the Robber Hood gang as well as the artwork taken.

"No, this was our only stop." Tomislav glanced over the photos. "I have nothing to do with those."

"So other members of the Robber Hood gang were responsible for them, then?"

"Robber Hood? Who's that? I don't know what you're talking about," Tomislav retorted, then quickly clammed up, realizing they had already searched through his backpack.

"Oh, no? Then why do you have one of their cards in your bag? What does 'You only love what you've lost' mean?"

Tomislav stared at the wall, stubbornness etching his face. Inwardly, he groaned, wondering again why he was ordered to leave those blasted cards behind. He always wore gloves and tightknit hats to reduce the potential for DNA evidence. He was fairly confident the police couldn't link him to any of the other robberies otherwise. Luka Antic paid them well in case anything went wrong. Tomislav knew the risks and when to keep his mouth shut. Even if he did do jail time, it wouldn't be for more than a few months, and Dutch prisons were summer camps compared to their Eastern European counterparts.

"Is your friend also from Serbia?"

Tomislav turned back to the detective, one eyebrow raised. "Don't know. You'll have to ask him." He was glad he hadn't gotten to know Sebastijan well—precisely for this reason. They'd never worked together before so the police here and in Serbia couldn't link them. And they hadn't developed the sort of comradery that would motivate either man to do anything to save the other. Honestly, he didn't care what happened to Sebastijan.

The detective smiled back. "I look forward to chatting with P."

37 A New Lead

September 14, 2018

"Hi, Vincent. Bernard Visserman from Wassenaar police department here. I think I have a new lead to share with you—a live one."

Although pretty much everyone on the Dutch police force knew Vincent was investigating any Eastern European links to the Robber Hood thefts, few knew his home number, but he and Bernard had a personal connection. They'd met during Vincent's investigation into a Nazi-looted portrait painted by Pierre-Auguste Renoir, a painting he had tracked to the home of a private collector in Wassenaar. The man had no idea *his* Renoir had been taken from the de Rijke family in 1942, and he gave it back to the rightful owner as soon as he was confronted with hard evidence.

He and Bernard shared a gin after Vincent returned the portrait to the ninety-eight-year-old Holocaust survivor. She died a month later, but her family said the painting's return had finally brought her peace. That was exactly why Vincent loved what he did for a living.

"I'm all ears, Bernard." Vincent sat straight up in his lounge recliner and lay the folder of stolen art aside.

So far, he'd found no new leads to follow. His Eastern European network was reticent to share any details about the Robber Hood gang's identity or membership let alone the location of the stolen artwork. Vincent still didn't know if it was because of his last informant's gruesome demise, if Robber Hood was somehow managing to stay under the radar, or because there was no link to the Balkans.

What if Marko Antic's involvement was only a coincidence? Vincent, the police, and the museum's insurance agent all assumed

Marko's presence at the Amstel Modern robbery pointed to the involvement of the Antic crime family. But he did freelance. What if Robber Hood wasn't being run out of Eastern Europe but by a criminal organization based out of the Netherlands?

"We just arrested two thieves who broke into the Kronenburg Museum in Wassenaar," Bernard said. "They were in the process of stealing three Kandinskys when the museum's security guards caught them. One had a Robber Hood card in his backpack. They are Serbian and Albanian, and both are wanted in connection with other art crimes."

Vincent punched his fist high in the air in victory. *Yes,* he rejoiced internally. *Finally, something solid to work with.*

"I'm on my way."

38 Try Not to Worry

September 14, 2018

"Ivan, I need help," Pauline cried into the telephone. "The police want to question me about a museum robbery. I didn't have anything to do with it!" She was one of the many gifted painters Ivan Novak represented. She was also the person the three Kandinskys were supposed to be delivered to by Team Will.

"Shhh, try not to worry. I will arrange a lawyer straightaway. Where are you?" Ivan asked.

"In Wassenaar police bureau."

"It's going to be okay. Try to remain calm, and remember, do not answer any questions until the lawyer gets there. It shouldn't take long." Ivan wished he could follow his own advice. He sat down hard in his chair, his heart racing. He wasn't worried about Pauline because the police wouldn't be able to connect her to the Kronenburg theft. At least, not until they searched her apartment and found her sketches and prep work for the forgeries, which they shouldn't be able to do until they had cause to arrest her. He had to get to her studio right away and clear it out. He couldn't risk the police discovering her work. More importantly, he had to make sure Luka Antic did not find out about the forgeries. And he had to assume that whatever the police knew, Luka could find out. He had eyes and ears everywhere.

Pauline's sobs filled the line.

"You promise not to say a word until your legal counsel arrives?"

"Okay," she finally managed through her choking tears.

"I am hanging up now and calling a lawyer. Hang tight."

"Please hurry."

"Of course." Ivan broke the connection then swore in Croatian.

150

Only after he'd finished cleaning out her studio would he call in a lawyer. He hoped Pauline would keep quiet until the man arrived but knew he had no choice but to trust that she would. He paid her well in case of such emergencies. Ivan grabbed his wallet and keys then headed to his car.

39 Mistaken Identity

September 14, 2018

When Vincent arrived at the Wassenaar police station, Bernard and his team were preparing to head out. In one of the thieves' backpacks, investigators found a slip of paper with the initial *P* and a local address written on it. They had already brought the woman to the police station and interrogated her, but her connection to the two thieves was suspect. The men were resolute they'd met her at a bar in The Hague and didn't remember what her full name was. The woman living at the address was an older woman named Pauline, who swore she was home all night and didn't know either of the men. Her lawyer cried mistaken identity, especially when considering their flimsy evidence.

For the police, this disparity was enough to get the go-ahead to search her apartment and studio, both located in an artists' collective in neighboring Leiden. Bernard invited Vincent to tag along in the hope he could help them find a connection to the other robberies more quickly. The art detective knew more about the other Robber Hood thefts than any of the local police did.

On the ride over to Pauline's studio, Bernard filled Vincent in about the Serbian and Albanian thieves in custody and their prior arrests. No one could deny the growing number of connections to the Balkans. Vincent promised to ask his network about these two and share any information he found out with Bernard. Although he was pleased to find more leads to work with, he wondered who in the Balkans—other than Luka Antic—could organize such a large operation and keep it so hush-hush. His mind was blank. He would have to revisit Split soon and pose this question to his most trusted Croatian associates. They may be more willing to share information face-to-face than they were electronically.

Minutes later, two police cars pulled up in front of a nondescript apartment building. Bernard waited for his team of six to assemble before entering.

"Will you look at that," Bernard said as soon as he'd opened Pauline's studio door. His long, broad frame hid their view.

"What is there?" one of his investigators asked.

"Nothing." Bernard stepped inside, allowing the others to enter.

The first detective walked into the square space and whistled softly. "That's unexpected."

"What am I missing?" All Vincent could see was an empty, unused studio. Years of paint splatter covered the walls and tabletops, the only memento of their recent use. The muff slightly acidic smell told his nose that the windows hadn't been open in quite a while. He stuck his head under the table and noticed a puddle of turpentine responsible for giving the air a sour sting. Whoever worked here last hadn't bothered to clean up after they'd finished using the space. He looked around again when the turpentine's liquidity struck him as odd. It would usually evaporate quite quickly. After touching the paint on the walls to test his theory, red and green flecked his fingertips. This studio wasn't unused. It had been recently cleaned out.

"According to the arresting officer, the artist was working on a painting hanging on one wall when he arrived," Bernard said in response to Vincent's question. "He also reported seeing numerous sketches and paintings stacked up against the other three."

"That is peculiar."

Two detectives emptied the contents of a bag of garbage left behind yet found nothing but torn up sketches and old paint.

Bernard clapped his hands together. "Okay, boys. Let's take a look at her apartment. I hope it hasn't been cleaned out as well."

They walked down a flight of stairs to the artist's living space. All breathed a sigh of relief when the door opened and her possessions still filled the rooms. The small area was divided into a living room, kitchen, small bedroom, an office, and a toilet-shower combination.

The detectives donned latex gloves before splitting up to

methodically search her small apartment, opening every dresser drawer, closet, and box they came across.

Bernard handed a pair of gloves to Vincent. "Why don't you start in her office?"

Vincent began with the filing cabinet. He scanned the scraps of paper shoved into the long drawers, creating themed piles on the floor as he went along. After an hour of flipping through old gas bills, rental contracts, sales agreements, and rejection letters from galleries, he stumbled upon a folder marked Gallery Novak. Inside were several sales contracts for oil and acrylic paintings sold through galleries owned by Ivan Novak. According to this information, her work sold best in Split, Copenhagen, and Madrid. *Another Balkan connection*, Vincent thought.

Bernard poked his head into the doorway. "Are you having any luck in here?"

"This woman, Pauline, is still working as an artist. According to these documents, her last painting sold two weeks ago. And this contract states she has another show in Dusseldorf next month."

Bernard shrugged. "So? What's your point?"

"Let's imagine for a moment that your thieves were bringing the Kandinskys here. Don't you think it's odd they were bringing stolen artwork to an artist?" Vincent asked.

His friend nodded thoughtfully. "You're right. It would certainly fit in with the theory that Robber Hood intends to ransom back forgeries to the museums. What is the gallery's name?"

"Gallery Novak. It's a chain of fifteen owned by one man, Ivan Novak."

"Huh, that's funny. Ivan Novak is who she called after being arrested. He arranged for a lawyer to represent her. It took ages for him to show up, though."

"What? Oh, no." Vincent leaned back on his haunches and sighed. "If she called Novak to arrange her legal counsel, that means he was probably the only person who knew she was in custody. What if he cleared out her studio before calling the lawyer?"

Bernard crinkled an eyebrow. "Okay, I agree he had the opportunity. But why would he have done that?"

Vincent shook his head. "I don't know. Do you think you can find out more about him? He may be involved somehow. If the Robber Hood gang is forging artwork, it makes sense to have a crooked gallery owner involved."

"Whoa, be careful with your accusations, Vincent. We can run a background check on Novak, but representing artists is not illegal. For all we know, he might have thought we would impound the artwork she's supposed to be showing in Dusseldorf and took it with him. It's probably just a coincidence."

Vincent shrugged casually, trying to keep his growing enthusiasm in check. "Could you bring him in and question him about the missing artwork from Pauline's studio?"

Bernard smirked. "Hmm, I don't know about that. And even if we did, I can imagine he would deny having taken anything. And I can't see a judge granting us a warrant to search his galleries based on a few what-ifs. Until we have more than a hunch, we can't do much for you."

Vincent sighed, knowing there was no point in arguing. He knew he could find out more about Ivan Novak than the police could, anyway. But before he wasted time researching the art dealer's background, he reckoned it was time to take a trip to Split. If his network of informants weren't going to get in touch virtually, he would go see what information tea and vodka could produce.

40 Plan B

September 15, 2018

Ivan hated being on the move like this, confined to cheap hotels close to the freeway instead of choosing his temporary homes based on the luxury they offered. But with so many jobs in progress, he wanted to be ready to assist the Robber Hood teams and his artists at the drop of a hat. It had worked out well in the case of Pauline. He was at her studio thirty minutes after her call and had cleared everything out an hour later. His central location in a soulless business hotel on the outskirts of Utrecht also made his collection trips more efficient. As soon as a copy was ready, he moved it and the original to his storage facility. The unit was already half full.

The Kronenburg mess was extremely frustrating but not impossible to bounce back from. He was 1.4 million euro short. It took him a few hours to find an appropriate replacement, a piece of artwork that his team could forge in the little time they had available. Ivan knew Luka's Turkish client wouldn't react well if they delivered the artwork too late.

Ivan was surprised Luka hadn't already called if only to vent his rage. Of course, it wasn't Ivan's fault the museum had increased security, but he doubted Luka would be so understanding. That was one of the reasons why Ivan had planned the robberies so close together, in the hope the slow-moving, government-subsidized institutions would not have time to improve their security. He had forgotten to take into account the speed at which private museums could work. Not that Ivan would ever admit that to Luka. Instead, as soon as he returned from clearing out Pauline's studio, he set to work solving the problem left by the Kronenburg botch up.

Luckily, he didn't have to worry about lying to his gallery

employees about his whereabouts. Since his daughter's death, he had taken a step back from the day-to-day operations, choosing to spend his time scouting for new talent for his galleries to represent.

The handpicked directors of each of his fifteen galleries were all experts in their field. Most had worked for him their entire careers, slowly moving up the figurative ladder from assistant to junior curator and further until they reached the top. Ivan still led the monthly Skype meetings, during which all of his directors discussed their future exhibition plans and the newly recruited artists the others should help promote.

Ivan stared out at the freeway below, a blur of lights in the heavy rain showers that signaled the beginning of autumn. He just reviewed his anonymous letter to the editor ranting about the importance of improving museum security and complaining about Dutch politicians' lack of action, making certain he didn't repeat the arguments he'd already used in the previous four. These letters and his frequent call-ins to local radio stations were just more ways of diverting the media's attention from the mafia. He had hoped the Robber Hood press release would keep the media completely preoccupied, but he didn't dare send it out until he knew this last robbery was successful. *Patience is the key*, he reminded himself. *And hurrying leads to mistakes.*

As the iPad in his lap dimmed then went to black, Ivan didn't bother waking it back up. He could email the letter to the editor later tonight. Moments later, his phone rang. *Finally*, he thought as he picked up. Steeling himself against Luka's anger, he answered brightly, "Hello, I've been expecting you to call."

Luka Antic responded with a string of Croatian expletives before finishing up with a hoarse, "Fix this mess. The deadline is looming."

"I already know what we are going to do."

Luka was silent a moment, waiting for Ivan to continue. When he didn't, the crime boss growled into the phone. "Well, what's your plan?"

Ivan smiled, knowing Luka hated having to ask. He expected people to do their best to read his mind and serve his every whim. "A village called Naarden. They've made a recent discovery that will fill the hole left by the, um, botch up." The Milson Museum showcased a collection of modern paintings assembled by the American couple Tanya and Larry Milson. Their artwork still filled the walls of their former home, located in a sleepy little village in the center of the Netherlands. Ivan recalled from his last visit how it was surrounded by pastures on one side and regal estates on the other.

"Good. Send me the details."

"I've already contacted Team Tuck. They know what to do and where to go once successful."

Luka went silent again, and Ivan reveled in it, knowing Luka hated not being in control.

"Okay, let me know when it's finished," was Luka's brusque response before he hung up.

Ivan laughed until his sides hurt. After he regained his breath and wiped away his tears, he woke up his iPad and surfed to the Milson Museum's website. Featured on the homepage was an image of the newsworthy sketch by Vincent Van Gogh recently discovered in their collection. Or rather, recently verified by the Van Gogh Museum as the real thing. A zealous researcher had found a miniature version of the sketch hastily drawn into the margins of a letter written by Vincent to his brother Theo.

Ivan zoomed in on a publicity shot of the Van Gogh sketch, the directors of the Van Gogh Museum and Milson Museum on either side. It was of a farmer doing backbreaking work in a field, loosely sketched with charcoal on paper.

It isn't much to look at, Ivan thought, *but it will be easy enough for Gabriella to copy.* And though it may not be worth 1.4 million, he knew Van Gogh's name carried with it a prestige that many a shady collector treasured. Most museums holding his work were incredibly well-secured, precisely because Van Gogh paintings were among the most expensive—and, thus, sought after—in the world. He was confident Luka's Turkish buyer would be satisfied with this replacement.

If all went as planned this time, Team Tuck would meet him tomorrow night at a truck stop on the A2. After the handoff, Ivan would drive straight through to Maastricht. Luckily, Gabriella and

Anthony were finished copying the Amstel Modern artwork. He bet she could finish the Van Gogh charcoal in a day, two tops. Once he delivered the sketch to Gabriella, it would be time to initiate the next phase of his plan. He only hoped all his artists would be able to complete their assignments on time.

Being so close to the finish filled him with dread and elation simultaneously. Vengeance was so close. He wouldn't let anything get in his way.

41 Rotten Flowers

September 17, 2018

"Hey, gorgeous. I'm back, safe and sound," Jacob said.

Zelda practically melted at the sound of his deep voice and lovely words. "It's great to hear your voice," she whispered so as not to disturb her colleagues.

Zelda was back at the Amstel Modern for the first time since her accident. As happy as she was to catch up with her friends and get lost in collection research again, she missed him already. After a week together, their goodbye early this morning was quite emotional even though both knew it was temporary. They had already decided they would take turns visiting each other every weekend until his project was complete. He had even put out feelers to a few Dutch universities about potential teaching positions he'd heard were opening next September. But for now, Jacob had to get back to Cologne, and she had promised to return to the Amstel Modern. It was time to focus on their immediate futures again. She glanced at the clock, surprised it was only ten o'clock. "Wow, you made really good time."

"I just walked in the door and couldn't wait to call you."

"Aww, you're sweet. I know it's only been three hours, but I miss you, too." She could hear him walking around his small apartment, the wooden floors creaking with every step. He must be unpacking his bags, she reckoned. "Is your housemate back?"

Jacob shared the apartment with a graduate student named Aaron, also working as a collection researcher at the same ethnographic museum. His housemate had recently hooked up with a German girl named Helen and hadn't been back to the apartment—to sleep anyway—since.

"No, he must still be at Helen's place. It doesn't look like he's been here much since I left."

Zelda giggled, happy for the young researcher. She'd met Aaron once, and he was so shy that he had trouble looking her in the eye when he spoke. She couldn't imagine him getting up enough nerve to ask Helen out. But then, they did meet at a beer garden, so alcohol probably played a role. "That's adorable. Good for him."

She heard Jacob open a door. "Aww, now that is sweet. You shouldn't have," he said.

"Shouldn't have what?"

"The flowers." Zelda could hear the floorboards creaking again. "Oh, you really shouldn't have. They stink. It looks like they're already starting to rot and all over my bed, too. Hmm, probably better use a different florist next time."

"Jacob, honey, I didn't send you flowers. Do you have an admirer I should know about?" Zelda said it half-jokingly, but a stab of jealousy filled her soul anyway. Not without reason since her last boyfriend had been unfaithful. She was starting to believe she and Jacob were meant to be together. The idea of him having a girlfriend on the side made her skin crawl.

"Ha, ha. Of course not, silly. Oh, wait. There's a card, and it says welcome home. Maybe the museum sent them. Let me open it up. Hang on a second." He set the phone down, and Zelda could hear the paper rustling.

Jacob picked up the phone again but said nothing. His ragged breathing sounded ominous.

"Jacob, are you okay?"

"Is this a joke?"

She had to strain to hear him. His voice was a strangled whisper. She tightened her grip on the phone. "What does it say?"

"Tell Zelda to keep her mouth shut and keep searching."

Zelda's whole body began to tremble.

42 Grasping at Straws

September 17, 2018

Vincent de Graaf glanced around the conference room table, taking in the stricken faces of the Amstel Modern's board of directors, department heads, and curatorial staff. No one said a word. All were still reeling from his update into Robber Hood's identity, the multiple unsolved robberies since the Amstel Modern had been burgled, and the involvement of three thieves with ties to Albania, Serbia, and Croatia. Vincent figured the rumors surely circling the Amstel Modern's halls were not nearly as farfetched as the reality.

He was embarrassed to admit that neither he nor the police had the first clue as to where the paintings could be. To his chagrin, his network in the Balkans remained remarkably quiet about these heists. Vincent hoped by going to Split that his contacts would have shared a tidbit of information that could lead him further. Yet during his weekend of tea and vodka, he had learned nothing new regarding the Robber Hood gang or stolen artwork's current location.

His inquiries into Marko Antic's whereabouts also lead nowhere. No one knew what he was up to at the moment, only that he was away on a job. His uncle Luka was at his cabin in the woods, presumably getting in touch with nature.

The only pieces of news he had picked up during his weekend in Split involved his investigation only indirectly. Vincent's news that one of their own was leaking information about the attempted Wassenaar robbery to a Serbian criminal organization still had the Dutch police rattled. It wasn't the first time informants were discovered in the Dutch police force—the European mafia had their tentacles everywhere—but the timing set everyone on edge.

The only good news he'd received so far had come from the insurance company. Their decision to offer a fifty-thousand-euro reward for any information leading to the artworks' recovery was encouraging. He had alerted his network about the finder's fee as well as gave them the names of the two men arrested during the Wassenaar break-in during his quick visit. The reward was large enough to inspire the more opportunistic to talk, he hoped. Now that the bait was set, he just had to wait for someone to get in touch. And if no one did, he may have to look further afield than the Balkans. In time, all the pieces of this puzzle would fall into place. They always did.

The Amsterdam police were also following up a new lead, even though it sounded unpromising. A collection assistant working for this very museum claimed to have seen one of the stolen paintings in an artist's loft in Amsterdam. Vincent knew Detective Prins had visited with Julie Merriweather, the Amstel Modern's director, this morning. Vincent would have to call him later and see if Prins had found out anything useful.

After a lengthy silence, one of the Amstel Modern's board of directors spoke up. "What can you tell us about the Robber Hood cards? We understand they were also left at the other robberies. Do you have any leads as to who they might be or their motives?"

"I have asked my network in the Balkans about them, but no one has come forward with more information. At least, not yet. I can tell you that they are not a known protest group or criminal organization, at least not one based in the Balkans."

Julie Merriweather piped up, "The Dutch police are leading the investigation into Robber Hood's identity. After that Belgium theater company's prank, they are also looking into any European organizations that may profit from such a stunt."

He nodded in understanding as another member of the board exploded in anger. "Those theater makers should be arrested!"

A month before the Robber Hood thefts began, the news was filled with reports that a Picasso sketch, stolen six years earlier from the Kunsthal in Rotterdam, had been found buried in a field outside of a small Romanian village. A Dutch author received the tip and a treasure map that led her and a local news crew straight to the sketch. However, what she unearthed was a poorly executed fake of the Picasso. One created by a Belgium theater company as part of an elaborate publicity stunt to promote their new show, a mystery about stolen artwork and forgeries.

Because their leads were nonexistent, the Dutch police were not ruling out anything—any motive, person, or organization. Vincent knew several detectives assumed Robber Hood hadn't released a press release or bothered to create a social media presence because the thefts were a cruel joke and the pieces would be returned, unharmed, any day now.

Vincent wished he could agree. Deep down, he couldn't shake the feeling that Luka Antic was involved. Whether it was because of the facts in front of him or his own need to implicate the Croatian mafia boss in the crime, Vincent was not yet certain.

Julie Merriweather was addressing the board of directors. He tuned back in to hear her say, "Do know our staff is scouring the websites of auction and art galleries across Europe in case the thieves are attempting to sell any of the work." Her smile was warm and confident. He couldn't imagine the pressure she was under to do *something* even though there was little anyone could do but wait for a lead to pan out or an informant to come forward. "As soon as the police—or Vincent—have a solid lead on the locations of the artwork, I will call another meeting. Until that time, we have to stay vigilant. Let us all pray this nightmare will soon be over."

Several attendees shook Vincent's hand or patted his shoulder on the way out, thanking him for being so proactive and encouraging him to keep searching for their artwork.

Julie hung back, waiting until they were the last two in the room. She gestured tiredly to a chair before sitting. "I need your honest opinion. Do you think there is any truth to this being a publicity stunt?"

Sitting so close to her, Vincent now noticed how withdrawn her thin face was. He shifted uncomfortably in his chair. "The Dutch police are investigating every lead, including that possibility, yes, but you would do better to ask them. I'm focusing my investigation on any Eastern European connections."

Julie bit her lip. "Do you think someone working here is involved? The police informed me this morning that they are investigating one of my collection assistants. But if it is a prank or the mob, then she couldn't be involved, could she?" Julie's tired eyes searched his face for answers he didn't have.

"The police are far better equipped to answer your questions," he said stoically.

"Yes, of course." She rose then shook his hand firmly. "Thank you for your time. Please, do keep me informed of any progress you make."

"Of course. I hope to be in touch soon."

43 A New Lead

Vincent de Graaf followed Julie Merriweather out of the conference room and then turned right toward the front entrance as she turned left back to her office. He had just rounded the corner when a tall woman with long auburn hair smashed into his shoulder and knocked the briefcase out of his hand.

"Oh, sorry. I didn't see you there." The young woman picked up the case and held it tightly to her chest instead of returning it. She stared up at him with desperate intensity. Her cheeks were puffy, and her eyes were red. "No, actually, I'm not sorry. Are you Vincent de Graaf?"

"Yes, I am." The woman's Dutch was heavily accented but understandable. He couldn't tell if she was American or South African.

"Can I please talk to you—alone?" She raced into the now-empty conference room, his case still in her hands. "It will just take a minute."

Vincent tempered his annoyance and followed his bag. *Who was this attitude-filled young woman?* "Can I have my briefcase back?"

"Are you still investigating the stolen paintings?" she asked, her eyes locking onto his.

"Yes."

"Have you found Gabriella yet?"

Vincent cocked his head. "I'm sorry. Who are you?"

"Zelda Richardson. I'm a collection researcher here. I saw one of the stolen paintings in my neighbor's apartment—Gabriella. But then someone hit me over the head, and when I woke up, she and the Pollock were gone. And when I got out of the hospital, this guy

166

I've never met showed up at my apartment and started asking all sorts of questions about Gabriella. But I don't know where she is! I went to the police. They don't know where she is either but did tell me that the guy who came to my apartment was probably involved with the robbery here. And then someone sent Jacob dead flowers with a warning telling me to keep searching for Gabriella. Dead flowers! But I don't know how to find her, and the police don't believe me. I don't know who else to turn to. I know you're looking for the artwork. I thought maybe you had found Gabriella. Or knew where she might be?"

Vincent stared at the jabbering American, dumbfounded. "*You* are Zelda Richardson?" He recovered quickly, adding, "I didn't realize you were working today." He didn't recognize Zelda from the photo in her file, though she had just been admitted to the hospital when the photograph was taken and most of her face was covered in blood.

The woman's cheeks flushed. "Why do you know who I am? Can you help me, or did I just get myself into more trouble?"

Vincent did his best to keep his facial expression open and his tone light. "I know your name because I read the police report about your neighbor's disappearance. It sounds like you took quite a hit to the head."

Vincent hoped she didn't see through his lie. He had read the report but had also heard of Zelda because of the Amsterdam police's recent decision to investigate her background and possible involvement in the thefts.

"Let's sit." He made sure to lean back in his chair and cross one leg over the other in an effort to come across as relaxed and open.

Zelda sat across from him, perched on the edge of her seat, her arms firmly crossed over his briefcase.

"Okay, let's take a step back, shall we? Who came to your apartment and threatened you? What can you tell me about him?"

"His name is Marko Anti or Antic? And the police said he works for a criminal organization in Croatia and that he's somehow involved with our robbery."

"What!" Vincent's shrill yelp surprised them both. He willed himself to remain calm. "Are you certain Marko Antic came to your apartment?"

"Yeah, twice. The police showed me his mug shot and told me all about him."

Vincent's pulse raced. Why had no one on the police force told him? There was no mention of Marko in the reports he had read, though those were about her assault, and she said Marko visited after she'd gotten out of the hospital. Visions of stakeouts were already filling Vincent's head. This was Christmas come early—and almost too good to be true. Vincent knew he had to temper his enthusiasm lest he act rashly and blow this chance.

"Did he leave a way for you to contact him?"

"Not really. He's sent me several messages and called a few times, but when I try to call him back, the numbers aren't in service."

Vincent wanted to jump up and dance around the room. He could hardly believe what he was hearing. This young researcher had a direct link to Marko Antic! This was the chance of a lifetime. He had to use her connection to his advantage and think up a way to rouse him out of his hiding place. And if Marko was so desperate to find Gabriella that he was pressuring this girl into helping him, then this missing artist was a lead worth pursuing.

"What exactly did Marko say—"

A knock on the conference door made them both turn. Julie Merriweather's secretary popped her head inside. She smiled at Vincent before blurting out, "Zelda, Julie wants to see you—right now." She held the door open and waited for the collection assistant to join her.

Zelda turned to Vincent, a pleading look in her eyes.

"Can you give me a call after your meeting? We really need to talk," Vincent said while scribbling his mobile and office telephone numbers down.

Zelda exchanged the briefcase for the slip of paper and held it tightly. "Thank you," she said sincerity evident in her voice before she rushed out the door.

Vincent hoped Zelda would still want to talk to him after her

168

meeting with the museum's director. He was fairly certain Julie was about to fire her after interrogating Zelda about her connection to Gabriella or the Amstel Modern theft. If the police were asking questions about Zelda's work history and background, Julie would find an excuse to get rid of her, if only to appease the board of directors. How could she not? The museum had already suffered enough. Any more whiffs of scandal and Julie would probably lose her job. *It is too bad*, he thought as he exited through the bookshop. *Zelda doesn't seem like a bad kid.*

44 Moving Forward

September 17, 2018

Zelda had never seen Julie Merriweather mad. It wasn't a pretty sight.

"You told us you were assaulted last week during a robbery," the Amstel Modern's director said. "However, we did not know you sustained the injury in the apartment of a woman the police suspect of being involved with the theft of our museum. Or that a suspect in the crime came to your house—twice—after you were released from the hospital."

Zelda wanted to be belligerent but chose shamefaced instead. "I didn't know Gabriella was involved with the theft. And that Marko guy is after her, not me."

"The police also said you believe you saw one of our stolen pieces in her studio. Why did you not mention it to anyone here?"

"I had just woken up from being unconscious for a day. The doctors warned me my memory would be faulty for quite some time. The police didn't believe me when I told them about the Pollock; they figured I imagined it. So I didn't think you would, either."

"Well, the police do now, or at least, they are searching for the missing artist to further investigate your claim."

"Good. I hope they find Gabriella so she can sort this all out."

"Gabriella. Is that the thief's name?"

Zelda stuck her chin out. "It's my neighbor's name—the missing artist."

Julie stared at Zelda, her jaw clenched. Zelda got a bad feeling in the pit of her stomach.

"You seem very protective of her, and your possible involvement in her disappearance raises cause for concern. Until the police have found Gabriella or ruled out her involvement, I am going to ask you not to come back to work."

"Wait—are you firing me?"

"No, not officially. You'll be on an unpaid leave of absence until this mess is sorted."

"You really don't think I—"

"I don't know what to think," Julie cut in. "But this place is already a rumor mill. Now that the police are asking about your work history and responsibilities, your presence here will only escalate things. I am trying to move forward with our upcoming exhibitions. Until the police or Vincent de Graaf finds the woman or artwork, I cannot have you working here."

"But I didn't do anything wrong!"

"I have to think of the museum first, Zelda." A heavy knock made their heads turn. A large man, almost as wide as Julie's office door, stepped inside. He wore the standard black suit worn by all the security personnel. "Excellent timing. Aart will escort you to your desk, Zelda. Please show him anything you wish to take home before you put it into your backpack."

Zelda stared at her wide-eyed before her temper got the better of her. "I cannot believe this! I did not steal anything, nor did I help anyone else do so."

Julie gazed at her calmly. "Let's hope the police find the artwork soon. Until then, please understand I have no other choice. I hope to see you again, Zelda."

45 Teaming Up

September 17, 2018

The buzzing intercom brought Zelda out of her stupor. "Yes?" was all she could manage.

"Vincent de Graaf. Do you still have time to meet?"

"Sure. Fifth floor." As Zelda buzzed him in, she glanced at her watch. He was here in record time.

Zelda caught a glimpse of herself in the hallway mirror and grimaced. The skin around her eyes was still dark and puffy, though no longer the shiny black it initially was. Her clothes were still soaked from the rainstorm that followed her home, so fitting for her mood. Her wet hair was ragged and stringy. The elastic holding it back had snapped, exposing the shaved patch around her wound.

Figuring she had about sixty seconds before the art detective arrived at her door, she quickly changed into dry clothes and pulled her hair into a ponytail. There was no time to fix her makeup, so she could only hope her sorry state increased Vincent's empathy. He was her only hope of finding Gabriella and getting out of this mess.

The police still hadn't located the missing artist, and no one was asking for a ransom. Zelda was becoming convinced that Gabriella had disappeared of her own fruition. And if that were the case, she didn't have the first clue as to where to look. If only they could find her, Gabriella would be able to explain to the police and Amstel Modern that Zelda had nothing to do with either the robberies or Robber Hood.

Zelda still didn't know if she could trust her memory or not. Did she see the stolen Pollock in Gabriella's apartment? Or did her mind transport it there?

It was so frustrating. The intense headaches were finally gone yet chunks of her memory still hadn't returned. She hoped the doctor was right, and she would soon recall everything that had happened to her and in the correct order.

But if she didn't see the Pollock there, why did she want to call the police? And why was Marko Antic looking for Gabriella?

A hard knock on her apartment door brought her back to reality. She hurried to open it, automatically looking through the peephole before she did.

"Hi, Mister de Graaf. Please come in." Zelda held open the door for the art detective. She forced herself to smile. "The living room is on the right." She followed him inside. "Thanks again for meeting with me."

As Vincent de Graaf sat on her couch, Zelda took the chair across from him.

"Zelda, your story has made me curious. I'd like to hear more about what happened, and then we'll see if I can help you locate your friend. I can't make any promises, but frankly, I am starting to believe it would be in my interest to find Gabriella, as well. The timing of her disappearance and your claim that you saw a stolen Pollock in her studio makes her a person of interest. And Marko Antic's interest in her whereabouts can't be a coincidence. The police have connected him to the Amstel Modern robbery. And the fact that Marko wants to find her badly enough to put pressure on you makes me believe that she is involved with the robbery, as well."

"I really don't know if I saw the stolen Pollock in her apartment."

Vincent held up his hands in mock surrender. "You're right. We don't yet know exactly how Gabriella is involved, but we do know that Marko Antic is after her. That fact makes me believe you did see the Pollock in her studio."

Zelda nodded tersely. "Well, we will have to ask her when we find her. Who is this Marko Antic exactly? The police said he worked for a Croatian crime figure."

"Marko is the favorite nephew of Luka Antic, the head of a powerful criminal organization based out of Split, Croatia. I've run into Marko on other investigations. He has a reputation for pulling off audacious art thefts and has a nasty habit of disappearing whenever a job is done. But this time, he's left us a direct line. That interests me immensely. I'll be honest with you, Zelda, I want to exploit that connection. I'm not quite sure how yet, but if he wants to find Gabriella so badly, I think we need to start there."

"I figured it was something like that. You reacted so strongly when I mentioned Marko's name. Okay, as long as you help me find Gabriella, I don't care what you do to Marko. I just want her to help me clear this mess up so I can get my life back."

"What can you tell me about Gabriella Tamic?"

"She's a successful painter, and her work is shown all over Europe. She has a large circle of friends, who I think are all artists. We've collaborated on a few pieces and visited several galleries together, but we aren't really close, so I can't tell you much more about her personal life. We talked about art and shows we enjoyed, but that was it. As far as I can tell, all she does is paint, visit exhibitions, and travel to her openings."

"What about her family?"

Zelda shrugged. "No idea. She told me she grew up in Croatia, in a small village close to Split, but I don't know where exactly. Her mom married a baker when she was a teenager, and they moved to another country. I honestly don't remember where—she only mentioned it once. She doesn't like the stepfather much and left for art school shortly after."

"Did she have a sibling or boyfriend she might be staying with?"

"She never mentioned any siblings or one specific boyfriend to me. Honestly, I got the impression Gabriella didn't want to be tied down to anyone. She's quite pretty and really smart. I think she could get whoever she wanted."

Vincent sat with one leg draped over the other, his arm casually thrown over the back of the couch. Zelda wished she could be so relaxed. He gazed at her evenly as he spoke, just as the police did. It made her so nervous not to see his emotional reaction to their conversation.

"That's it?" he asked. "You don't know the names or addresses of any of her friends or family?"

"Nope, no one," Zelda snapped. She added, in a calmer tone,

"That's why I need your help. I really don't know where to look for her."

"Any chance you have a key to her apartment?"

Zelda brightened up, "In fact, I do. We swapped right after I moved in. But the police already searched it."

"Shall we take a look anyway?"

"Sure, yes." Zelda was suddenly energized by this promise of action even if it didn't lead anywhere. She sprinted to her bedroom and grabbed the key to Gabriella's apartment before Vincent changed his mind.

46 Letters from Home

September 17, 2018

Zelda switched Gabriella's hall light on and entered her neighbor's apartment.

The first thing she saw was the trail of blood—her blood—leading from the living room to the kitchen. Zelda leaned against the wall and closed her eyes, telling herself not to faint. Once she regained her composure, she stepped carefully over the red streaks and into the living room.

Vincent de Graaf whistled softly. "Whoa, they really did clear out the place." He gazed at the blood trail but said nothing.

Zelda was glad she wasn't alone. Being confronted with this empty space brought a surge of bad memories and dark visions. She hardly recognized Gabriella's apartment. It was always so vibrant and colorful thanks to a mishmash of half-finished paintings stacked around the room, waiting for that last burst of inspiration before her talented friend finished them off. There was always one on her easel and a few hanging on the wall, but now, all of Gabriella's artwork and painting supplies were gone, making the room seem large and empty. Only her books and furniture remained. Zelda opened her desk and dresser drawers, not surprised to see that most of her clothes were also gone.

Vincent walked around like he owned the place, unencumbered by bad memories that might slow his pace. He felt along the walls for suspicious cracks, knocking on any panel that seemed loose. He made his way across the rectangular room, kicking at the floorboards with his heels. He moved the few pieces of furniture left behind, carefully examining them for any hidden compartments or items taped underneath. He searched through her empty drawers, flipped over cushions, and felt along every edge and ledge. The few scraps of paper he did find stuffed between the books were nothing more than shopping lists.

Halfheartedly, Zelda searched through Gabriella's clothes and toiletries but found nothing that might lead them to the artist. She blew a strand of hair out of her eyes, realizing nothing personal was left to find. Exerted from the effort, Zelda sat down on the couch and closed her eyes. How she wished she could ask Gabriella's friends about where she might have gone, but she was on a first name basis with only a few and didn't know where any of them lived.

Only after Vincent started searching Gabriella's bedroom did Zelda hear him exclaim, "Yes!"

She followed his shout of joy and found him bent over a small table, upon which rested an old-fashioned telephone and two telephone books.

When he heard Zelda enter, he held up a tiny silver key. "This was underneath the phone. Do you know what this might open? Her storage unit or bicycle, perhaps?" He turned it over in his hand. It was smaller than a standard door key yet seemed familiar.

Zelda came closer, concentrating on the shape. As Vincent twisted it, the light caught it just as an idea flashed through her mind. "I think I know what that is." She pulled her key ring out of her pocket. "Is this the same size?" She held up one of her keys. They were almost identical. "It's to her postbox, which is downstairs by the front entrance. Every apartment has one. It must have fallen off her key ring."

Vincent grinned. "Let's take a look."

Gabriella's postbox was filled to the brim. They each took a handful of mail and carried it back upstairs. After spreading it out on Zelda's kitchen table, they sorted the advertisements from bills and personal letters. Gabriella had received a plethora of invitations to exhibition openings in galleries across Europe. Out of the forty or so pieces of actual mail, only three were personal letters. They'd been sent a week apart, all from the same address.

Without a modicum of discretion, Vincent carefully opened all three envelopes, removed the handwritten letters inside, and began reading.

He skimmed the first letter before looking up at Zelda, a grin splitting his face. "Another Balkan connection. This is in Croatian. Mine isn't that great, but it appears to be a fairly mundane family update."

"Wait, you can read Croatian? Is your family from the Balkans?"

"No, I've been taking classes for a few months now. I admit it's not a language spoken by most, but it is integral to my business. Much of the artwork stolen in Western Europe ends up in the Balkans at one point or another."

Zelda was flabbergasted. "I had no idea it was such a hotbed for stolen art."

"That's why I'm opening an office in Croatia next year. Two of my English colleagues have already set up offices in Serbia and Albania. Hence, the lessons in Croatian, so I can communicate more effectively with my local contacts."

"You mean criminals." Zelda almost whispered.

Vincent puffed out his chest. "Sometimes. Look, art crime is extremely profitable, and organized gangs are heavily involved in its theft and forgery. The people moving in those circles aren't tipping us off about stolen art because they are culture lovers. They share information in exchange for lighter prison sentences, reward money, or to get rid of their competition. I listen to whoever has the information I need and don't concern myself with their day job. If someone can lead me to a piece of stolen art, I am willing to look the other way. All I care about is recovering the artwork." Vincent gazed sternly at Zelda. "And right now," he continued, his voice softening in tone, "my gut tells me we should take a trip to Luxembourg."

"What? Why Luxembourg?"

"Because Gabriella's mother lives there, and all three letters are from her. She mentions her work as a cook in a hotel in Clervaux. It's a small town in Luxembourg. We might be able to arrange a casual run-in with her at her work and find out if she knows where Gabriella is. You should come with me. You want to find Gabriella as much as I do."

Zelda bit her lip. "Yeah, I do. I guess I didn't expect to do any of the investigating. But you're right. I need to find her and don't have a job tying me down right now."

Vincent looked away as he asked, "What do you mean?"

"The director of the Amstel Modern has put me on an unpaid leave of absence, at least until the police are convinced that I am not involved in the robbery."

The detective grunted but said nothing.

Zelda's eyes narrowed. "Is that why you were so surprised to see me at the Amstel Modern? Did you know the police were investigating me?"

Vincent remained silent for too long.

Zelda rolled her eyes. "Great."

"Well, this gives you even more reason to want to clear your name. If we can find Gabriella, you might get your job back."

Zelda bobbed her head, knowing he was right but still embarrassed. *Wouldn't it be wonderful if Gabriella is at her mom's place?* she thought. Then Zelda could have her friend call the Dutch police and clear up all these misunderstandings. It was too late to save her apartment, but she could still save her job and her future. No museum on the planet would hire anyone suspected of being involved in art crimes. If she ever wanted to do what she'd spent the last three years training to do, she had to clear her name. "So what are you going to say to Gabriella's mother if we do find her?"

"Well, you can say that we are in Clervaux on vacation, knew the mother lived there, and just wanted to say hello."

"Wait. *I* can say that? I thought you were the investigator?"

"In this case, you have a personal connection with the mother."

Zelda stared at him blankly.

"You're friends with her daughter. It would be more natural for you to lead the conversation. If she asks who I am, you can say I'm your boyfriend, and we're enjoying a weekend away. I know I'm a bit old for you, but we can fake it for a few minutes." Vincent grinned. "Clervaux is a popular tourist destination and is the starting point for several beautiful hikes. It's not strange that we would be there on vacation and happen to stop by the hotel she works at. Especially if you say that Gabriella told you about it."

Zelda frowned. "Why don't I just ask to say hi to Gabriella? I can say I thought she was visiting her mom."

Vincent smiled. "Even better. Her reaction will tell us if she knows her daughter is missing or not." He patted her on the shoulder. "See? You're a natural."

"As long as she doesn't ask personal questions about Gabriella, I guess it would work. I really don't know her that well. And Gabriella never talked about her mom."

"You said that you collaborated on an art project. Perhaps Gabriella mentioned the project you were working on together to her mom?"

"Maybe." Zelda twirled a string of hair around her finger, contemplating. "But if Gabriella wanted to vanish, her mother might be helping her. She might lie to us."

"Yes, that's quite possible. But that's why I want to drive down and talk with her in person. Her reaction will help us decide if she is lying or telling the truth. That's also why I need you, as her friend, to do the talking. I am an outsider and have no connections to Gabriella. You're her neighbor and friend."

Zelda nodded. Everything he said made sense. She could feel a spark of hope burning inside.

"You'll be fine," Vincent said again, clearly trying to reassure Zelda. "Besides, it's only a few hours ride. And Clervaux is beautiful. It's worth visiting at least once."

Zelda didn't care if Gabriella was in Clervaux or Timbuktu. All she wanted to do was find her friend. Right now, she was the only person who could give her life back to her. "Okay. When do you want to leave?"

47 Breaking Routine

September 18, 2018

Marko sat on the terrace of Café Chaos, slowly sipping a *koffie verkeerd* in the bright morning sun. From here, he could see the entrance to Het Sieraad and Zelda's bike. If she followed her normal routine, she would leave for her work in twenty minutes. He took another large bite of his breakfast, chewing slowly so he could enjoy it longer. The café served deliciously simple Dutch food for a good price. Their farmer's omelet, full of thickly cut bacon and fresh vegetables, was heavenly. Since discovering this place during his first stakeout, he had been back often. Partly to keep an eye on Zelda, but really, it was the food that made him a regular. He figured he better enjoy it while he could since his last job was tomorrow night in Naarden, and then he was finished with this Robber Hood business.

Getting back to Croatia would be good. He hoped to take a week off and hit the coast before the autumn weather cooled the Adriatic Sea. Although he wouldn't be surprised if his uncle had plans for him lined up already. He'd been grooming Marko to take over his organization, one branch at a time. Luka claimed to want to retire, but Marko knew the old man wouldn't be able to step back completely. His uncle had been at this for far too long to live a pensioner's life. Marko knew he would miss the adrenaline kick, which was too bad because Marko had so many ideas on how to streamline the organization, cut back on costs, and concentrate their resources and collective knowledge on fewer businesses. But until Luka was dead, Marko didn't think he would be able to implement all the changes he desired. The old man's sway was far too strong.

A black Volvo pulled up to the small square in front of Zelda's building, right where a flower seller was trying to set up his stall. The man didn't get out to buy flowers but remained behind the wheel and made a call. After he'd hung up, the flower shop owner knocked on the Volvo's window. The man rolled it down, and the two began an animated conversation. Whatever the flower seller said only seemed to amuse the driver. When the flower seller started gesturing more wildly, the driver rolled his window back up to the seller's enormous irritation. Marko laughed aloud when the man began pounding on the Volvo's window, ignoring several customers as he gave the driver a piece of his mind.

Marko turned around to find the waitress, currently helping a table behind him. He signaled for another coffee as the Volvo's motor revved, and the flower shop owner stepped back, shaking his fist as the car pulled away.

Marko raised his empty cup in salute as the Volvo sped away, only noticing that Zelda was in the passenger seat as it passed.

48 A Walk to Paradise Garden

September 18, 2018

Zelda stood before W. Eugene Smith's *A Walk to Paradise Garden*, trying to ingrain this glorious image onto her mind. Two children walk hand in hand through a tunnel of trees. Up ahead was a clearing in the forest, a shower of light spilling down the path before them. The way the two innocents held each other's hand tightly as they headed off into the bright sunlight—symbolic of their bright futures—worked powerfully on Zelda. She could feel a tear forming in one eye as she gazed at the hopeful image, strategically placed at the end of the *Family of Man* exhibition in Castle Clervaux. Now thirty-one years old, Zelda couldn't help but wonder if she would ever be a mother to such beauties. She and Jacob had been together for sixteen months now, but she was still getting used to being a couple and sharing a living space. The idea of being a parent terrified her.

"The light really makes the image, doesn't it?" Vincent de Graaf said as he sidled up next to her.

They had arrived in Clervaux, Luxembourg, four hours ago in search of Gabriella's mother, Elaine. They had headed straight to her workplace, Hotel Koener, and ordered a late lunch from their restaurant. A friendly waitress informed them that Elaine had the day off and wouldn't be back to work until the next morning. After enjoying their sandwiches while gazing out at the Clerve River and a poignant monument to fallen soldiers, they set out to find Elaine's home.

Vincent used his phone to navigate the steep and windy streets to Rue Ley. No one answered the door, so they decided to try again later, closer to dinner time, which left them three more hours to kill in Clervaux.

Zelda had never been here before but had googled it on their drive up. The small town was a touristic hotspot thanks to its lovely location in the Luxembourg Ardennes. The Museum of the Battle of the Bulge and *Family of Man* exhibition were also big draws. She was glad they'd had time to visit both.

The long drive down from Amsterdam had been more pleasant than Zelda expected. After leaving the flat, pasture lands dominating the Netherlands, it had been a treat to wind their way through the rolling hills and budding mountains of Northern Luxembourg. The trip made her realize how much she missed driving through the Cascade Range back in Washington State. The foothills of the Ardennes weren't nearly as tall as the Cascades, nor were the valleys as deep, but they were closer to them than anything she'd seen in Europe so far.

Clervaux nestled in a bend in the Clerve River, on a small spit of land rising out of the middle of a heavily forested valley. Narrow, cobblestoned streets wound up the steep slopes to the pinnacle where an enormous white castle was. The structure dwarfed the medieval-looking homes covering the sides of the terraced hill.

Vincent led them up the quiet, curvy streets—most too narrow for cars. They passed a handful of locals, all of whom pretended not to see Zelda or Vincent. The brick walls used to terrace the steep hillsides were covered in an explosion of flowering vines and trees. Birdsong dominated, only occasionally interrupted by the revving motor of a truck climbing the steep Route de Marnach, a regional freeway running along the outskirts of town. To Zelda, this place was the epitome of serenity.

They climbed further, moving ever closer to the enormous white structure balancing on the top of the hill. In the bright sunshine, its white-plastered walls shone like a beacon. When they reached it, Zelda stood still to catch her breath while taking in the imposing medieval castle before her. Built in an *L* form, the building's shape created an open half-circle, which had been turned into a public park. On either side of a small patch of grass was a tank and cannon, both remnants of the fierce battles that took place in this peaceful valley in World War II—the Battle of the Bulge.

Since its restoration in 2013, the castle was home to the municipality of Clervaux and its museums. A large sign informed visitors that the *Family of Man* exhibition was on the right, and the Museum of the Battle of the Bulge was to the left.

While Zelda scrutinized the tank, surprised to see how small such a thing really was, Vincent made a beeline for the War Museum. Miffed that he expected her to follow him around, she finished her extensive examination of the tiny war machine before joining him. In the movies, tanks seemed to be vast and roomy inside, but she had trouble imagining two soldiers squeezed into the one before her.

When Zelda did finally follow Vincent, she was pleasantly surprised to see the War Museum was a wonderful compilation of parachutes, uniforms, artillery, rations, letters home, traffic signs, weapons, and other memorabilia all crammed into a series of subterranean spaces. Next to many of the objects were small yellow notecards, telling the story of its former owner. Not only did they personalize the objects displayed but they also helped make the atrocities of war even more real. Zelda was captivated.

What a sobering but educational visit, Zelda thought as they exited the museum.

When Vincent proposed they continue to the neighboring *Family of Man* exhibition, Zelda hesitated. The war displays had been quite draining.

But she was thrilled he pushed her to join him. The collection of 503 photographs taken by 273 artists from 68 countries was curator Edward Steichen's reaction to World War II. Devised to showcase the commonalities that bind people and cultures around the world, *Family of Man* highlighted the best of humanity. Steichen, a Luxembourg native, curated this iconic exhibition for the Museum of Modern Art in New York in 1955. It was so popular that it toured the world, ending in Luxembourg in 1966.

To Zelda, his message was loud and clear. The photos and groupings reminded viewers of the good in their fellow man, and how—deep down—we are all the same. Some of the images were dated, but Zelda couldn't help but applaud the wonderfully idealistic views of its creator. And in her already emotional state—thanks to the War Museum—the collection of images moved her to tears.

She and Vincent had just finished their tour of this temple to photography and mankind, and *A Walk to Paradise Garden* was the finale.

"What do you think?" Vincent asked.

"It's really worth the visit," Zelda said, keeping her head turned away until she could get her emotions under control. The last thing she needed was for Vincent to think she was a sniveling idiot.

"When you're ready, why don't we stop by Elaine's house again? If she's not home, we'll try again after dinner."

"Sounds good. I'm ready to go."

On their way out, Vincent walked straight through the gift shop without glancing at the many books on photography or their selection of related knickknacks.

Zelda couldn't resist buying a mini camera for her key chain. When she pushed on the tiny shutter button, the sound of a camera motor rumbled, and the flash went off. It was so bright that it was blinding.

They walked back outside into the warm autumn sun. The trees' leaves were already turning red and yellow, and from their high vantage point, the steep valley walls looked like crimson flames rising to the heavens.

Vincent was already halfway down the street when Zelda noticed he'd not stopped to admire the surrounding forest. She sprinted to catch up with him. They walked down then back up the cobblestoned lanes. Lavish lamps created from curled wrought iron hung on most corners, and though the homes were well maintained, they were clearly ancient. Most garden walls were crumbling and the grass was pockmarked with patches of settled ground.

As they approached Elaine's home for a second time, Vincent asked, "Are you ready?"

"Yep. As ready as I'll ever be."

This time, her knock was quickly answered by a small, frail-looking woman dressed in the same shade of gray as her hair. Only a bright red scarf kept her from resembling a ghost. Her eyes widened when she opened the door as if she were surprised to see strangers.

Zelda gave the birdlike woman a winning grin. "Hello. How are you? I am Zelda Richardson, and I live next door to your daughter Gabriella in Amsterdam," Zelda babbled in English, not entirely sure how to start the conversation despite roleplaying with Vincent on the ride down.

The woman relaxed visibly at the mention of her daughter's name. She gave Zelda a careful grin before her eyes darted nervously over to Vincent.

"Oh, and this is, um, my boyfriend, Vincent. We're here on vacation, and Gabriella mentioned she was here visiting, so I thought it would be fun to say hi. We stopped by your hotel, but the waitress said you were free today and gave us your address." The smell of a marinated roast wafted outside. Zelda glanced at her wristwatch and saw it was almost six p.m. She hoped they hadn't interrupted the woman's dinner preparations. "Oh, gosh. I didn't realize it was so late. We're getting up early for a day hike so wanted to stop by before we get ready for bed. I hope we didn't disturb you."

"No, of course not. It's always lovely to meet a friend of my daughter's. Please, come inside," Elaine's mother said loudly, smiling brightly.

Zelda suspected every neighbor in the vicinity was listening in. She glanced next door and saw a curtain move. *Not much happens here*, she thought, not that she cared. Zelda was grateful they were being let inside so easily. Away from prying eyes, she would also feel more comfortable lying to Gabriella's mother. She and Vincent had discussed different approaches, but now that she was standing across from this tiny old lady, Zelda was having trouble being so indifferent. Gabriella was her daughter, after all. And she was missing.

They followed the woman into a living room richly decorated with tapestries, quilts, and framed embroidery as well as photographs of her daughter, herself and an older man. Zelda assumed the man was Gabriella's stepfather. They'd never really talked about their families let alone shown each other pictures of them. Heck, if Zelda hadn't raided Gabriella's mailbox, she never would have known that her mother lived so close by. The scent of roasting meat was stronger in here, and the smells made Zelda's stomach rumble.

"Are you really friends with my daughter?" The woman's welcoming smile had vanished. Her accent was thicker than Gabriella's, though just as melodious. Despite her fragility, she gazed up at Zelda like a hawk.

"Yes, we've lived next door to each other for three months and have worked on a few projects together. I make stained-glass windows, and she paints them."

Elaine nodded, her frosty reserve melting slightly. "She mentioned you or at least that she was painting glass windows. She sent me a photograph of one last month. It was quite pretty. How lovely to meet you! How can I help you? Did my daughter really tell you to stop by when you were in Clervaux?"

Zelda shifted a bit in her seat. "She mentioned that she was planning to visit you at the same time we'd be here. I thought it would be fun to say hello, that's all." Zelda felt like such a fraud— the woman's smile was genuine.

Elaine laughed. "My girl's always on the move. No, Gabby's not here right now. I swear that she's afraid moss will grow on her feet if she stays in one place too long."

Zelda relaxed visibly and chuckled along. "Oh, so you know where she's at?"

"Of course, she's preparing for her next show. The last time we talked, she was hurrying to finish several paintings so they would have time to dry before being shipped to Venice."

"Venice?" Vincent and Zelda asked simultaneously.

"That's where the show is being held. Gabriella must have flown down early to help prepare the exhibition. I know she often helps her art dealer hang the shows she's participating in. Her eye for composition and color is quite extraordinary, and he trusts her implicitly," Elaine said, her motherly pride showing through.

Zelda and Vincent exchanged glances, neither daring to tell the mother the whole truth. If Elaine didn't know that Gabriella was missing, they didn't want to be the ones to inform her of that fact. Whatever happened to Gabriella, the state of her apartment and Zelda's concussion suggested she may not have gone willingly. All they could do was try to find her—if she were still alive and willing to be found.

Vincent joined the conversation, asking, "Do you know the name of the dealer representing her?"

"Of course! It's Ivan Novak. He has galleries all over Europe."

Zelda noticed Vincent freeze momentarily when Elaine mentioned Novak's name, but recovered quickly. "His galleries are world renown. Your daughter must be quite talented to be represented by him."

Elaine blushed. "He signed her as soon as she graduated and has shown her work in his galleries all over Europe. He's even sold five of her paintings to museums in Austria and Norway."

Vincent whistled appreciatively. "That is impressive."

Elaine beamed with pride.

"When did you talk to Gabriella last?" Vincent asked as casually as he could.

"Two weeks ago? Let's see. She called on my morning off so it would have been Thursday."

A day before Gabriella disappeared, Zelda realized.

"Do you think you could give her a call and see where she's at?" Zelda asked. "She just took off without telling anyone where she was going. I really thought she was here with you."

"If you tell her Zelda is looking for her, I'm positive she'll want to talk to us," Vincent pressed.

Elaine looked at Vincent quizzically. "Why would I do that?" The older woman stood up, her guard rising again. "I told you where she is. Who are you really? What do you want with my daughter?"

Zelda began to panic.

Vincent rose and started walking toward the door, and Zelda followed suit. "I'm sorry if we bothered you," he said. "Thanks for talking with us. Clervaux is quite beautiful."

"Wait, why did you come here?" Elaine grabbed Zelda's arm.

Zelda could have easily pulled loose from the old woman's grip but didn't want to make matters worse than they were. All they needed was for Elaine to call the cops. She turned to face Gabriella's mother as Vincent put his hand on the doorknob. "I am her neighbor, Zelda Richardson, and we did collaborate on several windows. Could you please tell Gabriella that I said hi the next time you talk to her? We didn't mean to upset you. I'm just worried about her; that's all."

The woman's brow furrowed, but she bowed her head in agreement.

As Zelda walked quickly to catch up to Vincent, she glanced back at Elaine's house. The older woman was still in the doorway, watching them walk away. Just before Zelda turned back around, she swore she saw Elaine take a picture of them. But when she looked again, the door was closed.

49 Sweating the Small Stuff

September 18, 2018

Ivan knew he should be thrilled—the Milson Museum robbery went off without a hitch, Gabriella was already hard at work on the Van Gogh sketch, and the rest of the artwork was already in his storage unit. He could begin the arduous process of packing up everything destined for Venice.

He looked around the storage unit, now partially filled with pairs of modern artwork leaning up against the walls and a stack of wooden boxes in the middle, calculating how long it would take him to complete his first task. He had two days to crate half of them up, which should be more than enough time.

Yet now that the first phase of his plan was almost complete, he couldn't help fretting about the next step. The Robber Hood press release was already saved in his email, ready to be sent to a hundred media outlets at the touch of a button. *When* was the most pressing question. He didn't want to send it out until Gabriella was done copying the Van Gogh sketch. Too much of his plan depended on the timing, and right now, he knew patience was more important than pressuring Gabriella to hurry up. Her work needed to be as perfect as possible for the final phase to work.

The only potential chink in his plan was his inability to find out where and when Luka would deliver the artwork to his Turkish contact. It was crucial he knew both details.

How was still the problem. He had to assume Luka's men would check the paintings for any electronic tracking devices and possibly repackage them before sailing on to Turkey. The man was paranoid to the extreme—and rightfully so. There were enough people and organizations after him to justify it.

Ivan refocused his thoughts on the task at hand. After he had crated up half of the art, he would have a few hours to arrange the rest. He wanted it to look appealing when it was found. He was confident the photographs of it would be shared around the world.

50 White Lies

September 18, 2018

As they walked back to the car, Vincent seemed to be struggling internally as if he dared not share his thoughts aloud.

"Do you believe Gabriella is in Venice?" Zelda asked, venturing a guess.

"Honestly, I'm more curious as to where the art dealer Ivan Novak is."

Zelda stopped in her tracks. "Why would you be interested in him?"

Vincent turned around and doubled back to her. "He represents another artist I think was involved with the botched Kronenburg Museum robbery. I also have reason to believe that copies of the stolen artwork are being made. Two artists—both represented by Novak and both with possible connections to the Robber Hood thefts. It could very well be that your friend is helping paint the forgeries and that Novak is preparing to sell them. It's almost too much of a coincidence to be anything else." He grabbed her gently by the shoulders. "Zelda, I think the dealer may be the missing link I've been searching for. I want to follow this lead as far as it goes."

"I still can't believe Gabriella would be involved in any of this."

"We don't know what her role in this is or even if forgeries are being created. But I would like a chance to find out more about Ivan and his galleries before you tell Marko Antic about his connection to Gabriella."

"But if I tell Marko about Novak now, maybe he'll leave Jacob and me alone. Especially if I tell him that her mom thinks Gabriella is with him in Venice." Even as she spoke the words aloud, Zelda wondered if it were true. Would Ivan's name and location be enough for Marko to leave her and Jacob be?

"If you tell Marko about Venice or Novak, I doubt we'll get the chance to question Gabriella. If Marko is so desperate to find her, I imagine he will kill her once he does."

"Oh, my God!" Zelda screamed out her mounting frustration. "I want my job back but not enough to condemn someone to death in the process." She pounded her fists against her temple. "Okay, it sounds like we have to find Gabriella first. So that means going to Venice, right? What are we waiting for?"

Vincent stood with his hands on his hips, staring at her. "First of all, you need to calm down. The mother thinks she's in Venice helping Novak prepare an exhibition, but we don't know for certain if either of them is actually there. And even if Gabriella is in Venice, she may not want us to find her."

"Then what do we need to do next?"

"As soon as we get back to Amsterdam, I'll see what I can find out about him, his gallery, and the artists he represents. Right now, I want to get on the road. Would you get in the car?"

Zelda hung her head. "Okay."

As soon as they were on the freeway, winding their way back to Amsterdam, Zelda asked, "So what do you propose I do, exactly? I have to tell Marko something. I don't know how far he will go with his threats, but I don't want to test him."

Vincent nodded, keeping his eyes on the road the whole time. "Look, I understand your concern, but I have to ask you not to contact Marko until we've had a chance to question the dealer. He doesn't know we went to Luxembourg, right? Can't you wait a day or two before you answer his calls?"

Zelda stared outside, contemplating his words. The darkness enveloped everything, and if it weren't for the frequent streetlights, the road they were on would be plunged into nothingness. She needed to find Gabriella, and right now, Novak was their only lead. As tempting as it was to tell Marko about the dealer and Venice straightaway, Vincent was right. If Marko found Gabriella first, Zelda would never get her life back. In his last message, Marko said she had twenty-four hours to respond. Could she risk ignoring him for another forty-eight hours? His aggression was scary, and she feared his next visit would end in violence.

"I don't know if Jacob or I have two days, and I'm not willing to risk it." Zelda pulled out her phone and replied to Marko's last message before Vincent could change her mind.

"What did you tell him?" Vincent asked, his voice breaking in anger.

"That I met with Gabriella's mother today, and she told me her daughter was in Bali for a month-long workshop."

"Nice. Smart thinking."

Zelda smiled. "Thanks."

Moments later, she received a reply. "Don't believe the mother. Keep searching."

"Damn it! Marko doesn't buy it. He says I have to keep searching for Gabriella."

"As soon as we're back in Amsterdam, I'll look into the art dealer's background and see if I can find any connections to Eastern European criminal organizations or the Robber Hood thefts."

Zelda stared out the window, fuming in anger. For the second time in a week, she felt cornered and helpless. She hated feeling like this. She was done being the victim. It was time to take action. She picked up her phone and surfed to Gallery Novak's website. She dialed the number of their Venice location without saying a word to Vincent.

"Gallery Novak, Isabella speaking. How can I help you?"

The woman's Italian accent made the standard English greeting sound like music. Zelda adopted her snottiest tone, "Yes, hello, I am calling for Ivan Novak."

Vincent tried to swat the phone out of her hand, but Zelda pushed her body up against the passenger-side window, keeping her mobile out of his reach.

"I am sorry, but Mr. Novak is not available. Can I connect you with one of our sales associates?"

"Do you know where I can reach him?"

"No. He is traveling at the moment. Can I leave a message for him?"

"No. A friend of mine recently purchased two paintings by a young artist he represents, Gabriella Tamic. I wish to purchase four. Ivan helped her personally. She said he was quite passionate about Gabriella's work."

"Of course, madam. I understand."

Zelda knew a snotty bitch like the one she was pretending to be would never be satisfied with being helped by a mere salesman. Not when the owner was also available to serve her every whim.

"Mr. Novak will be in the gallery on Friday. Can I make an appointment for you to meet with him then?"

"I will be there at ten in the morning," Zelda responded.

"Excellent," the woman responded as if Zelda's rudeness was par for the course in her job. "And who may I ask is calling?"

Zelda's haughtiness flew out the window. *Shoot!* She glanced around in panic, searching for inspiration when a bright yellow van with a mural of the Alps painted on its door passed their Volvo. "Van—essa, Vanessa von Trapp. The third. See you Friday!" She hung up the phone and puffed out her cheeks. "Well, that was easier than I expected."

Vincent glared at her. "Zelda, what did you just do?"

51 Tying Up Loose Ends

September 18, 2018

Luka Antic scowled at his phone. Marko had just let him know that Zelda Richardson was no closer to finding Gabriella than his men were.

Gabriella was the only loose end in an otherwise perfect plan. Was she copying artwork for Ivan Novak or not? He trusted Marko implicitly, but his nephew never did get the chance to double-check what he thought he saw in her studio. Yet if Gabriella wasn't copying artwork for Novak, why did he move her and her paintings out of her Amsterdam studio and then deny doing so?

If only he could ask Novak directly about Gabriella's current whereabouts and the paintings Marko thought he saw. But that was a risk he wasn't willing to take. In three days, all of the artwork—his down payment for the most important business transaction of his life—would be collected for transport to Turkey.

So much was riding on this deal. He had already reached agreements with several sellers in the Netherlands, Germany, and Sweden for most of this first shipment. It wouldn't be a problem to move the rest of the merchandise. He couldn't chance Ivan doing something stupid or rash. This transaction would secure the future of his vast organization, and he'd be damned if Ivan Novak's greed would destroy that. Until he knew otherwise, he had to assume the art dealer was having copies made. And no matter when or to whom he sold the copies, there would always be a chance that Kadir would find out about their existence and question the authenticity of *his* artwork. Then Luka would be to blame, not Ivan.

But right now, Ivan was the only person who knew where all the stolen artwork was. As soon as the deal was done, there would be enough time to take care of Ivan.

He didn't expect much from Zelda Richardson, but he wasn't ready to cut her loose, either. Her connection to both the artist and museum were almost too coincidental to be just that. He would string her along until he had dealt with Ivan. Then he would get rid of her and her boyfriend, Jacob. 'No loose ends' was a motto he had adopted long ago, one that served him quite well.

52 An Unexpected Vistor

September 19, 2018

"Ivan? My mom just called. My neighbor, Zelda Richardson, came by her house last night. Zelda said she was in Clervaux on vacation and thought I was there visiting. But that can't be true because I never said I was going down South. Besides, I make a point never to discuss my family with any of my friends. Zelda couldn't have known where my mom lives. Would the Amstel Modern have sent her to my mom's house to look for me? But if they did, that must mean they know I'm involved."

Even with the bad connection, Ivan could hear Gabriella's voice trembling. He suspected tears were already forming.

"Wait. Are you sure it was Zelda? Maybe it was someone pretending to be your neighbor?" Ivan kept his voice firm.

"I thought so too, but mom took a picture of her visitors and sent it to me. It's definitely Zelda, though I don't recognize the man she was with. It's not her boyfriend."

"Can you send the photo to me?"

"Sure." She hung up and sent him the image. A minute later, she called back. It gave him just enough time to recognize the man in question, and Ivan's heart sank as he realized what her companion's presence meant.

"Do you know who he is?" Gabriella asked.

"Yes. Vincent de Graaf. A private investigator who specializes in the recovery of stolen art." He knew de Graaf by reputation. He was tenacious and had a strong network of informants in the Balkans. Did one of the victimized museums hire him? Or was he helping the Dutch police with their investigation into the Robber Hood thefts? So many scenarios were running through Ivan's mind. "Gabriella, I have to ask you again. Are you certain Zelda did not see the artwork on your wall?"

"I really don't know. I don't think so, but I hardly remember anything about that day—until I woke up here in Maastricht."

When Ivan had arrived at her studio, Gabriella was slipping in and out of consciousness. If only she had been awake enough to explain to him that Zelda was there helping her, he probably wouldn't have hit the girl. What a mess. He told himself to keep cool and not panic. They were so close to finishing this job. He was tweaking the press release when Gabriella called. It was scheduled to go out at five a.m., just in time for the morning news programs to pick it up. Once the press release went viral, he hoped new tips about Robber Hood's identity would overwhelm the police force and that the national media would focus on museum security. That would make moving the artwork so much easier.

"Why would Zelda be working with de Graaf? I can't imagine the Amstel Modern would ask a collection assistant to help him with his investigation," he mused aloud.

"It doesn't make any sense. I still don't know how Zelda found my mom."

"De Graaf must have helped her with that. But why? Why drive all the way down there to talk to her? Unless he believes you are in Clervaux. I'll ask around and see what I can find out about both Zelda and de Graaf's involvement. As long as you stay in Maastricht, he won't be able to find you. How is your latest project going?"

"I finished it last night. It'll be dry by the time you drive down."

"Excellent. I'll see you in a few hours."

Ivan was about to hang up when Gabriella asked, "And what about Luka Antic? What if he goes to my mom's house?"

"He wouldn't have sent Vincent de Graaf to talk to your mother, and you know it. Besides, Luka has no reason to search for you. Your part of the story is finished—at least in his eyes."

53 Going Viral

September 21, 2018

Sipping his third coffee of the day, Ivan hit refresh and skimmed through the six new articles posted seconds earlier. He hadn't gotten a wink of sleep. Thirty minutes ago, at one minute after five in the morning, the first news blogger reported on his press release. Since then, it had been picked up by every news agency in the Netherlands and across most of Europe. It was gratifying to watch the flood of mystified reactions pouring in.

Ivan was incredibly relieved to see his plan was working. So far, the news reports universally focused on security, a need for more funding for cultural institutions, and how best to prevent such audacious robberies in the future. He hadn't seen a single mention of suspected involvement by criminal organizations, Eastern European or otherwise.

Now all he had to do was pack his bag and meet his private jet at the airfield. It was the easiest way to get himself and so many pieces of artwork to Venice in time for the delivery. His crates wouldn't arouse suspicion. He always used the same company to move his artwork from one gallery to the next. If all went as planned, he would be enjoying a Venetian sunset along the Grand Canal tonight.

Ivan refreshed the screen once again, and three more articles appeared. He clicked on the newest link and reread Robber Hood's manifesto.

You only love what you've lost...

When governments slash cultural subsidies, they leave their national institutions—those dedicated to culture, art, and

201

history—vulnerable to mold, insufficient conservation, thieves, and corporate sponsors. Museums aren't businesses. They are storehouses of knowledge and our history.

They are soft targets that need protecting, not monetization.

Don't let our cultural institutions become empty, dusty warehouses.

Lucky for you, we're the good guys. Your art is safe for now. If you improve your security, your loved ones will be returned to you.

Your politicians claim culture is invaluable and priceless, so here's their chance to prove it. If the Dutch parliament pledges two million euro in subsidies to help museums improve their security, all of the stolen art will be returned. They have two weeks to act. If they don't, they will have no one to blame for the art's destruction but themselves.

This was a warning. Criminal organizations are stealing our culture to fund their drug buys, terrorist campaigns, human trafficking routes, and arms deals. It is time the politicians we elected—at both a regional and national level—step up and take responsibility for our history's protection and conservation.

Our future generations are counting on it.

54 Sally's Coffee Hour

September 21, 2018

Zelda listened in awe to the banter on the radio. Though she only had two hours before she was to meet Vincent de Graaf at Central Station and travel to Schiphol Airport with him, she had trouble keeping her mind on what possessions to pack. The discussion about the Robber Hood press release and museum security was so heated that the host and guests kept interrupting each other, making their conversation difficult to follow. The Robber Hood gang turned out to be a radical group of cultural crusaders just as their messages implied. Zelda still couldn't quite believe it but was glad they finally made their manifesto and artnapping demands known. If she couldn't find Gabriella, maybe the situation would resolve itself upon the return of the stolen artwork. That is if it *was* returned.

Although the Robber Hood gang had not named all the artwork they had stolen during their twenty-seven-day spree, several institutions had already come forward this morning to acknowledge their loss. The list was astonishingly long and growing by the hour. Because of Robber Hood's demands, the police also decided to release all seventeen of their messages to the press, as well.

Zelda listened as Sally Sanderson, host of *Sally's Coffee Hour*, took back control of the conversation. She was in top form this morning. "Harold, there is so much more we can do! Our cultural treasures are sitting ducks, and no one will take responsibility for protecting them. Until there is an increase in security—I'm talking cameras, security guards, motion sensors—we might as well leave the door open as one of the Robber Hood's cards stated. They do have a point, you know. Heck, we might as well hand over the *Night Watch* to the first yo-yo that asks for it."

A deep, booming voice responded. "Sally, we can't turn

museums into fortresses. They need to remain accessible for all. Heck, the Van Gogh Museum was already one of the best-protected institutions in the Netherlands, and a pair of small-time crooks managed to break in—with a ladder no less—and escape with two multimillion-dollar paintings in a matter of minutes! Being accessible means being a soft target. It's a risk I'm still willing to take. We have to restore our faith in humanity. You don't want all our cultural institutions turned into the Jewish Historical Museum, do you? They have metal detectors, armed security guards, bullet-proof doors, and cameras, and that's just to get inside. I can imagine many visitors decide to skip it once they see—"

"Museums should raise ticket prices and dedicate the extra funds to improving security! There's no way the government could, or would, subsidize all of the changes needed," a third guest chimed in.

Sally ignored her, preferring to keep her spears pointed at Harold. "My faith in humanity was corrupted long ago, Harold. To say that trust is the solution to the theft of our national treasures is quite naïve—if not stupid—in my humble opinion. We're lucky this Robber Hood gang does have their heart in the right place. Most art crimes are committed by thieves planning to sell them to buyers who want them as a bargaining chip, trophies, or to use as a down payment in some illegal dealings. Groups such as ISIS and the Taliban use the profits from stolen art to fund acts of terrorism, for God's sake! Doesn't that make better protection for these paintings and objects worth fighting for?"

"You can't expect the government to—" The third guest valiantly tried to cut Sally off, but the radio host barreled over her.

"If we demonstrate a willingness to improve our museums' security, they'll give the art back. Their message is worth listening to."

"And the two million in subsidies Robber Hood demands? Where's that supposed to come from?"

The show's host laughed heartily. "It's a drop in a bucket compared to what is truly needed to get anything done. But it's better than nothing."

"You're suggesting we give in—"

"No, Harold. I'm suggesting we *do* something. If our politicians don't take any measures to improve museum security, what then? Are we just supposed to sit back and let any idiot steal our history?"

"You can't give in to Robber Hood. Otherwise, every protest group in the world will pull a similar stunt to ransom their opinion into law by forcing our politicians to do their bidding."

Harold may have a point, Zelda thought, but on the whole, she agreed more with Sally. Maybe we need a Robber Hood to get anything done. The average taxpayer or politician didn't care about art crimes—at least, not until it was literally too late.

Without more governmental funding, most cultural institutions would not be able to modernize their facilities enough to protect their collections adequately. And after years of filling in the gaps left after slashed cultural subsidies, the private sector was tapped out. As long as museums were expected to preserve, restore, conserve, and display priceless artifacts and artwork with limited funding, they would never have enough left to pay for multimillion-dollar security systems. They might as well open the door and let looters inside.

Zelda wondered what would happen if the politicians couldn't agree on a solution in time. Would the Robber Hood gang go through with their threat? Would the destruction of forty relatively unknown pieces of art really rile up the Dutch public enough that something would be done? Or once the shock of the destruction had subsided, would public interest wane and politicians become concerned with other, more pressing issues? Zelda feared the latter. And once again, the cycle would continue…

55 Amsterdam of the South

September 21, 2018

The moment Zelda stepped off the staircase leading away from Piazzale Roma, she was at a loss for words to describe the beauty of Venice. The water was liquid opal, the architecture opulent. Bridges soared over the wide *Canal Grande*, gravity-defying structures made of carved stone. Plying its choppy waters were watercraft of all shapes and sizes.

Zelda wove through the clusters of tourists standing outside of Santa Lucia Train Station to reach the water's edge. Zelda wanted to pinch herself; she was actually in Venice, gazing at one of the most famous canals in the world. A cluster of gondolas caught her eye, slowly bobbing in between the speedboats as they paddled rich tourists up the canal. Zelda couldn't help but marvel at the gondoliers' striped shirts and sunhats as well as the glossy blackness of the boat's sleek hull. She pulled out her camera to take a few pictures when Vincent caught up to her.

"We aren't here to sight-see, Zelda," he said, grabbing her hand and pulling her through the dense crowd.

"I know," she replied quickly, vowing to return to Venice one day soon to do just that.

They had flown to this island city in the afternoon to ensure they would be on time for their early morning appointment with Ivan Novak. Zelda was thrilled to have a night in Venice even though Vincent emphasized it would be spent working on Vanessa von Trapp's character, accent, and motivations. Zelda didn't care. She'd always wanted to visit the 'Amsterdam of the South' and was thrilled to be here, no matter how long their trip ended up being. Everywhere she looked was sparkly water, beautiful boats, and

206

people—masses and masses of people.

Zelda started to scale the steep Ponte Scalzi when Vincent tugged at her arm. "We should take a vaporetto. It will be faster."

"A what?"

"A water taxi. We can buy a ticket over there." He pointed to a row of ticket machines positioned inside a small bus stop floating in the Grand Canal, a few feet from the bridge Zelda wanted to cross. While waiting for line one to arrive, Vincent said, "I booked us into a hotel close to the Rialto Bridge. It's nothing fancy so don't get your hopes up, but it's clean, which is saying something around here."

Rialto Bridge! Zelda couldn't believe they were staying in a hotel so close to such an iconic landmark or that she was about to sail on Venice's famous Grand Canal.

They jostled with a surge of tourists to get on their floating taxi. Vincent pulled her to a small open seating area at the back of the vaporetto. "We'll have the best views from here."

Vincent was right. Their short boat trip took them along richly decorated palazzos that seemed to be sinking into the canals, thin bridges rising overhead, and several busy markets. Too soon, their vaporetto docked next to a wide bridge that resembled steps across the water. Its white stone façade glimmered in the early afternoon sun. It was the only bridge Zelda had seen with sheltered market stalls built into one side. She felt like a sardine as they pushed their way off the boat and over the Ponte di Rialto. There were so many tourists shopping at the glass, jewelry, and T-shirt shops lining one side of the famous bridge that she wasn't confident they would make it across. She'd heard about Venice's issues with overcrowding but experiencing it firsthand made her agree with the locals that a tourist tax was in order.

Vincent led her over to the other side, then down a dark alleyway a block away from Rialto Bridge. Their room was tiny but meticulously decorated. The curtains, bedspreads, and walls were all covered in brightly printed fabric with traditional designs. The explosion of color was a delight for the senses. Their light source was a chandelier made of transparent blown glass, each peak topped with a colorful glass flower from which light emitted. When Zelda lay down on the bed, she felt like a princess.

What she initially took to be one bed was two, albeit pushed so close together she and Vincent could spoon if they wanted to. Considering she wasn't paying the bill, Zelda didn't feel in a position to complain. She lay back, arms folded behind her head, and dreamt of living here.

"Don't get too comfortable. I want to scope out the gallery before it gets dark."

Zelda sat up, tossed her jacket onto the bed, and slung her bag across her shoulder. "Okay. You lead the way."

He led them to another vaporetto, but this time, they got off at the Accademia. Zelda rushed up the Ponte dell' Accademia before Vincent could stop her. When she crested the wide bridge soaring over the Grand Canal, she gasped in awe. On her right was a massive white-domed church—the Basilica di Santa Maria della Salute according to a tour guide standing close to Zelda, pointing out the highlights for her group. On her left, the iconic clock tower on Piazza San Marco rose high above the richly decorated buildings lining both sides of the canal. This was the money shot, the photo of Venice everybody wanted to have. Zelda snapped a few selfies, and then Vincent begrudgingly took a few more for her before finally ushering her off the bridge and toward the Dorsoduro neighborhood.

Zelda followed Vincent through one gorgeous street and square after another, past fairy-tale palazzos and grand churches, often begging him to slow down so she could take just one photo. Every corner was a postcard. Gallery Novak was situated in a residential neighborhood full of colorful, crumbling mansions, dainty staircases over thin waterways, and open squares filled with tourists and locals dining. Gondolas and speed boats played peekaboo with them as they crisscrossed over hidden walkways and Escher-like bridges. The soft colors, the chipped paint, the constant presence of water—it was more beautiful than she could ever have imagined.

Once Vincent was satisfied they both knew the general layout of the neighborhood, he steered them toward the Calle San Gregori, the street where Gallery Novak was located.

The buildings on the street were tall, grand structures with latticed stone worked into the fronts and backs. Most had apartments above and shops below, the majority occupied by expensive art galleries, jewelers and glass shops. Zelda noticed those on the left side butted up against the Grand Canal. Through tiny alleyways and gates, she could see most had a pier extending out the back with boats worth millions of euros tied up to them with a simple rope.

"It should be at the end of this street on the left." Vincent pointed straight-ahead. A few feet later, they saw the sign for Gallery Novak. It was one of three shops on the ground floor spaces of one long building. It wasn't a palazzo, but the façade was old and just as beautiful. The neighboring shops sold antiques and Murano Glass.

They sauntered past, pretending to study the artwork through the large windows. In reality, both were more interested in the woman turning off lights and locking doors at the back of the space. When she pulled on her jacket and turned toward the front door, Vincent said, "Come on, we don't want her to notice us."

He led Zelda further up the street toward the Campo della Salute, a small square made of white marble. Towering above them was the dome-shaped church they had seen from the Accademia Bridge. At its base was a pier full of gondolas. Zelda snapped a dozen pictures of the gleaming black boats and smartly dressed gondoliers before Vincent nudged her forward.

"I want to show you something," he said.

He led them past the Fondation Pinault then along a half-submerged waterway to the end of a narrow strip of land—the Punta della Dogana. At the tip was a tiny triangular space already full with tourists standing around, gazing out over the blue-green bay. Piazza San Marco was on their left and straight-ahead was an enormous church floating in the water. Zelda was captivated. She let the wind blow across her face, reveling in the hazy views across the open water.

Vincent pointed straight at it. "That's the Church of San Giorgio Maggiore. You can take an elevator up to an observation deck. If you get the chance, I recommend it. The views are spectacular."

Zelda muttered her appreciation, unable to put into words the joy she felt. Standing on this point, which was almost the same level as the churning sea, while gazing out to these iconic islands and structures was magical.

Too soon, Vincent steered them back toward the hotel. He wanted Zelda to bone up on Gabriella's oeuvre so she could play her part to the fullest tomorrow. And he wanted to do more online research as well as call a few Croatian contacts. Hours before they'd left Amsterdam, he'd found a report about Ivan's daughter, Marjana, and her apparent suicide. She worked as an art restorer for a company owned by Luka Antic until an accident forced her to stop painting. An accident—his network said—Luka was personally involved with.

It was a weak link for sure, one that left Zelda wondering whether Ivan was working with Luka or against him. Either way, Vincent was convinced the dealer was worth talking to, which made him even more anxious about her performance tomorrow at the gallery.

Zelda didn't quite understand why Luka was so important to Vincent. He continually stressed that his job was about recovering the artwork, not arresting any thieves. But in this case, he seemed to want to tie Antic to the Robber Hood crimes. She got the feeling that something happened between them, something personal that may be affecting his judgment. However, she was so grateful for Vincent's help in finding Gabriella that she didn't pressure him by asking about it.

They were following signs pointing to the Accademia vaporetto stop when Zelda spotted an unusual metal gate. It reminded her of a series of birds' nests woven out of fine metal strands. The threads were patinaed black, but time had removed some of the stain, revealing a golden glow beneath. Tucked inside several nests of metal were chunks of glass in a rainbow of colors.

Zelda pulled out her camera and took several shots of it while Vincent watched. "What do you think of the gate?" he asked.

"It's incredible. If I owned a Venetian palazzo, I would order one of these," Zelda said with a laugh.

"I doubt you could afford one."

"What's that supposed to mean?"

"Peggy Guggenheim commissioned an American sculptor, Claire Falkenstein, to make this entrance gate to her home before it became a museum."

"Seriously?" Zelda peeked inside and saw a small cobblestoned square that now served as the entryway to the Guggenheim Museum, home of one of the most exquisite modern art collections in the world. This trip was so last minute that Zelda hadn't bothered looking up the addresses of any museums she might have wanted to visit, figuring they wouldn't have time to see any of them anyway. If she had, the Guggenheim would have been at the top of her list. A long, snaking line of impatient-looking tourists filled the small square. "Oh, I guess it's pretty popular."

Vincent joined her at the gate and peered inside. "Yeah, you could say that. I think the average wait time is two hours." He looked at his watch. "It's closing in an hour. Do you want to take a quick look?"

"But you just said..."

Vincent laughed. "I know a guy..."

And indeed, he did. Three years ago, he had helped recover one of the Guggenheim Museum's Alexander Calder mobiles, stolen five years earlier from the Leerdam Glass Museum while it was on loan for a Calder exhibition. Vincent only had to ask for his friend, the museum's head of security, and they were skipping the lines—to the frustration of several grumbling tourists ahead of them.

They headed straight to the piece Vincent had recovered, one of the only Calder mobiles displayed in a public museum made from wood, string, and metal. The rawness of the material added an edge to his work Zelda had never seen before. The shapes and their positioning reminded her of the solar system, with moons, stars, and planets rotating around the sun. It was fascinating. They then walked quickly past masterworks by Constantin Brâncuşi, Georges Braque, Salvador Dali, Joan Miró, René Magritte, Jean Arp, and more. Zelda's brain had difficulty processing all that beauty. The lightning-fast visit only motivated her to make returning to this enchanted city a priority.

On the way back to their hotel, they dined on the water. Zelda ate fresh seafood and sipped excellent vino while enjoying the twinkling night lights reflecting off the water and sounds of street musicians, accompanied by drunk tourists singing on their way home. Her appetite waned a bit when Vincent pointed out a rat sneaking away from a nearby table with a bread roll.

Soon enough, they were back in their tiny hotel room. After hours of preparing for the morning meeting, they both called it a night. Zelda couldn't help but watch Vincent sleep as her mind raced. She knew she should be concentrating on tomorrow's meeting and locating Gabriella, yet she was mesmerized by how his chest moved slowly up and down, and his breathing sounded like a gentle breeze. She knew he was married, and she was so happy with Jacob. It was just odd to be sharing this room with him here in one of the most romantic cities in the world. She wished he were Jacob instead.

In the morning, her jangling nerves wiped away any residual notions of a Venetian tryst. Besides, she could never hurt Jacob like that. He was her soulmate.

Getting dolled up in her new clothes brought her no joy, and it took forever to apply the kind of makeup that Vanessa von Trapp would wear. By the time Zelda joined Vincent for breakfast, she was so jittery her hands wouldn't stop shaking.

Vincent grabbed her shoulders and looked her in the eye. "It's going to be fine. You are going to be great. All you have to do is get Ivan to talk about Gabriella, and we're golden."

Hand in hand, they walked back toward Gallery Novak. The warmth of Vincent's touch calmed her thoughts and steeled her nerves. For a fleeting moment, she felt as if this nightmare was about to end.

56 Venetian Betrayal

September 22, 2018

Zelda felt like a fraud decked out in her new clothes, standing outside Gallery Novak. A wobbly fraud on spikey heels, ones not meant for walking through the cobblestoned, uneven streets of Venice. She caught a glimpse of herself in the gallery's plate glass window and cringed. A clown looked back at her. She had to consciously stop her hand from scratching at the thick layer of makeup suffocating her skin.

Their plan was simple. 'Vanessa' would act like a spoiled American socialite with money to burn. She would ask extensive questions about Gabriella's background under the guise of wanting to buy four of her works—if 'Vanessa' deemed the artist was worth investing in. Vincent kept reminding her to remain haughty at all times. Zelda thought back to the many gallery openings she had attended and found inspiration in the actions of some of the more important guests, confident she could mimic their behavior for a few hours.

After Ivan showed her the artwork, 'Vanessa' would tell him she wanted to meet the artist—after all, she was planning on dropping two hundred thousand dollars on Gabriella's work. How Ivan reacted would determine their next steps.

While Zelda was inside playing the role of her life, Vincent would be outside the gallery, pretending to be a tourist infatuated by the canal the shop was located on.

But now, standing outside of Gallery Novak, their plan didn't feel simple at all. An impeccably dressed woman with long, curly black hair sat behind a wide desk, placed discreetly at the back of the square space. Her outfit and makeup put Zelda's to shame. Behind

213

her was a long wall of smoky glass. Zelda and Vincent figured that was the office and that Ivan Novak was probably sitting back there waiting for Vanessa von Trapp to arrive.

At ten past ten, 'Vanessa' opened the gallery door. She gave one fleeting glance at Vincent, who was steadfastly ignoring her, then disappeared inside. "I am Vanessa von Trapp," Zelda announced in the most dismissive tone she could manage.

The gorgeous woman behind the desk rose with a smile. "Of course. I will tell Ivan Novak you are here. May I offer you a cappuccino?"

"Yes, thank you." When the woman disappeared behind the glass partition, Zelda sauntered over to the nearest painting and took in the abstract rendering of the Doge's Palace at night. The flat perspective and bright, unnatural colors reminded her of the Fauvists. Zelda wasn't sure if she liked it but did find the painting fascinating.

"Good morning, Miss von Trapp. That is one of Gabriella Tamic's pieces, the artist you are interested in. It's part of her *Ode to Venice* series. She's painted several of our landmarks in her unique style."

"Oh, that's interesting..." Zelda turned to greet him, and the smile on her face vanished when they made eye contact. "You! You were the one who hit me!"

Zelda grabbed the older man by the lapels and shook him as hard as she could. Ivan was smaller than she was and much older. His head bobbed around like a rag doll. His eyes were wide with fear, not recognition.

"Where is Gabriella? What did you do to her?" Zelda's screams brought Ivan's gallery assistant and Vincent de Graaf into the action. The Italian woman tugged on Zelda's dress and scratched at her arms as she cursed at her in Italian.

Vincent raced inside and pulled Zelda's fingers loose from Ivan's lapel. "Enough. Let him go, Zelda!"

As soon as he was free, Ivan Novak stepped back and smoothed down his hair. "I was told you are a collector interested in buying Gabriella's work. Who are you really?"

Zelda glared at him. He didn't seem to remember her at all. "I'm

Gabriella's neighbor. Don't you recognize me? You assaulted me three weeks ago. I'm doing better now, thanks," Zelda said, unable to leave the sarcasm aside.

Novak's face remained completely neutral. He rebuttoned his jacket then wiped a speck of lint off, avoiding Zelda's gaze as he answered. "We have never met. I am quite certain of that. I think you should leave."

"What did you do to Gabriella?" Zelda cried. She surged forward, but Vincent held her back.

"Leave it," he whispered in her ear.

"I don't know what you think happened, but Gabriella is fine." Ivan locked eyes with Zelda, his cold stare startling her. "She's back in the Netherlands, preparing for her next show, an *Ode to Barcelona*. If you were really her neighbor, you would know that. If you do not leave right now, I will call the police."

As Vincent pulled her toward the door, Zelda glared at Ivan but said nothing.

Once outside, she broke free from Vincent's grip and raced to the Campo della Salute. She stopped at the water's edge and stared out at the gondolas. "Why didn't you do anything? I don't care what he said. That is the man who hit me!"

"Zelda, I believe you. But he would never admit it to you, me, or Vanessa von Trapp," he said in an attempt to raise a smile. It didn't work. "I'll follow him today and see what I can find out. If he does know where Gabriella is, I bet your performance will spur him to visit her. Or at least get in touch with her."

Zelda wanted to cry. They were no closer to finding Gabriella or the stolen Pollock. She didn't believe for a second that Gabriella was back in Amsterdam. Where could she be hiding? Anywhere in this vast city of interconnected islands, Zelda realized. They could search for months and still not find her, especially if she didn't want to be found. "I guess we have no choice. It's just—what the?" Zelda couldn't believe what she was seeing. "Vincent, look! Ivan's getting away!"

Vincent followed Zelda's finger, pointing to a speedboat racing up the Grand Canal, Ivan Novak behind the wheel.

The detective raced through the crowds, following the boat along the water's edge. He was retracing their steps from yesterday, though now at top speed. Zelda followed the cries of anger Vincent was inciting as he pushed his way through the throng of tourists gawking at the glorious scenery.

Ivan's boat was faster. By the time Zelda reached the land's end, Vincent was already there, his telephone's camera zoomed in as far as possible, documenting Ivan's actions. The art dealer had tied up to a large yacht called *Sunset Dreams* bobbing in the Bacino San Marco, anchored directly in front of Isola di San Giorgio Maggiore, an island on the opposite side of the bay. They watched through the screen as Ivan boarded the yacht. Two burly men climbed down to his vessel and swiftly lifted twenty-five crates up onto the yacht. On deck, there seemed to be a disagreement between Ivan and the yacht's captain. The art dealer made a call, then handed the phone to the boat's captain. Moments later, the captain ordered the speedboat to be cut loose, then the yacht pulled away and quickly headed out toward the Adriatic Sea.

"Shit!" Vincent screamed.

A mother standing next to him covered her young child's ears and glared at him in disapproval.

Zelda looked up to him. "What now?"

Vincent stared out at the horizon, his eyes locked on the rapidly disappearing yacht.

"Time to call in another favor."

57 You Only Live Once

September 22, 2018

Count Giovanni Bonato's baritone voice boomed through the phone. "Vincent, my dear fellow. I've got the information you requested."

"That was fast. Thank you for making it a priority."

"Of course! I am always happy to lend a hand. Gallery Novak owns the speedboat as you suspected. However, *Sunset Dreams* is the property of a rental company owned by Tekin Enterprises, based out of Marmaris, Turkey. I'll send you the details by text."

Vincent gave Zelda a thumbs up. He quickly scribbled on her notebook. 'Search for flights Venice to Marmaris, Turkey.'

Zelda pulled out her iPad.

"That's great, Giovanni. It gives us a solid lead to follow."

Vincent had called on Count Bonato, a Venetian aristocrat whose mother lost her family's art collection during World War II. Vincent was instrumental in the recovery and restitution of seventeen of the thirty-one looted paintings. The family was forever grateful. During his five-year-long investigation, he had grown particularly fond of Count Bonato. The older man was the epitome of kindness and grace with a sharp wit to boot. He was also the owner of a multimillion-dollar cruise ship company and an avid boat collector. He had the connections to check the boat's registration numbers as well as a fleet of vessels Vincent hoped he might be able to use to get them out of their next bind.

"Give me just a moment." Vincent put his hand over the receiver as Zelda thrust the iPad's screen in front of his face. She'd found a short list of flights, none of which had available seats until three days from now. *It must be high season*, he thought, which meant the ferries would be booked out as well. Vincent knew they needed to find a way to get there faster.

"Count, I hate to impose on your goodwill even further, but would it be possible to borrow one of your boats?"

"For a trip to Marmaris, I presume."

"Indeed."

"Certainly. Let me check and see which vessels are available. I'll call you back as soon as I know more."

"YOLO? Seriously?" Zelda stopped in front of the gangplank and stared up at the sleek yacht, appropriately named *You Only Live Once.*

Vincent shrugged. "It's what was available."

When the captain told them it would take approximately thirty-five hours of sailing to get there, Zelda's first thought was to take a long nap. She hadn't gotten a decent night's rest in weeks. Yet despite her cabin's luxurious interior, she couldn't sleep a wink. The events of the past few hours kept her mind abuzz.

Gabriella's art dealer assaulted Zelda then whisked her half-comatose friend away. Zelda was having trouble wrapping her head around that fact. Did Gabriella go willingly? Did her disappearance have anything to do with the stolen Pollock? It must, she reckoned. Otherwise, why would a Croatian mobster be interested in finding Gabriella, one who was involved with the Amstel Modern robbery?

Zelda hoped their trip to Turkey would bring them answers. All she wanted to do was get Marko out of her life, the police off her back, and go back to work.

An hour before dinner was served, Zelda finally fell into a restless sleep. She awoke to a crew member knocking on her door, asking if she would prefer red or white wine with her meal.

"Red, please," she muttered loud enough to send the man scurrying back to the kitchen. After a long stretch, she rose, groggy and disoriented. It took her a while to dress for dinner.

When she finally arrived in the dining room, she was amazed at the size and lavish interior. Large windows provided unobstructed views of the open ocean. The paneled walls and ceiling were a rich red cedar with swirls in the highly polished grains, which reminded Zelda of abstract paintings. The plush couches lining the walls were covered in a royal blue as were the chairs. Zelda was surprised to see the table was large enough for a party of sixteen with two places were set. Her meal was covered to keep it warm while Vincent was already halfway through his steak. She took her seat and stared out at the setting sun lighting up the sky with streaks of red and purple as it slowly disappeared under the horizon.

"How do you know so many rich people?" she asked Vincent as she unfolded her cloth napkin and lay it in her lap.

He laughed heartily. "My job, I guess. Most of my clients are wealthy. Otherwise, they wouldn't have the means to hire me to find their missing artwork or antiquities."

"It doesn't seem fair that only the rich can hire someone like you to help recover what is rightfully theirs."

"Sometimes I help families who aren't able to afford me, but if I took on every pro bono case I was contacted about, I wouldn't have time to earn a living."

"Sorry, that was rude of me. Of course, you need to make money. You have rent to pay and groceries to buy just like the rest of us. What you do is just so specialized, and there aren't many people out there who have the right kind of training and contacts to find lost or stolen artwork."

"No offense taken. Luckily, there are several of us working in the field. But you're right. There aren't that many private investigators specializing in art crimes. It's too bad there aren't more. It is time-consuming and often frustrating but finding a piece and being able to return it to its rightful owner is quite a kick and extremely rewarding."

"I can only imagine." Zelda looked at Vincent with new respect. It must take a tenacious investigator to track down stolen artwork. He'd definitely proven himself a man of action and well connected. She hoped he could work the same magic in Turkey. After a few sumptuous bites of the cauliflower couscous salad, Zelda asked, "Why do you think Ivan is heading to Marmaris?"

"I'm still trying to work that out. I spent the afternoon talking to several of my Croatian associates, and so far, no one knows how Ivan fits into the picture. Other than the rumors about Luka's involvement in Marjana's accident, I can't connect Ivan to his criminal network or any other in the Balkans. He seems to be clean."

"I heard you say something yesterday about the Balkan Route. What is that exactly?"

"Cocaine and heroin are often smuggled by boat from Turkey into Europe through Croatia and Albania. Interpol calls it the Balkan Route. There are rumors that Luka Antic is expanding into heroin or cocaine. It could be the stolen art will be used to pay for drugs. You heard me asking one of my contacts if they'd seen any movement on the Balkan Route that could be tied to Luka. So far, he's heard nothing. But if Luka and Ivan aren't working together, it might be Marko Antic who is buying the drugs, which could result in a bloody interfamily feud, depending on whether or not Luka Antic has given Marko his blessing. There are still so many possibilities."

"Do you think the artwork is on the yacht?"

"Yes, I do. The crates moved from Ivan's boat onto the yacht were the right size and number. I just hope we're not too late, that we see what Ivan does with the stolen art and we can recover it before it vanishes."

"What if we can't find Ivan or the yacht, and the artwork disappears forever?" she asked, her mind racing with scenarios, each one more horrifying than the next.

Vincent shook his head. "I don't know. Right now, I want to focus on the positive." He pushed back from the dining room table. "I'm going to give one of my contacts a call. I just remembered something he told me last week that could be useful."

Zelda hoped with all her might that he was right. They needed all the luck they could get.

58 Hitching a Ride

September 24, 2018

An hour before the *Sunset Dreams* was to dock in Marmaris, Ivan rose and enjoyed a leisurely breakfast on the deck. The morning sky was an orange glow above a sea of dark blue, sharply divided by the straight horizon. It reminded him of a Mark Rothko painting come to life. He meditated on mother nature's artistic abilities until their boat turned inland. When the mouth of Marmaris Bay was in sight, Ivan called Luka Antic as promised.

"We're about to dock."

"You made good time."

"What should I do now?" Ivan hitching a ride to Marmaris wasn't part of Luka's plan. He knew Luka was not pleased that he was on board, but when he'd called the crime boss from the yacht in Venice, he only had to tell Luka that Vincent de Graaf was nipping at his heels, and he was allowed passage.

De Graaf's unexpected visit to his gallery had been a blessing in disguise. So far, he had been unable to find out where Luka was meeting with his Turkish contact or when. For his plan to work, Ivan needed to know the location and timing of the handoff, preferably before their transaction was complete.

Revenge was so close that he could taste it. Sleep was impossible. He spent every waking moment reviewing the facets of his plan, brainstorming the strengths and weaknesses of each step. This was his only chance to get Luka back; his plan had to be perfect.

Only then could he be free of the crushing guilt he felt whenever he thought of Marjana. Ivan wondered if hurting Luka would be enough to lessen his pain or if he could overcome his own role in his daughter's downfall.

"Your job is finished," Luka said. "The money has been transferred to your account. I have already informed the captain you will be disembarking as soon as you dock. Do you think Vincent de Graaf followed you?"

"I don't see how."

"Excellent. Say, why not stay a day in Marmaris? We can meet after the deal is complete and celebrate," Luka said, his tone unusually jovial.

Ivan's heart raced. "Certainly. When is it taking place exactly? Are you in Marmaris now?"

"You did good, Ivan. I'll be in touch," Luka said then hung up without answering Ivan's questions.

"He must already be there," Ivan muttered aloud.

One of the crew members approached with another mimosa. "Sir, we will be docking in twenty minutes. Do you require help packing your belongings?"

Ivan only had a small satchel with him, and the crew knew it. He played along anyway. "No, thank you. I'll take care of it as soon as I finish this drink." He took a long sip of the orange juice and prosecco mix, savoring the bubbles.

59 Two Birds, One Stone

September 24, 2018

Luka Antic watched through binoculars as the *Sunset Dreams* entered the bay and sailed to the Setur Netsel Marina. He was already nervous enough without Ivan Novak poking around where he shouldn't be. Was Vincent de Graaf really in Venice? Or did Ivan lie to get onto the boat, to stay with the artwork and see where it went? His curiosity was troublesome.

He lay down the binoculars then stared out toward the mountainous island rising before him in Marmaris Bay. He wiggled his toes around in the tiny pebbles covering the beach. He would have to come back here on vacation one day. Marmaris was his kind of place with the right mix of bars, alcohol, drugs, and scantily-clad women. Sitting here on the water's edge, the sound of lapping water calmed his nerves ever so slightly. Next to him stood a glass water pipe. He picked up a long tube attached to its middle and sucked hard. Three deep puffs set his mind spinning as the tension dissipated from his body.

Ivan was supposed to hand over the crates in Venice and return to Amsterdam, not hitch a ride to Marmaris. He'd been asking too many questions about his Turkish contact's identity as well as the location and specifics of their upcoming transaction. It shouldn't have interested him, but Ivan steered every conversation back to the artwork's handover.

To top it off, Ivan didn't seem suspicious when he asked him to stay in Marmaris and celebrate with him. In fact, the art dealer seemed downright pleased by the invitation. Given their history together, Luka hadn't expected Ivan ever to want to share another drink with him again.

A horrifying thought had entered his brain during their conversation and refused to be quelled. Could Ivan be working with the Dutch police or Vincent de Graaf? That would explain the constant questions, forced joviality, and unusual interest.

Now that Ivan was in Marmaris, Luka could spin it to his advantage. It would be far easier to get rid of the gallery owner here in Turkey than it would be back in Europe. And the sooner he did, the more confident he could be that Ivan would not be able to sell any of the copies that his artists may have made. Dead men don't make deals, and he couldn't imagine the art dealer would have entrusted any forgeries with his staff. The risks were too high. He probably had them stashed in a warehouse or storage unit back in the Netherlands.

Luka stood and stretched before stepping into the warm water of the bay. He floated on his back, letting the waves crash over his belly and massage his legs with their powerful pull. Retirement was only a few years away. If things with Kadir worked out the way he hoped, this transaction should be the beginning of a lucrative business relationship, one that would help his organization solidify its position in a larger, more profitable market. In the world he lived in, one needed to constantly evolve to stay on top.

He closed his eyes and breathed in the thick salty air. The laughter of playing children and roaring motors of watercraft crisscrossing the bay lulled him into a trance as the sunlight warmed his skin. It was heavenly here. Who knew, perhaps when he finally did retire, he would buy an apartment in Marmaris.

As soon as his transaction with Kadir was wrapped up, he'd have that drink with Ivan, and then get rid of him. His bodyguards would find a way to dispose of the art dealer's corpse. Afterward, he would stop at a realtor's office. *Two birds with one stone.* Luka smiled. This was turning out to be an extremely productive trip.

60 Exploring Marmaris

September 24, 2018

When Zelda walked onto *YOLO*'s deck, the suffocating humidity enveloped her like a warm blanket. They were cutting across the Mediterranean Sea as they approached the mouth of Marmaris Bay. Rocky mountains dotted with pine trees stretched down to the water's edge, their craggy feet flowing into the blue water. Zelda sucked in the salty air and watched as dolphins played in their boat's wake. It was early morning and soft pinks and oranges reflected off the rolling waves and colored the sky.

Vincent was already relaxing in a lounge chair, enjoying the stunning views. "The captain will drop us off in Marmaris but can't stay. They need to go to Kos."

"Good morning to you, too," Zelda said as she sat down next to him. "So, what's your plan?"

"Find the *Sunset Dreams* and watch it in the hope that the art hasn't yet been moved. They shouldn't have arrived much earlier than we did. Our captain's been cruising at top speed the entire journey."

"What, no favors to call in?"

Vincent chuckled. "No, not here. Unfortunately, I'm going to have to do this the old-fashioned way."

"You mean we."

"No, me. Zelda, I shouldn't have brought you to Marmaris. You aren't an investigator. We still don't know if Luka or Ivan Antic are involved. Both men are extremely dangerous, and I don't want to see you get hurt."

"If we don't find the stolen artwork, I don't get my life back. No museum will ever hire someone suspected of being involved in a robbery. Please, let me stay and help you."

"No! Zelda, I can't let you. You should fly back to Amsterdam. There are two airports reasonably near here. Once I have a better handle on this situation, we'll book you a flight back."

"I am not leaving Marmaris, Vincent! It's your job to find the art, but it's my life and future that are on the line! If you won't let me help, then at least let me stay so you can keep me updated."

Vincent scrutinized her for quite a long time, clearly weighing the pros and the cons. "It's a deal. But you have to stay out of the way, okay? I'll fill you in on anything I discover, but you must promise to let me do the investigating." He sat up straighter, stretching to his full height, and gazed at her sternly.

"Agreed," Zelda said solemnly and stuck out her hand to make it official.

"As soon as we dock, I'm going to look for the yacht. Why don't you find us a hotel close to the marina? Nothing too expensive. My expense account is limited."

As their yacht entered Marmaris Bay, Zelda couldn't help but gawk at the long, crescent-shaped beach and azure water. From the YOLO's deck, Zelda could see the entire town. Marmaris was a sprawling metropolis situated in a deep valley and encircled by tall, craggy mountain peaks with a mix of modern skyscrapers and residential homes lining the waterfront. They approached from the right, cruising past Setur Netsel, a public marina on the far end of town, then around a small hill jutting far out into the bay. The outcrop was covered with a mishmash of ancient buildings and topped with a miniature castle, complete with turrets. Unlike Clervaux Castle, this one appeared to be made of yellow marble.

On the other side of the hill was a giant statue of Atatürk surrounded by a half-circle of Turkish flags—a field of red with a crescent moon and white star floating in the middle. Docked close by were schooners decorated like pirate ships. Two were made to look like Jack Sparrow's Black Pearl. Signs indicated that all offered daily cruises around the bay.

As they sailed past the city center, the architecture became progressively modern. The far-left end of town was a forest of new hotels, most of them as tall as skyscrapers.

The captain wanted to dock at the public marina, but Vincent convinced him to take them further into the city center. Vincent had to assume Ivan was already in Marmaris and that his yacht was tied up to one of Setur Netsel Marina's many piers. He wanted to be dropped far enough away that Ivan wouldn't notice their arrival.

Zelda thought Vincent was crazy to make such a request, but she soon realized that in Marmaris, finding a place to tie their yacht up was not a problem. Once they reached the middle of town, there was a pier, jetty, or dock placed every few feet. Some were owned by hotels, and others were public, but all were appropriate options for the captain to allow Vincent and Zelda to disembark.

The captain pulled up to an empty pier in front of a trio of glass skyscrapers. Zelda was glad to be on dry land again. She loved watersports but always had trouble adjusting to the constant rocking motion when sailing. Between the hotels and the strip of beach ran a long promenade along the water's edge, which they soon learned connected one side of Marmaris to the other. The beach itself was filled with umbrellas, lounge chairs, and drink tables. Only a few Western tourists splashed around in the water, most preferring to lay out and smoke hookahs while they stared out to sea.

After the captain sailed away, Vincent pointed back to the right. "The marina is that way."

"Okay, let's go," Zelda said.

The wide sidewalk was a gray strip surrounded by red-brown earth. Thick shrubs with white and purple flowers grew like weeds, their blossoms scenting the air with a sweet perfume. Despite the strong breeze, Zelda was sweating. It had to be at least a hundred degrees Fahrenheit and humid. Every step was an effort, and the thick air felt like a shackle weighing her legs down.

The promenade was popular with tourists and locals. Most walked at a leisurely pace, enjoying the shade provided by the multitude of palm trees lining both sides. Children, oblivious to the sweltering heat weaved between their parents, chasing each other on steps and bicycles.

The contrast between the Western and Turkish tourists was astounding. Most Western men strode around in speedos and flip-flops, proudly displaying their pasty white or fire-engine red skin. Their better halves sported bikinis and short-shorts that left nothing to the imagination. Walking alongside them were Turkish families, the women in headscarves and formless dresses, the men in white T-shirts and long pants. However, all the children she and Vincent passed were dolled up in swimsuits featuring a multitude of Disney characters.

Hiding in the shade were bunny rabbits and feral cats. It seemed as if they'd passed hundreds on their short walk. She'd yet to see a rat. Perhaps they were a solution to Venice's vermin problem, Zelda pondered.

As they continued along the boardwalk and approached the old city center, one-story buildings housing snack bars, beer bars, sports bars, cafés, tattoo shops, hair extension salons, shoe stores, and clothing boutiques replaced the skyscraper hotels. A half-hour after disembarking from the *YOLO*, they reached the Atatürk statue. Both briefly admired his friendly smile and enormous size before continuing along the waterfront. As they approached the hill, a large sign caught both of their eyes.

"What does Grand Bazaar mean?" Zelda asked.

"It looks like a covered market. It must be huge. You can see how it splits into streets further back."

Next to the Grand Bazaar's entrance was a street leading up the hill. The neighborhood was a mishmash of old structures that almost appeared stacked on top of each other. Although they must have been built as residential homes, most had signs hanging off them advertising hotels, cafés, bars, and apartments, several of which looked promising. She also noticed a large sign pointing up, leading visitors toward the castle at the top.

Vincent said, "The entrance to the marina is just on the other side of this hill. I'd like you to find us a place—preferably up there, as high as you can. A balcony overlooking the marina would be ideal. Why don't you send me a text with the address once you've booked us in? I'll get in touch as soon as I'm able."

"No problem. What are you going to do exactly?"

"I'm going to look around the marina and see if I can find the *Sunset Dreams*. Wish me luck!" Vincent was already striding away, a man on a mission.

Zelda followed the sign leading toward the castle. Narrow streets and alleyways snaked upward, crisscrossing at random intersections. Souvenir shops displaying postcards, glass hangers, scarves, jewelry, and ceramics were in abundance. Several Turkish flags flew off a building close to the top, which Zelda assumed was the castle.

She walked into the first hotel she found on the marina side, but it was booked up. The next one was ridiculously expensive for the poor condition of the rooms. And the third one only had one single room left. Zelda continued searching until she ended up back at the top of the hill. She crossed over to the right side and walked into the next hotel she found. Her persistence was rewarded with two single rooms at a reasonable price. When she threw open her hotel room window, she could see the marina and the entire harbor from there. When she leaned over the railing, she realized the castle was only a few streets away. *Vincent will be pleased with me*, she thought as she sent him a message with the hotel's address.

Now that she'd completed her task, she didn't know what to do. She briefly contemplated sitting on the balcony with a book but realized this was a once-in-a-lifetime opportunity. Turkey had never been on her bucket list, but now that she was here, she might as well make the most of it. Besides, Vincent didn't want her in the way. After a quick shower to wash the sweat off, she headed back out to find lunch and explore Marmaris.

Halfway down the hill, Zelda happened upon an unusual terrace. To help counter the unrelenting heat, the café had hooked up a series of tubes that sprayed mist over their customers, and large fans helped distribute it evenly. Zelda took a seat directly under one of the jets.

After a delicious serving of skewered lamb, she decided to check out the Grand Bazaar and buy souvenirs for Jacob and her parents, who were talking of visiting over Christmas. Something from Turkey would be a lovely surprise.

It was indeed a large market that covered four city blocks. She'd never been in such a massive one before. The small, interconnected alleys seemed to form a maze one could easily get lost in. In the larger streets, there were fountains with strange statues of Western tourists shopping. Zelda realized the sculptor didn't have to look far for inspiration. All the alleys and shops seemed to be full of Westerners haggling over prices.

When Zelda was somewhere in the middle, a piercing cry startled her so badly she almost dropped a ceramic vase. A man's voice singing a high-pitched melody broke through the market banter. Zelda realized there must have been a mosque nearby and figured it was a call to prayer, but to her Westerner's ears, it sounded like a hauntingly beautiful song.

She wandered through the streets and alleys. The shops and stalls were numerous, yet most sold the same knock-off brand clothing, shoes, pottery, jewelry, leather bags, and belly dancing outfits. Those made for children were especially popular. She settled on ceramic tiles and glass hangers featuring a white eye floating on a field of blue.

"To protect," said the salesman.

Zelda bought three, figuring she could use all the help she could get.

61 Stake out in Turkey

September 24, 2018

It took Vincent thirty minutes to find the *Sunset Dreams*, docked at the end of the farthest pier in Setur Netsel Marina. Its position and the many security guards made it impossible to stroll by and get a closer look. As soon as he tried to enter the marina, he was stopped and questioned by two guards stationed at one of six guard houses dotted around the large parking lot for million-dollar yachts. The city was a popular destination for wealthy Westerners and Turks. While they partied in the nearby Bar Street, most left their boats and crews behind with the knowledge that their possessions would remain unmolested. Less expensive boats were forced to park along the waterfront and take their chances.

Vincent tried to bluff his way inside, but when the guard asked which boat he was a crew member of, the name that popped into his head—*Good Times*—was of a boat tied up two piers away from his target. At least when he sauntered over to *Good Times*, he would be able to get a bit closer to Ivan's yacht. Unfortunately, he only saw the same crew members as he did yesterday and no sign of Ivan or the crates before the crew of *Good Times* came out on the deck, and he switched direction again.

When he didn't board, the security guards began to approach him. Vincent walked out of the marina as quickly as he could, then raced to the right instead of back over the bridge to Bar Street. Running parallel to the marina was a short street filled with designer name shops—Burberry, Gucci, Hermes, Dior, and many other top designers. He followed the Turkish Rodeo Drive to the end where he noticed a sign for Robert's Coffee Shop.

He followed the arrow down a small alleyway between Gucci and Dior and out to a large café with a terrace overlooking the marina. After ordering a Turkish coffee, served with a saucer of milk, a glass of water, and a tray of bonbons, Vincent took a seat along the railing and turned to face his target. He put on his sunglasses in case Ivan walked by and opened a book on his phone. Experience taught him always to be prepared to sit and wait.

Try as he might, he couldn't keep his mind on his book. Was the stolen artwork still on board? He had to assume so until he had reason to believe otherwise. He still didn't know what Ivan was planning to do with it, but he was positive the art dealer was running away from him in Venice. If it wasn't because he was transporting stolen art, why would Ivan have taken off like that? All he could do was wait for Ivan to make his next move. With a little luck, Luka or Marko Antic would show up, as well.

After three hours of waiting, nothing had happened. No one had exited or boarded the yacht or any others on that pier. Apparently, their rich owners were living it up in town while the punishing heat kept the crews indoors. The café was also pretty quiet with most tourists not knowing it existed.

"Hey, man, we're closing now," Robert, the café's young owner, said.

Vincent had ordered several drinks, snacks, and a large lunch to justify his presence, tipping well every time. He preferred to pay as he went in case he needed to leave in a hurry. It turned out to be the perfect place to stake out the yacht. Unfortunately, the café was focused on the breakfast and lunch crowd.

"No problem. I'll get out of your way. I might see you again soon," Vincent said, smiling at the wait staff as he left. If Ivan were still in town tomorrow, he would be back to Robert's café. There were almost no places he could hang around without drawing the marina guard's attention, especially now that they thought he worked on the *Good Times*.

After a last look at Ivan's yacht, Vincent headed back toward Marmaris. A pedestrian bridge was the only link to town. A father and son were fishing off it, and Vincent watched as the older man lovingly helped his offspring cast his line, smiling with pride when the young boy did it correctly. As much as he loved his father and cherished the good times they had, Vincent was glad he and Theresa felt the same way about children. He'd rather be chasing down leads than changing diapers any day.

Vincent charged ahead, walking down the wide boulevard that ran between the waterfront and the strip of bars and dance clubs geared toward the rich and affluent. Most had large terraces in front, and all offered cocktails and water pipes. *And more*, Vincent thought, confident that hard drugs would also be available in most. Large fountains and statues of tourists playing in the water interspersed the walkway. He stepped closer to one and let the spray cool him down while he watched paragliders and speedboats race across the open bay. Close to the marina's entrance was a lighthouse attached to land by a rocky jetty currently inhabited by fishermen. It would give him great views of Ivan's yacht, he figured. All he needed was a pole. Vincent checked the map on his phone for a nearby fishing supply store when he noticed Zelda had sent a message with the address of their hotel. It was straight up the hill — Zelda had chosen well.

A few minutes later, when he knocked on Zelda's hotel room door, she practically pounced on him. "Did you find the yacht?"

"Yep, it's in the marina, but I didn't see Ivan. I still can't imagine he would be making a heroin deal. Luka or Marko Antic must be involved. I can't wait to see which one shows up."

"Why are you so convinced the Antics are involved? Why couldn't Ivan sell the stolen art to someone?"

Vincent looked at her in puzzlement.

"I mean, Marko is desperately searching for Gabriella, who is represented by Ivan Novak. And from what you told me earlier, Luka may be responsible for Ivan's daughter's death. I doubt they are working together. What if Ivan is double-crossing the Antics somehow?"

Vincent wanted to slam his palm into his forehead. Being so fixated on Marko and Luka Antic, he had ignored an obvious alternative scenario. His Croatian associates assured him that Luka

233

was getting into the heroin business, and in a big way. What if his contacts were wrong, and it was Ivan who was about to make a drug deal, not Luka?

"Zelda, you're right. I hate to admit it, but I didn't consider that possibility. I really need to get back down to the marina and keep an eye on that boat."

How he wished he could ask her to help him with his stakeout. But he wouldn't be able to live with himself if anything happened to her.

"Wait. I have a surprise for you." Zelda grabbed the second set of keys and opened the room next to hers. As soon as she was inside, she raced over to a set of French doors. "Tada!" she said as she opened them.

The balcony looked directly down onto the marina. With a pair of binoculars, Vincent bet he could see Ivan's boat from here. This was the perfect vantage point. "Well done."

Zelda preened. "I thought you would be pleased."

Vincent pulled his binoculars out of his satchel then positioned himself on the balcony. When he sat down, Zelda took the seat across from him.

"What are you doing?" Vincent asked.

"Enjoying the views."

"Why don't you do that somewhere else? We probably won't be in Marmaris long. Have you smoked a hookah before?"

"Nope."

"It's worth trying once. Bar Street has plenty of options. Why don't you check it out?"

Zelda chuckled. "Okay, I'll get out of your hair."

"Thanks."

62 A Moment of Weakness

September 24, 2018

Ivan sat at the Back Street Café on Bar Street, next to the only bridge connecting the marina to town. He knew there was a chance Luka would arrive by taxi, but that entrance to the marina was heavily guarded. He had to hope that Luka would arrive by foot or boat.

After sweating away the afternoon, Ivan wished that waiting around for Luka to act wasn't the only option. He briefly contemplated calling Luka and asking where he was at but knew it was too suspicious. Luka was already irritated by all of his questions about his Turkish dealer and the location of their final transaction.

He had no other option but to wait. He had to send his next message after the art was in the Turk's hands but before Luka left with the heroin. Otherwise, Luka could escape, or the Turk could pretend there was no deal. No, as tempting as it was to act now, he had to wait for Luka to appear. As soon as he did, Ivan could set the final phase of his plan into action. But not a moment sooner.

Exhausted from another sleepless night, he ordered one strong Turkish coffee after another, but the caffeine did little except jangle his nerves even further. He would have to get up and stretch his legs soon if only to relieve his jitteriness. From Marmaris Castle, he should be able to see the marina and bay, he figured.

In a moment of weakness, he took out his wallet and flipped through the pictures of his little girl—Marjana as a baby, a toddler with her first tooth, riding her first bike, winning her first painting contest. Moments he cherished immensely. Tears stung his eyes, so he picked up a cloth napkin to wipe them away, jostling his wallet in the process. It fell open to a photo of Marjana and Gabriella, both dressed as princesses or maidens as they preferred to be called. At ten years old, the girls were obsessed with the *Adventures of Robin Hood*. Ivan read Marjana every folktale he could find featuring the fearless do-gooder and the love of his life, Maid Marian. He held the photo closer, his little Marjana, his beloved one. When the girls were little, he used to take them to Trakošćan Castle, outside of Zagreb in Northern Croatia. It was a fairy-tale structure surrounded by a thick forest and lake, perfect for evoking images of sheriffs, thieves, and kings. The girls loved to reenact his stories about knights and princesses when they were there. At Marjana's insistence, he would play Robin Hood to their Maid Marjana and Maid Gabriella.

Ivan squeezed so hard on the photograph that it wrapped around his thumb as a wave of regret and despair washed over him. His perfect little girl was so full of potential. Marjana could have done anything she set her mind to, and he led her right into the arms of Luka Antic, who caged her spirit and destroyed her destiny. If only his fatherly pride and Luka's false promise hadn't blinded him. He should have known better than to trust Luka. And when she needed him most, he wasn't there for her. Ivan looked skyward as he pressed his fingernails into his palms until his skin bled, anything to keep his screams silent. He let out a long breath that calmed his soul. It was time to avenge his little princess, his perfect Maid Marjana.

63 Hookah for One

September 24, 2018

Zelda headed down the hill to Bar Street. She stopped at the first café offering an apple-flavored smoke and took a seat on the terrace under a parasol. The waiter brought over the enormous water pipe with a single tube attached to the side of its mouth. On top was a flat bowl wrapped in aluminum foil. The waiter used tongs to place five blocks of burning coal on top, then bowed slightly before departing. Unsure of what to do, she watched as other patrons picked up the tube and sucked on it. She followed suit and soon her mind was buzzing.

She took another drag and watched the bubbling water. Zelda let a gigantic cloud of apple-scented smoke trail out of her mouth, watching abstractedly as it twirled and rose before dissipating in the warm air. It smelled delicious, like an apple orchard in bloom. Her buzz and the cool breeze were a pleasant relief from the punishing sun.

She was inhaling deeply as she took another puff when Ivan Novak walked right by her table. He was heading up the hill. In shock, Zelda chocked on the smoke, hacking terribly. A Turkish couple next to her frowned as the waiter brought her a glass of water. She gulped it back, finally recovering enough to say, "Sorry, this is my first time. I don't think it's for me."

The Turkish couple and waiter laughed heartily and started chatting in Turkish, ignoring her completely.

Zelda pulled out her wallet. "How much do I owe you?"

The waiter and couple were so engaged in their conversation, obviously at Zelda's expense, that he didn't respond. The art dealer was almost to the end of Bar Street. The hill above was a maze of small streets and tiny alleyways, all leading up to the castle then back down to the Grand Bazaar on the other side. In a few minutes, he would be as good as gone.

"Please, how much?" she pressed. When he didn't answer, Zelda took out fifty lire and shoved it into the waiter's hand before pulling out her phone and sprinting off after Ivan. "Vincent!" she screamed into her phone the second he picked up.

"I told you not to…"

"He's here! Ivan just walked by me. He's heading up the hill toward our hotel."

"Thanks," Vincent said, then hung up.

Zelda's sprint slowed to a crawl as she contemplated her next move. She knew that Vincent didn't want her help in case the Antics were involved. But if Vincent didn't catch up with him, and Ivan managed to slip away with the stolen artwork, she would never get her life back. No, she didn't care what Vincent said. She was going to see this through to the end.

64 A Quick Visit to Marmaris Castle

September 24, 2018

Zelda raced up Bar Street, weaving her way through the fountains, large Turkish families strolling arm in arm, and Western tourists photographing everything in sight. Farther up the promenade, she could see Ivan's white hair bobbing in the crowd. He was approaching the first of many crossroads, and she needed to keep him in sight, so forcing her legs to work harder, she ran at top speed until she was only a street away. Moments later, he stopped to buy a bottle of water. Afraid he might see her, she leaned heavily against a crumbling wall, grateful to catch her breath. When she dared to peek around the corner, Ivan was walking away, up the hill. Zelda followed as discretely as she could, doing her best to keep a street or two between them. The narrow roads wound around ancient homes, many with shops on the ground floor and hotels above. The crumbling structures seemed to be made of plastered wooden frames and most hadn't been painted in years. *It is a beauty in ruin,* Zelda thought as she got lost in the sights, almost forgetting her prey.

She rounded the next corner and almost ran into Ivan, who was, luckily, more interested in a leather bag than the plethora of tourists milling about. *Shoot!* Zelda cursed to herself. If he saw her here, there was no way he would think it was coincidence. She doubled back to a shop specializing in scarves and picked up a dark blue swath of fabric. To the saleslady's surprise, Zelda handed her the lire she asked for instead of negotiating for a lower price. Zelda used the woman's small mirror to adjust the scarf so that it covered most of her face and shoulders. Once satisfied, she put on her sunglasses then dashed out of the shop.

Ivan was walking out of the leather shop with a new satchel over his shoulder. Zelda wove through the crowd, telling herself not to run. When he turned right at the next intersection, Zelda realized he was following the bright yellow signs pointing to the castle above.

Where is Vincent, she wondered, *still at our hotel or in this maze of streets hoping to catch a glimpse of Ivan*? Zelda pulled out her phone and called his number. He didn't pick up. "He's heading to the castle!" she whispered into his voicemail.

A few turns later, Ivan reached the castle's entrance, and Vincent was nowhere to be seen.

Zelda froze, unsure of what to do next. She hadn't been inside and didn't know if there was another exit. Figuring Vincent would applaud her initiative, she waited until Ivan paid his entrance fee and disappeared before buying a ticket.

The castle was imposing and grand from the outside. From inside, it reminded Zelda of an inner-city garden collective. According to her ticket, this landmark also served as the region's archeological museum. Enclosed inside the castle walls was a square of grass filled with palm trees and park benches, ancient pottery, and carved stone icons that had been excavated in this region. Next to each artifact was a small text board identifying where the piece was unearthed and explaining its cultural importance. Signs pointed to exhibition rooms built into each of the four corners. Zelda assumed they would be full of more pottery and artwork. She approached the closest but realized it was a tiny space. If Ivan were inside, they would run into each other.

Instead, she headed for a series of staircases and walkways, which lead up to the top of wide walls. It was hard work, climbing in this hot sun, but the high vantage point provided excellent views of the bay, mountains, and the city center far below. The views were stunning. The blue water sparkled in the sun as boats of all shapes and sizes crisscrossing over the bay. Looming above were the gray-green mountains rising out of the islands sheltering Marmaris from the Mediterranean Sea. Overwhelmed by the bay's beauty, Zelda took out her camera and snapped several photos, momentarily forgetting Ivan. She walked along the wall, pausing to take pictures as she went when footsteps behind her made her freeze.

When Zelda dared to glance behind her, she was immensely relieved to see it wasn't Ivan. She put her camera away and reminded herself why she was here. Even though she would love nothing more than to sit here and while the day away, she had to find Ivan. If he wasn't in one of the rooms below, then there must be another exit, she realized. From here, she could see the entire inner square. Despite the punishing sun, she decided to wait a while and see if either Ivan emerged from one of the exhibition rooms or Vincent arrived to save the day. Just as she was about to give up on both men, Ivan emerged from the toilets, directly across from her.

Zelda didn't know what to do. All Ivan had to do was look up, and he would see her. She turned to face the water, hoping he wouldn't come up the staircase behind her. Unfortunately, Ivan did just that. He didn't notice her until he was about to pass her on the wide ledge.

"You!" Ivan Novak yelled. He picked up one of the ancient vases and threw it at her. As it shattered at her feet, he raced across the courtyard and out of the castle before Zelda could get down the stairs. When she finally reached the exit, she caught sight of her prey running down a steep street heading left toward the Grand Bazaar. Worried she would lose him in that maze, Zelda dialed Vincent as she set off in pursuit. He picked up this time.

"Zelda, where are you?"

"Ivan just left the castle. He's heading toward the market, the Grand Bazaar!"

"On my way," he yelled back.

Zelda could hear him through the phone and in person. "Vincent?" she called out.

He ran around the corner, straight into her. "Zelda! Which way did he go?"

She pointed straight-ahead, and he sprinted away. Zelda did her best to keep up, but he was too fast. The humidity and heat made it so hard to run.

A minute later, she saw Vincent standing at a crossroads in the market. "You go left, and I'll go right," he ordered. His face was flush with excitement.

She nodded, and he raced off again. Zelda scanned the mass of human bodies but didn't see Ivan in front of her.

"Damn it! Where are you, Ivan?" Zelda knew he wouldn't answer, but her frustration was boiling over. Her need to know what was going on was overwhelming. Where was the stolen artwork, and what was he planning to do with it? Were Luka or Marko Antic really involved or was this Ivan's show?

Seconds later, she saw her prey sprint to the right. Zelda tore after him, racing past shops selling the same cheap crap as their neighbors. As she tripped over a display of scarves, she caught sight of Ivan two streets ahead before he disappeared into the shadowy maze of similar-looking shops. Zelda could hardly believe how fast he was going, especially for his age.

She saw him up ahead, quickly approaching another crossroads in the maze-like market. Luckily, an aggressive salesman grabbed his arm and was pestering him to buy something, which slowed the art dealer down long enough for her to catch up. Sweat poured down her face as she jogged toward him, hoping the salesman's pushiness would distract from her approach.

"Hello, madam. Look, please. Good prices." Another shop keeper tried to grab her arm, but she twisted out of his grip. Unfortunately, the shopkeeper's yells alerted Ivan to her presence.

Ivan took off to the left; Zelda raced after him. It was a dead-end street. Up ahead, Ivan was rattling on locked doors, searching for a way out. But there was nowhere to go.

Zelda shouted, "Where is the artwork? Please, I need to know."

Ivan turned to face her. He bent over and rested his palms on his knees. "I can't tell you just yet. I've worked too hard to get everything in place. The art is safe for now. If you leave me alone, I promise you will get it all back. But only if you let me go." He panted.

"I don't believe you!" Zelda pulled out her phone to call Vincent. When she looked at her screen, Ivan charged right at her. He was swinging a heavy glass hanger in one hand, aimed right at her head. She raised her arms too late to block the blow, and the blue glass

242

connected with her temple and shattered. Zelda grabbed at her head, blood streaming through her fingers. She sank to her knees, the pain rapidly spreading through her body. Moments later, she fell forward onto the concrete floor and passed out.

When Zelda woke up, the humidity and heat made it hard to breathe. Concerned whispers in a language she didn't understand made her open her eyes to ambulance personnel surrounding her, pulling slivers of glass from her cheek and scalp.

"Try not to move," said the only female paramedic, her English accent so thick Zelda had trouble understanding her.

She closed her eyes and let her mind shut down.

When she awoke again, Vincent was standing over her, his arms folded tightly across his chest.

65 Bad Luck

September 24, 2018

Vincent couldn't believe his bad luck. Ivan Novak had escaped and hurt Zelda in the process, which was exactly what he didn't want to happen. He cursed himself for not putting her on the first flight back to Amsterdam the minute their boat hit the shore. Now Zelda was back in the hands of paramedics, and his only consolation was that her injuries weren't life-threatening. The glass hanger Ivan used to hit her shattered when it hit the side of her head, lessening the impact.

"Luckily for you that your skull is so thick."

"Ha ha," Zelda mumbled, her speech already slurred by the painkillers the paramedics had administered. They sat at a café table while the ambulance personnel were busy filling in the insurance forms. One of Zelda's hands held an ice pack to her head, the other to her jaw, both swollen and bruised from the hit. Vincent was relieved she didn't slip into unconsciousness for too long, knowing about the previous assault and her long-term stay in the hospital.

"Where's Ivan?" she asked.

"Excellent question." Now that Ivan knew they were in Marmaris, would he go underground and take the art with him? Or would he try to complete whatever transaction he was planning? Vincent still didn't know why Ivan brought the stolen art here. "What happened? Did he say anything before he hit you?"

As Zelda recounted her conversation with Ivan, Vincent felt a growing discomfort. What she was telling him was almost too strange to believe. Perhaps her head injury, so soon after the last, was to blame.

What did Ivan mean by the art was safe, and they would get it back if they left him alone? That didn't make any sense. He brought the stolen artwork here to Turkey, a land from which it would be nearly impossible to recover through official channels. If he were planning on returning it, why did Ivan go to all this risk to bring it here?

"Are you going to go to the hospital?" he asked.

"That's all you have to say? What do you think Ivan meant?"

"He's not your concern anymore, Zelda. None of this is. You need to take care of yourself, which means you either go to the hospital with these gentlemen or back to your hotel room to rest. It's your choice." He felt responsible for her getting injured, but Zelda was an adult and he wasn't the fatherly type so she could make up her own mind.

"Hotel. I just need to rest. The paramedics said there's no permanent damage. Once the swelling goes down, I should feel fine."

"Okay, let me walk you back."

After Zelda signed a few papers, they slowly ascended the hill back to their hotel. Once he tucked her into bed, Vincent returned to his room and grabbed his binoculars. He hoped for the best as he opened the balcony door, knowing Ivan would have had plenty of time to leave town by now. If he were lucky, Ivan had gone back to the yacht and called his buyer to finish their deal. But when would his buyer arrive?

He looked to the marina, focused in on the last pier and let out a yelp. The *Sunset Dreams* yacht was motoring out of the marina. "No!" He zoomed in on the boat's deck, hoping to see the art dealer on board. Instead, what he saw made him grab his camera. He zoomed in again on Luka Antic, standing at the railing next to an older Turkish man, both with glasses in their hands.

As Vincent snapped away, capturing the men laughing and toasting, he felt as jubilant as they appeared. Here was Luka Antic on the same boat as the stolen artwork! This was the perfect opportunity to recover the stolen goods and finally see the crime boss arrested. Vincent's frustration mounted when he remembered that he had no contacts in Turkey. Worse yet, because Turkey was not a full member of the European Union, the chance of getting Luka

245

extradited was virtually nil.

His contacts at Interpol were excellent, but would they be able to help him here in Turkey? He considered who he could call and how long it would take them to respond. Too long. By the time they got here, Luka could be halfway down the Balkan Peninsula.

He decided on Greece, instead. The captain of the *YOLO* told him the Greek island of Kos was only a forty-minute ride from Marmaris. Vincent bet Luka's yacht would cross into Greek waters shortly after they left Marmaris Bay and entered the Mediterranean Sea.

He searched online for the Greek Coast Guard and dialed. After several attempts, Vincent was connected with an English speaker. He identified himself as a detective and explained how he was working with the Dutch national police and that a yacht leaving Marmaris Bay contained forty pieces of artwork stolen from Dutch museums. The Greek agent quickly confirmed his story and offered the Coast Guard's full support.

"Excellent. How soon can you pick him up?"

"Once he reaches the Aegean Sea and Greek waters, so probably within an hour. Assuming he isn't heading to another port further down the Balkan Peninsula, instead. We'll watch his progress and pounce as soon as he's well within our territory."

Vincent put his hand over the phone and cursed silently. "Thank you. I look forward to hearing from you soon." He hung up, knowing he couldn't wait that long. There were too many variables and what-ifs. Luka was right there on a vessel full of stolen artwork. As long as the authorities stopped the *Sunset Dreams* while both were on board, there was no way Luka's team of lawyers could talk his way out of this mess. Vincent couldn't let him slip away again.

He had to keep track of the artwork, at least until the Greek Coast Guard could board his vessel. But even from his excellent vantage point, he would lose sight of them as soon as they went out to sea. Knowing he had only one choice, Vincent raced out of the hotel and down the hill to Bar Street. He jumped aboard the first unmanned fisherman's boat he saw and sped toward the yacht cruising ahead of him. To his relief, none of the tourists snapping photos along the waterfront blinked an eye, and no belligerent Turkish fishermen cursed him.

As stupid as it was, stealing a boat was the only thing Vincent could think of to track he artwork. If the *Sunset Dreams* turned right at the mouth of Marmaris Bay, it would sail into Greek waters within the hour, but if it turned left, the yacht might be heading further down the Balkan Peninsula and dock at another port in Turkey. In that case, he would need to call Interpol and see what they could do.

With the bay full of boats, he hoped to stay far enough behind Luka and his companion that they wouldn't notice him until it was too late. The yacht was much faster and more responsive than his trawler, but Vincent was able to cross through the maze of parasailers, banana boats, Jet Skis, party ships, turtle expeditions, and lumbering sailboats with ease.

As they approached the mouth of the bay, Vincent heard sirens approaching fast. *Did the Greek Coast Guard dare to enter Turkish waters to arrest Luka,* he wondered. Puzzled, he looked around, searching for the source. Behind him, two patrol boats were tearing out of the marina and heading straight for him. *Oh shit,* Vincent thought. Could they have seen him take the boat?

Vincent slammed his fist into the wheel. "Damn it!" he cursed aloud. Luka Antic was getting away—again.

As the marina's police boats circled his, Vincent raised his hands in the air. Two heavily armed officers boarded his boat. When one grabbed his arms to handcuff him, Vincent noticed the yacht began speeding up. His heart was in his hands as the *Sunset Dreams* exited the bay, its bow already veering to the right toward Greece. Vincent sighed in relief. There was still a chance that the artwork would be recovered, and Luka Antic would finally get his due.

66 Ivan's Final Message

September 24, 2018

Ivan stood on the bridge next to the marina, his eyes almost unable to believe what he was seeing. Vincent de Graaf stole a boat and was tearing after the *Sunset Dreams*. "No!" he screamed involuntarily, attracting the attention of a father and son fishing close by.

He was so close to finally exacting his revenge, and he couldn't let that detective or Turkish authorities screw it all up by arresting Luka Antic. Ivan ran to the marina and waved down the first guard he saw.

"A Western man just stole one of the fisherman's boats—there by the lighthouse. He's speeding away!"

Ivan pointed at Vincent's boat, and the guard followed his finger until he was positive which one the art dealer meant. As soon as he locked onto the fisherman's boat, he yelled into his walkie-talkie and raced toward two Turkish police boats moored close to the marina's entrance.

Satisfied they would deal with Vincent in time, Ivan ran back to the bridge to watch the chase. As soon as he knew Vincent was out of the way, he would make his final move. Ivan squeezed the railing tightly, praying the police caught up with him before the detective could climb aboard. Vincent couldn't arrest him, but if either Luka or his buyer sensed anything was wrong, the deal wouldn't go through, and all his work would have been for naught.

He watched as the police's patrol vessels easily caught up with Vincent and enclosed him, effectively cutting him off from the yacht. Tears of relief streamed down his face as Luka and his associates sailed on without attracting any attention from the authorities.

Ivan wiped the tears away and walked to the nearest bench. His heart was about to explode. As he pulled out his phone, his hand shook so badly he had to put it back in his pocket for fear of dropping it. He closed his eyes and thought of his beautiful Marjana.

The doctors couldn't agree if it had been a suicide or an accidental overdose. Whatever the official cause, Ivan knew it was the loss of her perfect hands that lead to her death.

In the beginning, having her working for Luka was ideal. At fourteen, Marjana's talent was already apparent, and by joining Luka's team of forgers, Marjana was paid royally to paint while she improved her already incredible skills. And he got an extra commission out of the sales of her copies, which was always appreciated. By merely practicing her craft daily, her painting improved so dramatically that she was soon able to reproduce a small Rembrandt that could fool local experts. Luka had big plans for his organization and needed an extra impulse of cash. Thanks to Marjana's skills, he was able to have his thieves steal Old Masters, pieces none of the other artists in his stable were able to copy properly and make a mint off her forgeries. Within two years, she became his golden goose, and his organization expanded exponentially. In turn, Luka treated her like a queen, even allowing her to paint her own works and sell them through Ivan's gallery under her name. Their lives were perfect until she got accepted into art school.

She was determined to stop forging and concentrate on becoming a real artist. She refused to believe that any self-respecting artist would also forge another's work. When Ivan confessed that some he represented did occasionally copy pieces for him, she turned on him in a way he never expected. She said he was as sick as Luka, a perversion to the business. And from that moment on, she refused to accept his calls or answer his emails.

If only she had been satisfied with her life. After the London School of Arts accepted her into their master's program, there was no talking sense into the girl. Marjana convinced herself that even Luka would understand why she could not let this opportunity go. Ivan knew better.

Luka got wind of Marjana's plans as he always does. He had the courtesy to warn her first, making it clear that there would be dire consequences if she tried to leave.

If only the train had been on time, she would have made it. But three of his men snatched her from the platform before she could board. When they dragged her away and threw her into a van, she refused to let go of the doorframe. When she began screaming for help, the driver panicked and sped away. One of her captors threw the door closed and crushed her hands. Even after too many surgeries and infections to count, she was barely able to hold a pencil let alone paint fine detail, and she never would again. The pills the doctors found in her stomach were a prescription for morphine. That was the only relief Ivan could hold onto—she was in no pain when she passed.

The day before Marjana was to turn twenty-one, her housemate found her in their bathtub. Was it suicide or an overdose? They would never know for certain. And it didn't matter anyway. Luka didn't pull a trigger, but he might as well have. It would have been more humane. Luka ruined her life, and now it was time for Ivan to return the favor.

His hands steadied. Ivan took out his phone and sent his final message to the world.

67 The Weakest Link

September 24, 2018

Kadir Tekin and Luka Antic watched from the deck of the *Sunset Dreams* as two police boats circled a fisherman's boat close by then led it back to shore.

"What a commotion. Why would a Westerner have stolen such a simple vessel?" Kadir asked.

"He must have really wanted to go fishing," Luka quipped. Internally, he was petrified. He recognized Vincent de Graaf behind the trawler's wheel seconds before he was stopped and boarded. How did the art detective track him to Marmaris? And did he know the stolen art was on board? Luka assumed he did not. Otherwise, Vincent would have screamed bloody murder when the Turkish police stopped him, demanding they search Kadir's yacht instead. But the police weren't interested in them at all.

Kadir watched him closely. "No matter. Shall we step inside? My nephew should have unpacked all of the artwork by now."

They descended to the lower deck. In a spacious living room, Kadir's nephew Taner had hung up all forty pieces. Luka was impressed by the collection Ivan had assembled. He hoped Kadir would be, too.

Taner smiled broadly when the men entered. "They are magnificent. Congratulations, Uncle. You have a fine foundation upon which we can build a world-class museum."

Luka laughed to himself. The boy had spent only a few minutes with the artwork yet had already declared it genuine. Forging the art was a missed opportunity, he realized. Taner probably wouldn't have known the difference, but Luka was not stupid. His life was far more valuable than whatever their forgeries would have brought him in sales.

Kadir examined each piece, allowing his art historian nephew to inform him about the maker, style, and the piece's importance in the artist's oeuvre. Luka could tell that Kadir really didn't care. He played along anyway, his ego stroked with every compliment. By the time Taner finished his long-winded presentation, Kadir was preening. And why shouldn't he? According to Taner, this collection showed the progression and development of the world's most important modern artists. It would most certainly secure the Tekin name in art history books as Kadir desired.

Kadir was walking on cloud nine by the time they sat down to a celebratory lunch. The two men discussed Kadir's grand plans for a museum in Marmaris to be opened in thirty years and run by his ten children. A local art gallery had already forged bills of sale for all of the artwork, making it appear Kadir purchased them legally. This allowed him to take full advantage of the loophole in the current Dutch law and guarantee that his children's ownership would be uncontested. Luka didn't care about the specifics as long as it made Kadir happy enough to want to work with him again.

Kadir was chatting away about the plot of land he'd already secured and his architect's initial plans when a crewmember entered and whispered into his ear.

Luka didn't understand what was said, but whatever Kadir had just learned instantly dampened his good spirits. The Turk turned to Luka.

"Please, excuse me. There seems to be a problem in the kitchen I must attend to." Kadir rose and stormed out of the room without waiting for a response.

Luka shrugged his shoulders. What could the cooks need from Kadir right now, he wondered. It didn't matter. He had delivered the artwork. When his host returned, he would steer the conversation toward the heroin shipment. His European contacts were eager to see his merchandise, and Luka had promised to deliver the first batch next week. He hoped there would be no delays.

When Kadir returned, his cold gaze told Luka that something

was very wrong. Instinctively, his hand went to his side, but he had turned in his weapon when he boarded.

"Do you take me for a fool?" Kadir asked, his voice a growl.

Luka cocked his head. "What do you mean?"

"It's all over the international and Turkish news. Did you think I wouldn't find out?"

Luka stood to face him. "I don't understand. Explain to me what happened."

Kadir turned on a television mounted in one corner. The news was live, and the camera zoomed in on the same artwork hanging in Kadir's lower deck, but this wasn't a shot taken from this boat. The reporter was standing next to a nondescript storage unit.

"How did…" Luka stopped mid-sentence.

Kadir turned up the volume so they could both listen to the on-scene reporter.

"Police opened this storage unit in Nijmegen twenty minutes ago, after a press release from Robber Hood announced that the stolen artwork would be found here. Experts are calling the art's return a miracle. Curators from all of the museums affected are now converging in Nijmegen to help with the verification process and to assess any damage the art may have suffered. A note left inside the storage unit reads. 'Improve your museums' security and protect your cultural heritage for future generations. Next time, we won't be so generous.'"

"I don't understand," Luka said. "They must be fake. But how? And why?"

"Indeed, Luka, why? This should have been the start of a mutually beneficial business relationship. Is it because I am Turkish? Do you think we are all stupid? Is that why you brought me forgeries?"

"These aren't forgeries! These are the pieces taken from…" The truth flashed into Luka's brain like a lightning bolt. Ivan Novak wasn't having copies made so he could double his profits. He was copying the artwork to get Luka back for his daughter. He should have known a father would never forget. "It was Ivan Novak! He must have switched the artwork," Luka babbled. "I wouldn't be so stupid. Ivan was the only one who had access to it all."

Two large men entered the room, and Kadir walked to the door. As he stepped outside, he turned to look at Luka one last time, his face a mask of disgust. "Your organization is only as strong as its weakest link. You should know that. Take this trash away and dispose of it."

The heroin dealer closed the door on Luka's screams of protest as one of Kadir's men pulled his arms behind his back. The other one wrapped his arm around Luka's neck and squeezed. He gasped for air, clawing at the massive bicep blocking his windpipe. His vision blurred, and he felt himself slipping away. He tried to cry out, but his lungs were empty. The last thing Luka felt was Kadir's bodyguard twisting his neck until it snapped.

68 Moving Too Fast

September 24, 2018

Kadir closed the door on Luka Antic's screams and went down to the lower deck. "Taner, you're fired. Get off of my boat. Now."

The young man looked at his uncle in shock but only nodded before darting away.

Kadir gazed at the worthless artwork before him as contempt and sadness now replaced his recent feeling of joy. His dream of seeing his museum open in his lifetime was shattered. The money he lost was nothing—a few months' profits at most—but the hope he vested in this particular collection, as a foundation for legacy, was gone.

Did he want too much? Had his desire overcome reason and turned to greed? Kadir knew he was not dreaming too big, only moving too fast. He was young enough, so his dream was not unattainable. For a brief moment, his legacy had been secure and knowing that had given him a feeling of invincibility.

He didn't care who switched the originals for forgeries. Luka was ultimately responsible for the delivery and should have chosen more loyal associates.

The opportunity Luka presented had been an unexpected gift. But his network of art thieves was not unique. He would have to discretely query his most trusted associates to see who else he may be able to work with.

Kadir stared out at the setting sun, trying to process this setback and figure out how best to move forward. He may not live to see his legacy fulfilled, but his children would. And that was enough.

69 Breaking News

September 24, 2018

When Zelda woke up, the sun was just starting its slow descent behind the mountains enclosing Marmaris Bay. She stretched out, careful not to move too quickly. Her temple and jaw felt broken and swollen. At least it wasn't as bad as the last time Ivan whacked her on the head.

After splashing water on her face and carefully brushing her tangled hair, she knocked on Vincent's door, expecting him to be watching the *Sunset Dreams* from his balcony. But there was no answer.

Zelda went out to her balcony and looked over. Vincent wasn't there, and his room was dark. *Did he return to the marina to get a closer look,* she wondered. She called his phone, but no one answered. She tried twice more until she realized he probably had his ringer off. Instead, she sent a text message. "Where are you?"

When no immediate answer came, curiosity and the desire to stretch her legs propelled her back down the hill toward Bar Street and the marina. The setting sun cooled the air and lessened the humidity, making it quite pleasant to walk around.

On her right was the bay, full of boats, many filled with tourists out enjoying a sunset cruise. Beyond the plethora of masts and sails rose the mountains. Thanks to the setting sun, their green flanks appeared gray and distant.

Bar Street was hopping, and all of the terraces were overflowing with drunken tourists. Rap and dance music blared out of many speakers. Zelda scanned the crowd as she passed, wondering if Vincent had chosen one of these bars as a lookout. Deciding they were far too lively and thus distracting, Zelda continued down to the bridge.

A lone security guard stood next to the guard house, taking advantage of the cool evening breeze. She veered to the left and walked up a small street filled with expensive clothing stores—which, at this hour, were all closed. Vincent told her about a café he'd sat at this morning, so she walked down a small alley and found Robert's Coffee Bar, but it was also closed. She stood on the empty terrace and stared out at the boats, wondering where Ivan's was parked.

A marina security guard approached her immediately. "Excuse me, Miss. The shops in this vicinity are closed. Do you work on one of the boats docked here? Otherwise, I will need to ask you to leave."

The guard's question gave her an idea. "I don't, but my boyfriend does. He's a crew member of *Sunset Dreams*. Could I pop by and say hello? He's not answering his phone."

The guard picked up his walkie-talkie and called it in. When a male voice responded in Turkish, the guard's expression became sheepish. "Miss, the *Sunset Dreams* left the marina today at 4:15 p.m. They paid their bill in full, which means they are not returning."

Zelda's mouth dropped. "What! Where did they go?"

The guard mistook her panic for rejection. "I'm sorry, Miss." He blushed and looked away, embarrassed by her fictitious boyfriend's heartless behavior.

"Damn it!" That meant the *Sunset Dreams* left the marina just minutes after she'd woken up to a circle of paramedics surrounding her in the Grand Bazaar. Did Vincent miss the handover because of her? But how did Ivan get back to the marina so quickly? Even if he were younger and fitter, it would have taken at least ten minutes at a full sprint. And in this heat and humidity, she reckoned fifteen would be more realistic, which meant Ivan wasn't part of the final transaction. But who was? And if Ivan wasn't involved with the sale of the stolen artwork, why did he hit her again?

The guard didn't know what to do with the seemingly scorned woman before him. "I am sure you're friend had a good reason for not calling you. These rich owners often arrive and depart on a whim. Perhaps you should call him again."

"What? Oh, I'll call him all right. Thank you for your help, sir."

The guard tipped his hat as Zelda walked back toward the hotel, crushed. Her mishap had ruined Vincent's chance of recovering the stolen artwork. If the yacht sailed away this afternoon, they could be anywhere by now.

Vincent must be in a bar getting drunk, she reckoned. Zelda checked her phone. Vincent must be furious with her because he still hadn't responded. She called him again, but he didn't pick up. Instead, she sent another message. "Please call me back. I am so sorry."

She touched the phone in her pocket absently, hoping it would begin to ring. Unsure what to do, she walked along the waterfront toward the city center. When she reached the Atatürk statue, her stomach started rumbling.

She bought a baked potato with everything on it—a popular snack—and sat down on a bench placed along the water's edge. Behind her was a playground full of kids swinging and sliding. Others stood in a long line to view the full moon through a telescope, many children anxiously clutching their lire as they waited impatiently for their chance. Now that the sun had gone down, the heat and humidity were finally dissipating, and the Turkish families were out in force.

After finishing her meal, Zelda continued down the waterfront, joining the many well-dressed Turkish families as they slowly strolled down the pedestrian boulevard along the shoreline. She walked out onto a short pier to better see the moon's reflection on the bay. The upside-down exclamation point reflected in the rippling water reminded her of an Edvard Munch painting.

She sat down in a lounge chair close to the shoreline and stared out at the multitude of stars above. The rippling water quickly lulled her to sleep. Zelda woke with a start, then headed back to her hotel. Vincent hadn't left any messages for her at the front desk. Once back in her room, she turned on the news.

Video footage of a badly-lit storage unit filled with artwork drew her in. As a camera panned across a room full of paintings, Zelda realized several looked familiar. She rushed to the screen to look more closely when the truth struck her like lightning. All six of the works stolen from the Amstel Modern were in among the rest. When the video cut to a close-up of a Robber Hood card, stating: 'Improve your museums' security and protect your cultural heritage for future generations. Next time, we won't be so generous,' Zelda yelled out in triumph.

She flipped to CNN International and saw the same video.

"In a highly unusual twist to a string of robberies in Dutch museums earlier this month, the Robber Hood gang contacted the media and police this afternoon, telling them in an email where to find the stolen artwork. An email, Sandra, can you believe it?" The anchorman glanced over at his perky blonde co-host.

"That's right, Will. Their message is a serious reminder of how extraordinary this situation is. According to the FBI, only ten percent of artwork stolen from museums is ever recovered. Art experts are examining the paintings now. Early reports indicate that they are all in pristine condition. Several of the pieces have been authenticated and are already on their way back to their respective homes."

"The storage unit was rented by a Croatian national named Luka Antic. Police expect to…"

Zelda's jaw dropped. So Luka *was* involved. Vincent must be thrilled to be right. But if the stolen artwork was in his storage unit in the Netherlands, what was in the crates that Ivan delivered to the *Sunset Dreams*, and who was the intended recipient?

She needed to talk to Vincent. It was approaching midnight, and he still wasn't answering his phone. Out of desperation, Zelda asked at the reception desk where the nearest police station was. She figured she'd better report him missing before she called the American Embassy in Istanbul.

As she walked to the police station, Zelda thought about her last conversation with Julie Merriweather. With the art recovered, she would be able to return to the Amstel Modern with her head held high. Wouldn't she? Zelda's feet stumbled. Or would the police still try to tie her to the robberies? How she wished Gabriella would get in touch with them if only to make the police understand that Zelda had nothing to do with any of the thefts or the Robber Hood gang. Would Gabriella resurface now that the artwork had?

Zelda had so many questions and hoped Vincent knew at least a few of the answers.

"Vincent de G-r-a-a-f." Zelda spelled out the art detective's name for the Turkish police officer.

"Your friend isn't missing. He's here in our holding cell."

"What? Why? Is he okay? Can I see him? Thank God he's alive!" Zelda knew she was babbling, but the relief at having found her friend was overwhelming.

"Yeah, you can see him. It's a slow night."

Zelda was surprised by the officer's casual approach to policing but didn't mind. Right now, she needed to talk to her friend.

Minutes later, the officer escorted Zelda to a visitor's room.

Vincent's shirt was torn and one pant leg ripped but, otherwise, he looked fine. In fact, he was grinning from ear to ear. Zelda looked around the room, perplexed by how clean and modern it was. She'd watched too many National Geographic specials on prisons abroad and had been expecting damp walls and rats scurrying about.

She tried to hug him, but the officer wagged his finger at her. "No contact."

Zelda sat down across from Vincent. "What happened?"

"I was arrested for stealing a fisherman's boat. I have to pay a fine. As soon as the wire transfer goes through, I'll be a free man again."

"But why did you steal a boat?" Zelda had trouble not interrupting Vincent as he rehashed the day's events, ending with the police arresting him while he tried to tail the yacht—with Luka Antic on board.

Vincent smiled and leaned forward so that his head was partially hidden from their Turkish guard. "I tipped off the Greek Coast Guard. They should have stopped and boarded the *Sunset Dreams* as soon as the yacht entered Greek waters."

"But, Vincent, the stolen art wasn't in those crates."

He nodded. "I saw it on the news."

"But if all the real art is in the Netherlands, what have we been chasing?"

"I'll know more once I talk with my contacts. But they might have been copies of the originals."

"You mean forgeries? Do you think Luka would be stupid enough to try to pay his Turkish drug dealer with fakes instead of the real pieces?"

"This wouldn't be the first time a Croatian mafia member tried to pass off a forgery as the real deal."

"Okay, but why did they return the originals now? I can't imagine the Turkish drug dealer Luka met with would have been happy to know he'd just accepted fakes as payment."

Vincent's grin widened. "I'm guessing someone double-crossed the Croatian. The timing was too perfect for it to be a coincidence."

"But who?"

"I don't know, but I have a feeling we'll find out soon enough."

Zelda contemplated the situation for a moment before her face drained of color. "Oh, my God, that means Luka Antic..."

"Is already sleeping with the fishes." Vincent's grin lit up the room. "We'll know for sure as soon as I can talk to the Greek Coast Guard. With a little luck, they should be able to tell us what is inside those crates and who is still alive and on board."

70 A Museum in Marmaris

September 24, 2018

Minutes after his yacht entered Greek waters, a Coast Guard vessel signaled the *Sunset Dreams* to stop. There was a report that artwork recently stolen from several Dutch museums was on board.

Kadir laughed as he escorted the police down to his lower deck. "Here are the artworks you speak of. All are copies of paintings I admire. The originals were found in the Netherlands an hour ago—I saw it on the news. I have committed no crime." The alcohol racing through his blood flushed his cheeks. It also made it easier for him to be courteous to these officers. Whoever screwed over Luka was trying to screw him over, too. Someone must have tipped them off. Otherwise, the Coast Guard would have had no reason to stop his yacht and search it.

The Greek officer in charge glowered at him but refused to respond. Once his men had inventoried all of the pieces on board and compared them to the list of stolen works, the officer called it in. After a heated conversation in Greek, he turned to Kadir, "Why do you have copies of the same paintings as those stolen by the Robber Hood gang?"

"I admire the Modernists. After the robberies made the international news, I feared the stolen works would be lost forever. So I hired several artists to paint them to save them for the world. I am building a modern art museum here in Turkey and thought they would fit nicely within the new displays. But now there is no need since the originals have been returned unscathed. Instead, these pieces will hang in my summer home."

It took the Coast Guard several hours to confirm the art stolen by the Robber Hood gang was really in Nijmegen. Only after curators working for the victimized museums had verified that all the pieces in that storage unit were indeed the same ones stolen, did the officer's demeanor soften. It also took the Coast Guard's legal team time to confirm that there was no law against owning copies of artwork—it was only when they were sold as the originals that a crime was being committed. Ultimately, the Coast Guard had no choice but to let Kadir sail on to Corsica for a much-needed vacation.

When Luka's phone rang later that night, curiosity made him answer. "Yes, who is calling?" he asked, assuming that was enough to let the caller know he was not Luka.

"This is Marko Antic. I am trying to reach Luka Antic. Is he with you?"

Not one to pussyfoot around, Kadir told him the truth. "He is no more. The merchandise he delivered was not up to snuff."

Marko was silent for so long that Kadir thought he had hung up the phone. "That is unfortunate," the Croatian finally said. "I saw the news report and am as confused as you are. I'm afraid he put his trust in the wrong person. One I will soon deal with. Such a mistake won't happen again. I'll bet my life on it."

"Why are you calling?"

"For confirmation, and to introduce myself. My uncle tried to expand too quickly and paid the price for it. I plan on streamlining the organization. I also intend to continue where Luka left off but believe smaller shipments are easier to manage. If you are willing to listen, I will do what it takes to make things right. I know what your taste in art is. Its procurement is my specialty. Spacing the jobs out over a longer period would be smarter. I know we can help each other. If we could meet, you will see that both of our organizations would benefit."

Kadir heard his thoughts mirrored in this young man's words. His legacy was still within reach. Best of all, he still may live to see the museum's opening. As long as museums were soft targets and art was a prestigious object for the rich, it was a thieves' paradise.

"I'm listening."

71 Bucket List

Ivan Novak, now Dominique Strausburg, boarded a plane bound for Mexico City. He scratched at his fake beard, not yet accustomed to its presence. His normally long, bushy locks were now shaved down to a military-style buzz cut. Fat pads hidden under a Hawaiian T-shirt and Dockers completed his disguise.

Anyone who knew him personally would never recognize him in this getup.

Belize, his final destination, had always been on his bucket list. The warm climate and Mayan history appealed to him. And the cost of living was much lower than in Europe.

Ivan Novak still existed and was the owner of Gallery Novak, which his lawyers were already in the process of selling off—one gallery at a time since no one had enough capital to buy him out completely.

Dominique would live off the profits, funneled to him via a series of overseas banks and holding companies.

He was certain Marko Antic would take over his uncle's role as family head as soon as Luka's demise was confirmed. Ivan couldn't imagine that the Turkish drug dealer would have let him live. He had to assume Marko would come after him—family honor would demand it.

Only after their plane was flying high over the Atlantic did Ivan have a chance to reflect on Luka's probable demise. The intense joy and relief he had expected to feel had not yet arrived.

He could never forgive himself for suggesting his precious Marjana work for Luka. Nothing could bring his princess back, but at least the man who destroyed her life was gone. That was a small consolation. He hoped, in time, it would be enough.

72 Miracles Do Exist

September 25, 2018

As soon as Vincent was free, he and Zelda went out on the town to celebrate with a kofta and lots of beer. He had arranged a flight for them back to Amsterdam for the next afternoon. They would have to explain why they had arrived in Marmaris without first obtaining the proper visa, but Vincent was confident his contacts would ensure their safe passage home.

It was during their lunch that Vincent received a message that made him shout in glee.

"What is it?"

"Luka's dead. And Marko has taken over." He leaned back in his chair and kicked one leg over the other. "I would have liked to see him rot in jail, but I have a feeling he would have gotten out of it somehow. No, this is more fitting."

"But Marko took over, so how can that make you happy?"

"Marko doesn't appear to be as psychotic as his uncle. And according to one of my Croatian contacts, he's not a bad painter, either. Maybe he'll help modernize the organization. If he starts using a set crew, as I suspect he will for efficiency's sake, it will be easier to track them and trace their thefts back to Marko's organization."

"I don't understand. Wouldn't it be better to roll it all up?"

"Don't be so naïve, Zelda. Killing Luka is akin to cutting the head off Medusa. I'm certain other young upstarts see Luka's death as their chance to make a move on the Antic family's market share. It will probably get bloody until things settle down, but from what I hear, Marko will be a capable replacement. And one who is more concerned about the bottom line than torturing people into working for him. Who knows, he might even get a few of the other crime families to work with him instead of competing against each other."

Zelda rolled her eyes. She'd rather be naïve than as hardened as Vincent.

"Hey, did you see the latest *Art Investigator* blog? Nik is even more cynical than I am."

"Gosh, I totally forgot to check." Zelda hadn't thought about the blogger since they went to Clervaux. It seemed like a lifetime ago, though it had only been a few days. Vincent handed her his phone, its browser already open to Nik's latest post.

Miracles Do Exist

Well, folks, I stand corrected. Miracles do exist. The artwork stolen by Robber Hood has been returned. I cannot emphasize enough how exceedingly rare this is. Our nation's museums should consider themselves lucky.

But do they deserve to have the artwork returned?

Robber Hood raised valid points about our museums and their protection. What have our politicians done to secure our artistic and cultural treasures of the past and present?

Telling a news reporter that you support more subsidies is quite different than introducing a bill to that end. So far, I haven't seen much new happening in our parliament. And if a politician did introduce such a bill, where would the money come from?

Everyone wants to protect culture and the arts until they have to pay for it. It's the same with education, emergency services, and healthcare.

And if by some miracle they do find the money, how exactly can museums best protect themselves from thieves? By turning themselves into fortresses?

I honestly don't think this will be a problem we have to face because as much as politicians like to grandstand, I doubt any will have the guts to introduce such legislation.

No, I'm afraid the next Robber Hood gang is already making their preparations. As long as artwork fetches so much on the open market, it will be a commodity desirable by the criminal underworld and rogue collectors alike. As long as our museums are not better equipped to protect their collections, they will continue to be targets. And easy ones, to boot. And the cycle will continue…

As Zelda read his latest blog, she couldn't help but agree with Nik's pessimistic outlook. Not only did security cost buckets full of money with little to no return on investment but it was also difficult for organizations to agree on how best to protect their cultural treasures. It was a sad reality that this was a necessary debate, one with no foreseeable resolution.

73 Next Assignment

September 27, 2018

Zelda and Jacob sat on the Tolhuistuin's terrace, enjoying the sunset lighting up the sky in shades of orange. From their table, they could see the city skyline, now a black silhouette. It was bliss to sit here quietly and enjoy the evening with Jacob. After she'd had a chance to fill him in on her trip to Venice and Turkey, he'd taken a week off work to be with her.

This morning, Gabriella had stopped by to apologize—to Zelda's great relief. Despite Zelda's stream of questions, the artist refused to tell her exactly what had happened or why. When she finally dared to ask about the Pollock, Gabriella left without saying where she was going. Zelda grabbed her friend as she fled and hugged her tight, knowing they would never cross paths again.

After dinner, she would pack a bag so she could ride with Jacob back to Cologne for a long weekend.

The police were still searching for Robber Hood, though not as intensely as before the artwork was recovered. As soon as all the art found in Nijmegen was verified as the originals, Zelda got her life back. Even though Gabriella refused to talk to the cops about what had happened, it proved unnecessary. Vincent de Graaf had explained to several of his contacts on the Dutch force how Zelda helped recover the artwork. That was enough for the police and Julie Merriweather. The Amstel Modern welcomed her back with open arms, though Julie made a point of avoiding her. Zelda doubted the director would be willing to hire her again. Not that Zelda could blame Julie. Any museum director would prefer to distance themselves from a robbery, and her presence was a daily reminder of all that had gone wrong.

She did note that extensive security improvements were being planned, which were expected to be completed before the museum hosted a Frieda Kahlo exhibition in 2021. Julie had already recruited several local businesses to help fund part of the new system she envisioned.

"Did you finish your presentation?" Jacob asked.

Zelda's university mentor, Marianne Smit, had called the day after she returned to Amsterdam with great news—her master thesis had been approved. All she had to do now was present it to a small group of interested museum professionals and fellow students.

"Yep, even the PowerPoint slides are in the correct order now. Can I make you my guinea pig later?"

Jacob took her hand and kissed her fingertips. "Anytime."

"Excellent!" She leaned over the table and brushed his lips with hers. "I think the presentation is long enough, though—" Zelda's ringing phone interrupted her. She was about to mute it when she noticed who was calling. "Oh, I've got to take this." She stood up and answered the call. "Hi, Vincent. How are you doing?" They had touched base the day after returning from Turkey but hadn't spoken since.

"Great, never better. My office in Split is a go."

"Hey, congratulations!"

"Thanks. Opening a second office is the right move in the long run, but in the short term, I'll need some extra help. I was calling to see if you would be interested?"

"You mean if I'd be interested in working for you? Yes, I am. What exactly do you need?" Zelda was thrilled he would consider hiring her to do anything. Although her university mentor had mentioned that a few assistant and junior curator positions would be opening up soon, all were part-time and temporary.

"Well, it wouldn't be as glamorous or exciting as our last adventure together"—Vincent chuckled—"but I am looking to hire an office assistant and researcher for the Amsterdam office. It's more about keeping the doors open and the phones manned. I get a lot of calls, though most are from those who can't afford my services. I'll also need your help with archival research for any local clients while

I'm in Split. Though let me make clear that I will take care of any leads that need to be followed up in person. You're not a detective and don't have a license to investigate or a weapons permit. Your work would be concentrated on helping me follow paper trails and searching for documents."

"Okay," Zelda said slowly, not exactly enthusiastic about his proposal. But right now, work was work, and she had bills, groceries, and rent to pay. And who knew, Vincent had an incredible network. Perhaps one of his associates would know of a great job for her. "It sounds interesting. Yeah, I think it could be a good fit—at least temporarily."

"Excellent. Glad to hear you're interested. I've already got a job for you lined up. Huub Konijn told me about the research you'd done for the Amsterdam Museum and their collection of Nazi-looted art."

"Oh, I hope he was positive," she said with a gulp. Zelda hadn't spoken with Huub since she left the Amsterdam Museum. Though they hadn't seen eye to eye during her internship, he had proven to be a strong ally.

"Yes, quite positive. In fact, he convinced me to have you help us with a special case. Why don't we meet up on Friday, and I'll tell you more about it?"

"Could we make it next Tuesday? I'm heading to Cologne for a long weekend. Though I must admit, you've got my curiosity piqued. Could you give me a hint?"

"You know how you were asking about pro bono work? A friend of mine called in a favor. Actually, he's a friend of both Huub and me. He's searching for leads on a painting, and I promised to see what I could find in our local archives. Since I'm going to be busy opening the new office, that means I would like you to poke around for me."

"Oh, that sounds mysterious. What will I be searching for?"

"A landscape by Johannes Vermeer. It was taken from our friend's family during World War II and since then, he can't find any trace of it—at least, not in the digital archives that he's accessed. His daughter recently found a new lead, and he's asked us to check it

270

out for him. He's hooked up to an oxygen tank and is wheelchair-bound, making a trip over here nearly impossible. Huub and I promised him we would take a look and see what we could find out."

Zelda felt tingles of excitement coursing through her veins. "I can't wait to get started." Working for Vincent might not be so boring after all.

THE END

Thank you for reading my novel!

Reviews really do help readers decide whether they want to take a chance on a new author. If you enjoyed this story, please consider posting a review on BookBub, Goodreads, Facebook, or with your favorite retailer. I appreciate it!

Acknowledgments

I am deeply indebted to my husband for his support and encouragement while writing, researching, and editing this novel. My son also deserves a big kiss for putting up with me writing another book.

I am forever grateful to my beta readers, Philip and Janice, for their constructive criticism. My editors, Rogena Mitchell-Jones and Colleen Snibson, also deserve a huge round of applause for helping to make this novel shine.

This book was inspired by several newspaper and magazine articles as well as my own visits to several incredible modern art museums in the Netherlands. None of the institutions named exist— with the exception of Vianden Castle—though several real works of art held in Dutch museums did find their way into this novel.

According to Interpol, a gang of art thieves dubbed the 'Balkan Bandits' and 'Pink Panthers' is a loose association of approximately thirty to fifty robbers spread across Europe who steal art, jewelry, and antiques for criminal organizations based in the Balkans. Other sources estimate there are as many as 250 thieves active in their network. Centrally placed managers handle the thefts' coordination and handovers. This gang is considered to be the most profitable and daring group of art thieves in the world.

Vincent de Graaf, the fictitious art detective in my novel, is loosely based on real-life art recovery experts working today— though Vincent is by no means a true representation of their profession. *Marked for Revenge* is, after all, a work of fiction. For those interested in learning more about the work of real art detectives, I highly recommend *The Rescue Artist* by Edward Dolnick. It's a nonfiction account of Charles Hill's recovery of Edvard Munch's *The Scream*.

The Association for Research into Crimes against Art (ARCA) blog is an invaluable research tool for those interested in learning more about art thefts and forgeries. *The Art Newspaper* is also an excellent resource.

While writing this novel, a rather tasteless and cruel publicity stunt involving a treasure map and a forged Picasso made the Dutch national and international news, one I couldn't resist including in my novel. You can read more about the 'discovery' of this fake *Tête d'Arlequin* by Pablo Picasso online.

The Netherlands is the only country in the world where a thief can eventually become the legal owner of stolen goods. The statute of limitations is thirty years when the art is stolen from a museum, public collection, or institution and registered as national cultural heritage. It's only twenty years if the art is taken from a gallery, private house, or art fair. To learn more about this quite shortsighted piece of legislation, read the article *Thief Becomes Owner* on Maastricht University's website.

Dutch artist Rob Scholte has publicly claimed that he and several successful artist friends were forced to forge artwork for the Italian mafia in exchange for studio space. Their fakes were then sold in a gallery owned by another friend in Amsterdam. When Scholte refused, he claims the mob placed a bomb under his car that blew off his legs.

For more information about drug smuggling and the Balkan Route, check out Europol and Interpol's websites.

Turkey is a fascinating country and well worth visiting. I was lucky enough to write all of the chapters set in Turkey while on vacation in Dalyan and Marmaris.

About the Author

Jennifer S. Alderson was born in San Francisco, raised in Seattle, and currently lives in Amsterdam. After traveling extensively around Asia, Oceania, and Central America, she moved to Darwin, Australia, before finally settling in the Netherlands. Her background in journalism, multimedia development, and art history enriches her novels. When not writing, she can be found in a museum, biking around Amsterdam, or enjoying a coffee along the canal while planning her next research trip.

Jennifer's love of travel, art, and culture inspires her award-winning, internationally oriented mystery series—the Zelda Richardson Mystery Series—and standalone stories.

The Lover's Portrait (Book One) is a suspenseful whodunit about Nazi-looted artwork that transports readers to WWII and present-day Amsterdam. Art, religion, and anthropology collide in *Rituals of the Dead* (Book Two), a thrilling artifact mystery set in Papua New Guinea and the Netherlands. Her pulse-pounding adventure set in the Netherlands, Croatia, Italy, and Turkey—*Marked for Revenge* (Book Three)—is a story about stolen art, the mafia, and a father's vengeance.

She is also the author of two thrilling adventures featuring Zelda Richardson. In *Down and Out in Kathmandu*, Zelda is volunteering in Nepal when she gets entangled with a gang of smugglers whose Thai leader believes she's stolen his diamonds. In her short story set in Panama and Costa Rica, *Holiday Gone Wrong*, Zelda's vacation turns into a nightmare when she gets entangled in a cultural heritage scam.

Her travelogue, *Notes of a Naive Traveler*, is a must read for those interested in traveling to Nepal and Thailand.

For more information about the author and her upcoming novels, please visit Jennifer's website (jennifersalderson.com) or sign up for her newsletter (eepurl.com/cWmc29).

Rituals of the Dead: An Artifact Mystery

Book two in the Zelda Richardson Mystery Series

"Simply magnificent, filled with intrigue and suspense, and a lot of wonder!" - Amy's Bookshelf Reviews

"Everything I like in a mystery: Compelling characters, international settings, a mystery steeped in culture and history." - Amazon review

"If you're looking for a mystery jam-packed with art and history, look no further. Zelda is a fun and inquisitive sleuth! I look forward to going on more adventures with her." - Amazon review

A museum researcher must solve a decades-old murder before she becomes the killer's next victim in this riveting dual timeline thriller set in Papua and the Netherlands.

Agats, Dutch New Guinea (Papua), 1961: While collecting Asmat artifacts for a New York museum, American anthropologist Nick Mayfield stumbles upon a smuggling ring organized by high-ranking members of the Dutch colonial government and Catholic Church. Before he can alert the authorities, he vanishes in a mangrove swamp, never to be seen again.

Amsterdam, the Netherlands, 2018: While preparing for an exhibition of Asmat artifacts in a Dutch ethnographic museum, researcher Zelda Richardson finds Nick Mayfield's journal in a long-forgotten crate. Before Zelda can finish reading the journal, her housemate is brutally murdered and "give back what is not yours" is scrawled on their living room wall.

Someone wants ancient history to stay that way—and believes murder is the surest way to keep the past buried. Can she solve a sixty-year-old secret before decades of deceit, greed, and retribution cost Zelda her life?

ONE
Rituals of the Dead

August 17, 1962

"Dip, scoop, pour. Dip, scoop, pour. Dip, scoop, pour." Nick Mayfield's dry lips cracked open as he repeated his mantra. Just a few more inches, then she'll float as the survival guide had explained. He leaned against the T-shirt and bits of plank filling the gashes in the sides of the canoe, willing the stream of seawater to stop pouring in faster than he could scoop it out.

The sun was slowly descending, growing in size as it neared the horizon. Bands of pink and orange streaked across the sky, intensifying in color by the second. The new moon was barely a sliver. In an hour's time, he would be plunged into darkness.

Nick squinted to orient himself, thankful he could see an emerald belt of jungle rising in the distance. He must be in Flamingo Bay, he reckoned, and not too far from land. Still, the expanse of blue-green water between him and the shore was vast. A strong wind tried to push him seabound. Only the weight of the water and a few crates of barter goods still filling its hull kept the canoe in sight of land. Nick sighed. He was in for a long paddle back once his boat was seaworthy again.

Nick stopped scooping to reposition the jeans tied to his head, arranging the legs so they covered most of his sunburned back. His thoughts turned to the eight rowers who had jumped overboard hours ago. Had they already made it to shore? Nick wondered for the hundredth time if he should have abandoned ship and swum back with them. Though his faith in his survival guide was unwavering, the water was rushing in extremely fast. The holes were too large to plug completely.

Nick gazed again toward the shoreline. He was a strong

swimmer. He knew he could still make it to land if he had to, but he wouldn't leave his boat unless there were no other options. His guide made it clear you should never abandon ship until all attempts to save it have failed. It was the captain's code. Okay, the real captain had jumped overboard hours ago, but still. It was Nick's collection trip that went amiss and his supplies now bobbing in the waves close to his crippled watercraft.

Nick shook his head in disdain, certain the locals had given up too quickly. They all sprang into the water and began swimming as soon as they had discovered the first leak. If only they hadn't moved that bag of beads, then the water wouldn't have filled the hull so quickly. Nick bashed his coffee tin onto the bottom of the canoe as he scooped, his irritation manifesting itself as Albert Schenk entered his mind. *That Dutchman should be here helping me*, Nick thought. His fever couldn't have come at a worse moment.

A few feet away, a gurgling noise made him jump. The second canoe finally took on more water than it could handle. As soon as the holes in both were found, he'd cut it loose along with the makeshift platform connecting them together like a catamaran. Nick's face paled as he watched its stern slowly rise until the canoe was perpendicular to the water's surface. The platform hung off it like a starched flag. Nick watched in fascination as it stood stock-still, seemingly frozen in space and time, before suddenly disappearing into the sea. Several large air bubbles broke on the surface, the only sign the boat ever existed.

Nick gazed down into the dark water and redoubled his efforts.

Inexplicably, a can of tobacco soon rose from where the canoe had gone under, and it bobbed next to him. *That airtight container would make a useful flotation device*, Nick thought, resolving to keep it in sight. Almost all of his supplies had gone under as soon as he cut the second canoe loose. The rest he had thrown into the sea in hopes of making his boat light enough that the two holes in the stern would rise above the water's surface. Not that he had to worry about wasting supplies. He had plenty more stored in Agats. Losing these trading goods was a minor delay, not a setback.

Nick laughed, splitting his lip further. Blood dripped down his chin as his thin bray drifted across the waves. *Just like capsizing and sinking is a minor irritation*, he thought, giggling again despite the pain.

Cracks of lightning tore across the broad sky. Thunder rumbled seconds later. The storm was closing in fast, Nick realized. He hadn't taken into consideration the storms that frequently whipped across the jungle. If the rain started soon, he would never be able to get the boat floating enough to paddle back. Especially with only one oar to help—the rest had floated away in the ensuing panic when his rowers discovered the gashes in both boats' sterns.

As a second streak lit up the sky, Nick cleared his mind and focused on nothing but his coffee can. Dip, scoop, pour. Dip, scoop, pour. He had to survive—he was a Mayfield. It was his destiny to do great things, not die in the open ocean. Dip, scoop, pour. Dip, scoop, pour. And as every Mayfield knew, he had his destiny in his own hands.

*   *   *

Available as paperback, eBook, and audiobook.

Down and Out in Kathmandu: An Art Mystery

PREQUEL to the Zelda Richardson Mystery Series

"Better than anything else I've read lately. This one was a joy to come back to daily." – Amazon VINE VOICE review

"A book I'd like to mention to any readers thirsty for some armchair adventure." – Beth Green of *The Displaced Nation*

"The author brings Nepal to life. The descriptive detail leaves no doubt that she has been there and done that, and the vivid prose takes the reader along for the ride." – Author Robert Krenzel

Zelda wants to teach children English and "find herself" in Kathmandu. Ian wants to get stoned and trek the Himalayas. Tommy wants to get rich by smuggling diamonds. How their stories collide will leave you on the edge of your seat!

Travel from the dusty, tout-filled streets and holy sites of Nepal to the sultry metropolises and picture-perfect beaches of Thailand, as Zelda and Ian try to outsmart the smugglers and escape Asia alive.

This fast-paced, thrilling travel mystery set in Nepal and Thailand is sure to captivate readers thirsty for some armchair adventure. Down and Out in Kathmandu: A Backpacker Mystery is the perfect book for lovers of dark humor, backpacker fiction and (mis)adventure novels.

Available as paperback, eBook, and audiobook.

Turn the page to read an exciting excerpt...

TWENTY-FIVE
Down and Out in Kathmandu

"Waiter, I said *double* whiskey; this one's got bloody ice cubes in it. Waiter!" Ian brought the worthless drink down hard onto the bar, spilling its contents onto the bloke sitting next to him.

"Look out. The's real leather," the man growled at him, grabbing handfuls of napkins and rubbing fanatically at his footwear.

"Sorry, mate. It's just the fucking waiter doesn't seem to want to serve me a proper drink. Sorry about your shoes." At least, that's what Ian tried to say. He was slurring his words so badly no one could understand him. He grabbed a few napkins off the bar and attempted to wipe the man's jacket off, missing him by centimeters and falling off his stool.

The man scowled at his Italian leather footwear, rubbing at his shoes for a full minute before helping Ian to his feet. As Ian righted himself, the man brushed off his shoulders and back. He stood in silence, awed by the man towering a good meter over him. Ian felt as if he were in the presence of a Greek god, Adonis come to life. The man's features weren't just sharp, they were chiseled. With his perfectly manicured eyebrows and coiffed hair, Ian could almost see the swimsuit models bouncing up behind him.

"It's okay. They are just shoes, after all." Even his voice was magnificent, a low rumble that could easily summon Zeus. The man looked down at Ian's backpack, now soaked in whiskey. "Are you all right? You look a bit down on your luck."

In a thick drunken slur, Ian informed his new acquaintance about the turn of events that had led him to this particular bar at this particular hour. "So after Veny ripped my heart out, I checked into this place just down the street, but when I lay down on the bed, it sounded like the walls were alive. I might be broke, but even I have my limits!" he exclaimed, rocking on the barstool.

The Greek god smiled slightly. So far, he had said nothing,

listening patiently while Ian spilled his guts. "Maybe I could help you find somewhere decent to stay—at least for tonight?" the stranger said.

Ian eyed the man unsteadily. The bloke was well dressed, perhaps too well dressed for a place like this. The man's clothes looked high-end, tailor-made even. Why was he being so friendly? He couldn't imagine that this guy would want to roll him. But then why would he want to help him out? After a moment's silence, Ian blurted out, "I ain't no poof."

The stranger laughed. "Nor am I. Just someone who knows what it's like to be down on your luck. I guess I'm trying to help a brother in need."

Ian looked at his new friend with renewed interest. After all, the man did speak the universal language of human decency in a most sincere way. And besides, what did he really have to lose? The way he felt right now, if this bloke killed him, he might be doing him a favor. "What did you say your name was?" Ian asked.

"Harim," he said, offering Ian his hand. "It's a pleasure to meet you."

*　　*　　*